Unleash your wild side with
Herotica®5

"Letter from New Orleans" by Catherine M. Tavel
A casual encounter on a New Orleans holiday
comes to a dangerously erotic climax.

"Under His Thumb" by Marcy Sheiner
A rock and roll icon awakens a young girl's sexuality—
and becomes the star of an obsessive erotic fantasy
that lasts for more than thirty years.

"The Appliance" by Michelle Stevens
The intimate relationship between a divorcée
and her deluxe, nonbreakable, three-speed lover
is altered by the touch of an aggressive stranger.

AND 20 OTHER TALES OF EROTICA
BY, FOR, AND ABOUT WOMEN

Marcy Sheiner writes fiction, poetry, essays, and journalism.
Her erotic stories have appeared in *Herotica 1, 2, 3,* and *4,*
Virgin Territory, On Our Backs, and *Penthouse.* She was editor and fiction editor at *On Our Backs,* and her nonfiction has
appeared in *Playgirl, Mother Jones, High Times, Girlfriend,*
and *Lilith.* She lives in San Francisco and is working on her
fourth novel.

HEROTICA® 5

A New Collection of Women's Erotic Fiction

Edited by Marcy Sheiner

A PLUME BOOK

PLUME
Published by the Penguin Group
Penguin Putnam Inc., 375 Hudson Street,
New York, New York 10014, U.S.A.
Penguin Books Ltd, 27 Wrights Lane
London W8 5TZ, England
Penguin Books Australia Ltd, Ringwood,
Victoria, Australia
Penguin Books Canada Ltd, 10 Alcorn Avenue,
Toronto, Ontario, Canada M4V 3B2
Penguin Books (N.Z.) Ltd, 182–190 Wairau Road,
Auckland 10, New Zealand

Penguin Books Ltd, Registered Offices:
Harmondsworth, Middlesex, England

First published by Plume, an imprint of Dutton NAL,
a member of Penguin Putnam Inc.

First Printing, February, 1998
10 9 8 7 6 5 4 3 2 1

LIBRARY OF CONGRESS CATALOGING-IN-PUBLICATION DATA:
Herotica 5 : an anthology of women's erotic fiction / edited by Marcy Sheiner.
   p. cm.
  ISBN 0-452-27812-0
  1. Erotic stories, American. 2. American fiction—Women authors.
3. Women—Sexual behavior—Fiction. I. Sheiner, Marcy.
PS648.E7H477   1998
813'.01083538—dc21   97-34058
                                          CIP

Printed in the United States of America
Set in Caledonia and Serif Gothic

*For Angie, who never dreamed
what she was starting when she showed me
the road to sin and salvation.*

ACKNOWLEDGMENTS

Thanks to Shar for her brilliance; Jamie for his technological expertise; and Leigh, not only for her hard work but also for pushing me to write about Mick.

CONTENTS

INTRODUCTION

Editing women's erotica is somewhat different from editing other kinds of writing. Sure, the nuts and bolts of spelling, grammar and punctuation, and of helping a writer tell the story in the best possible way, are the same as with any other fiction—but to be involved in the creation of sexually explicit literature by women is to be part of a collective exploration of female sexuality and the evolution of a relatively new literary genre.

Nearly seventy years ago Virginia Woolf put forth a theory of literature as a collective progressive endeavor. "[M]asterpieces," she said, "are not single and solitary births; they are the outcome of many years of thinking in common, of thinking by the body of the people, so that the experience of the mass is behind the single voice."

I can just imagine feminist and literary academics rolling their eyes at my evocation of The Canonized One in a discussion about pornography. Well, add another footnote, dearies—because the ideas Woolf talked about in *A Room of One's Own* are nowhere more applicable than in the field of women's erotica.

Woolf believed that it was solely because women lacked the time and space for writing that they had not developed a body of written expression. She predicted that "the habit of freedom and the courage to write exactly what we think" would lead, in the next hundred years, to the emergence of a female literary canon. And she was not a snob about what form this writing should take: "I would ask you," she exhorted women, "to write all kinds of books, hesitating at no subject however trivial or however vast."

There's no doubt that Woolf's predictions were on target with regard to mainstream women's fiction, feminist theory, and historical works. They are also turning out to be accurate with regard to women's erotica.

Would women be writing truthful stories about their sex lives and fantasies if the only forum for sexually explicit stories was *Hustler*? Not only wouldn't *Hustler* publish the kinds of stories found in *Herotica* and other women's anthologies, but without access to sex stories by other women, we might not feel inspired and/or courageous enough to tell our own.

One of the first pornographic stories I ever wrote was about a sexual encounter with a prisoner in a private room in a prison. Because the story was written for a male-produced magazine geared towards a largely male audience, I wrote it as a purely exciting adventure, omitting any of the fear and ambivalence inherent in such a situation. Were I writing that story today, for *Herotica* or for another women's anthology, it would read very differently.

It would also have my real name, rather than a pseudonym, on it. Recently I wrote a heavy-duty S/M story for a lesbian collection, and I put my real name on it, something I would not have done ten years ago. Were it not for the brave women who've trailblazed the genre of S/M literature, I never would have had the courage to do this. I believe that this is what Woolf was talking about—the influence we exert on one another's work.

The lead story in this fifth *Herotica* collection, "The Knitting Circle," also exemplifies Woolf's theory. The women in this story urge each other to talk about their sex lives, until their stories become interwoven and the knitting circle widens:

> The weeks and months went by, the needles moved steadily through the yarn, and we talked and talked. We branched out from the present and delved into the dim past of wild youthful flings and

into the fantasies of the man next door, the mechanic at the garage, the brawny young hulk who came to repair the roof. Pretty soon more friends began to show up Tuesday evenings. Some of them didn't even knit.

Similarly, working with authors to revise and shape their stories is a vital element in this ongoing sexual dialogue that women are engaged in. Participating in that dialogue is, for me, the most rewarding aspect of editing erotica. Some of the pieces I accept for *Herotica* need little or no revision, but others need that extra push to realize their full potential. Contributors have a wide variety of writing experience: some are professionals, some even specifically professional sex writers. Others have never written any kind of story before. The level of the author's experience, though, has little to do with whether or not the story needs revising.

I've found that when something's missing from a story, what's most often needed is for the author to go deeper. "Wouldn't this narrator feel afraid in this situation?" I might ask, and after a long pause the author confesses that in fact fear was what triggered the woman's arousal. "Write it into the story," I tell her, and we've all moved one baby step further along in our evolution as writers and as honest sexual beings. Each time we take a step towards greater truthfulness, each time a writer journeys deeper inside, she paves the way for more honesty from the next story, the next author, the next collection. And so we build upon our own and each other's work.

"This doesn't ring true," I tell another writer. "I don't understand why the narrator stays with him."

"Funny you should say that," she tells me, "because right after I wrote this story I decided to leave him." And then she'll tell me the tragic real-life saga that inspired the fiction, the details that never made it into the written story, because she thought they were "too heavy"; by the time we're through she can't wait to get to her computer to add another dimension to her piece.

Sometimes asking women to go deeper means pushing them to fully claim their story. As fiction, these stories are already assumed to be fantasies—yet many women are still afraid to present them without some caveat like: *This is a fantasy I made up for my lover*, or: *And then I woke up*. Getting a woman to give up the camouflage is a delicate operation; it's a big step for her to remove the protective veneer she's painted over a story that's probably intensely personal.

Even having been on the other end, and knowing as I do the value of this process, I'm still amazed every time a *Herotica* writer responds with enthusiasm to my suggestions. I'm impressed and grateful when she is willing to rework a story, sometimes for as many as four drafts. Writers of erotica feel a gut-level commitment to this group grope with words.

Even if an author thinks my ideas are off the wall, we're likely to wind up in some pretty interesting conversations, the kind not usually engaged in at your everyday editorial conference. One author was perfectly willing to embellish her story by adding some reflection on the psychic significance of the bondage scene, but she disagreed with my interpretation of exactly what that was. Perfect strangers, we ended up having an intimate phone conversation on "what bondage means to me." Another writer questioned whether or not a sexual position I suggested was technically possible, and our conversation dissolved in fits of laughter when I assured her that I could personally attest to its viability. There are stories where the sexual activity is shrouded in metaphor, and I've had to ask an author exactly whose cunt or cock is doing what to whose. Or I'll ask a writer to clarify her complicated description of a sexual position, and in finding the words to untangle the characters' limbs we'll end up trading sexual secrets and giggling like conspiratorial teenagers.

How Do We Write Sex? Let Me Count the Ways

One of the most common things I seek in a story is more sex—or, in some cases, any at all. More stories than you might expect are submitted to the *Herotica* series without a single paragraph of explicit sex written in. Sometimes the writer has never tried to write a sex scene, but is able to do so when encouraged. Others simply refuse—making me wonder just how they've interpreted the title *Herotica*.

Considering the abundance of erotic anthologies currently on the market, these writers aren't totally off base—some of these collections contain nary a naughty word. I used to maintain that there was no difference between the terms *erotica* and *pornography*, but I find I must yield to the inevitable. It's not that erotica is classier than pornography, or that porn objectifies and exploits while erotica is egalitarian and sensual, or any of that gobbledygook that the prudish invoke to justify whatever it is that excites *them*. In fact, it seems to me that with the growth and permutation of this literary genre, we're running out of words to describe it. Erotica and pornography aren't enough anymore: we're going to have to expand our language to encompass the growing varieties of sexual literature. The words we invent, though, shouldn't become labels that confer moral judgment. This is a practical matter, much like the Eskimos' need for a multitude of words to describe snow.

If *Hustler* is pornography and *Herotica* is erotica, it seems to me that we need a new term for fiction that talks about sex but is not explicit—perhaps "erolit" would do. Erolit would include those works that talk about sex and sensuality but are not as explicit as pornography or erotica. Personally, this kind of writing doesn't stir *my* juices—but it does serve a purpose. It's another form of sexual communication and another blow to sexual repression.

As noble as this purpose may be—and I do believe it's noble—the *Herotica* series is not erolit. We have made a conscious decision to be sexually explicit. I do not believe that heat has to be sacrificed for light—in fact, I think the two go together like thunder and lightning. I want an erotic story to hit me over the head with an unusual perspective—but I also want it to take me on a good hot ride.

The stories in this collection do just that. As always, they're wildly diverse—but one theme that popped up in this batch is the influence of cultural background on sexual response.

In "Fish Curry Rice," for instance, after we've been treated to an exquisitely detailed picture of Indian customs regarding the behavior of women of marriageable age, we see the narrator flouting them:

I swept my tongue across his nipples, and they wrinkled and red-dened. I struck them again and again until they were purple and bulging. The twin ridges of his ribs rising over his sunken stomach signaled the breath held in anticipation. I bit a nipple. He turned his dilating eyes on me, struggling to focus, pleading, laughing, challenging me to arouse him further.

In America, where race relations seethe with fire and ice, a white woman reflects on her attraction to black men in "In the Mood":

These lovers left her with sensual memories of black skin on white, black cock entering pink pussy.

In "Sauce," a decidedly hip no-nonsense butch who thinks she knows everything is surprised and seduced by a Southern belle:

Oh, she *was* a southern woman, in the best sense—slow, so slow. Play all the nuances, taste every subtle flavor, savor the textures. So I held steady while Veronica crept over me like a big voluptuous cat, rubbing and almost purring into my ear, teasing me, easing me to her magic bed.

And in "Dragon Cat Flower," a sexually experienced Chinese woman is transported, by making love to a Chinese man for the first time in her life, to a part of her ancestry long forgotten, as she discovers her totem animal:

With him inside me now, I thrashed freely, my long spine curving and twisting as we continued through a heavenly sky . . . curving like wisps of smoke, flying upon the air, dragons . . . I flexed my claws and held even tighter to him then, feeling my power.

Reading these kinds of passages, it's easy to forget that not so many years ago the notion of women writing at all was scandalous, and any woman who dared do so was subject to ridicule. Even now, in some quarters, a woman who dares to write the words, ideas and acts contained in these pages is at risk of ostracism or worse. I can't honestly say what Virginia Woolf would think of women's erotica, but I have no doubt that she would respect *Herotica* authors for having "the courage to write exactly what we think."

—*Marcy Sheiner*
Emeryville, California
April 1996

Joan Leslie Taylor

⁂

The Knitting Circle

At the knitting group we talk about many things, but our main topic is always sex. We've been getting together on Tuesday nights to knit and talk and laugh, and sometimes cry, for almost five years. We are all well above the age of consent, how shall I say? We are women of *un certain âge*. Not one of us looks to be the sort of woman to sit around telling tales of hard cocks, wet cunts, and orgasms that shake beds.

It all began the year Susie was knitting sweaters for her twin grandsons, and Emily decided to knit an afghan for her mother-in-law. Knitting takes full charge of your hands, but leaves your mind pretty much free; just sitting home alone, click, click, click, knit, purl, knit, purl, can be decidedly dull, so Susie and Em started getting together. Then Lenore heard what a good time they were having, so she bought some yarn and started coming over, too. I think they asked me mostly because they all have husbands and they liked the idea of coming to my house where there was no man lurking about so we could be wild and silly.

That's when the sex stories started. I had just broken up with a very fine lover named David. The sex had been terrific, but he'd been a jerk in all other ways. It was a relief to have him out of my hair. I just wished I could have kept him in my bed. Susie, Emily, and Lenore just drooled to hear me tell how David and I used to make love all night long, with him lapping away at my cunt, his gigantic hard cock in my mouth, him on top, then me on top, such wonderful gymnastics. I'd get hot just telling them about it, and they all sat there rapt and looking like their pussies were dripping all over my chintz furniture. They never wearied of hearing about David, but eventually, great sex or not, I got tired of talking about a man I disliked.

"Oh, tell us again about the time you went to the Olsons' barbecue and David brought you to orgasm in the hot tub, right under the noses of all the guests!" Lenore gestured with her knitting needle as if it were a baton and she were conducting the orchestrated ensemble at the Olson barbecue, me and David in the steamy, swirling water, David's finger up my cunt, the laughter and chatting of the slightly inebriated guests wafting around us in waves that seemed to make David's finger twirl and thrust with symphonic genius. Yes, it had been a particularly fine moment, even if that had been the same week David borrowed my car and left me stranded for hours, no warning, no phone call, no apology, and no gas in the car when he finally reappeared.

"Enough already. You've heard that story at least three times. I'm sick to death of David. Not another word. I want to listen to someone else's hot story."

At first they all protested that they were just nice married ladies with boring husbands. Well, yes, they did "do it," but there was nothing to tell. Susie flushed as red as the sweater on her needles, and Emily fidgeted so nervously in her seat that it was as if David's errant finger had lodged itself in her pussy from so much telling. She kept her eyes on her afghan, scrutinizing the stitches as if they were intricate lab science requiring all her concentration, but something in the way she always pronounced her husband's name made me think that she would definitely have tales to tell, tales worth listening to. So I pressed her.

"Emily, tell us about Derek. I bet he's really good in bed." I paused to give her time to bring the image to mind. She shifted again, and let her hair fall across her face, hiding her expression.

"We promise we'll never breathe a word outside this room."

"Yes, Em, do tell," crowed Lenore. I knew that for all her enthusiasm she would be a harder challenge. She probably had the most active sex life of any of us: a robust-looking husband who adored her, plus, I've heard on very good repute, a sometime lover at her office. I think the deception of an affair made her reticent, but I knew she wanted to talk, too. But not yet. First Emily.

With only a little more coaxing Emily told us about Derek and how they'd send the kids to his mom's sometimes on Sunday afternoons, then give each other massages which started with almond oil and ended with enough bodily juices to keep the two of them slipping and sliding, moaning and panting, fucking and sucking, and Emily coming all afternoon. Derek's forte, above and beyond being able to give a terrific massage, was endurance. Ah, we all sighed, as Emily whispered in a breathy little voice about how he could make her orgasm over and over again. How the best ones were after Derek had been slip-sliding his cock in and out of her wet, pulsing pussy for an hour or more.

"I'm afraid I'm slow to warm up," she said apologetically, "so it's a good thing I have Derek who can go and go . . . and go . . . ." Her voice trailed off in a sigh.

"Who warms up as quick as most men?" Susie interjected. "No one, I think. Not really. There's pretending to be hot and ready, oh, just a little lubricant, but good loving takes a patient man." Susie sounded like she was giving a Marriage and Family Life lecture, but she'd opened her mouth, so we teased her stories out of her, too. Then we got Lenore talking about her husband and after that her lover.

The weeks and months went by, the needles moved steadily through the yarn, and we talked and talked. We branched out from the present and delved into the dim past of wild youthful flings and into the fantasies of the man next door, the mechanic at the garage, the brawny young hulk who came to repair the roof. Pretty soon more friends began to show up on Tuesday evenings. Some of them didn't even knit. Ruby crocheted, and though she was no sweet young thing, but a slightly overweight, fortysomething, twice-divorced secretary, she always had at least two or more men panting after her. Samantha was a quilter, very healthy, very New Age, with children in their twenties still "finding themselves" while she footed their bills. She was always going off to some sort of festival or workshop at one of the power places of the earth, and coming home with tales of SNAGs (you know, Sensitive New Age Guys) we all wished we had around to adjust our chakras. Delilah brought yarn and needles the first time she came, but we all snickered to see the number 12 poles she had, along with a skein of baby-fine pink yarn that had the well-weathered look of having been in a drawer for a long time. She couldn't knit any more than I could do brain surgery, but we loved having her appear each week and pretty soon she gave the pink yarn back to her sister. A country-music star wanna-be, she had the clothes, including a whole wardrobe of Wonderbras, and the hair and the walk down pat, but she was still working on the singing part. She probably had the tamest sex life of any of us, but she made up the naughtiest tales of late-night rendezvous with cowboys in leather vests and very tight pants bulging over swollen members, throbbing to get into her sateen leggings.

One week a new woman came, a widow who had showed up at Lenore's law office after her husband died, for help in handling some trust documents. Lenore didn't really know her, but she said there was something about Olivia that made her want to find out more about her.

"She's extremely sexy but in a subtle way," Lenore told us. "If I were a man I'd be absolutely in love with her. She's older than we are, I guess about sixty, but the way she looks makes me think sixty is the perfect age we're all waiting to be. I don't know how she managed the last couple of years while her husband was so sick. She did everything for him, and I guess he had a pretty awful time at the end. After I got her trust straightened out and I knew she wouldn't be coming anymore, I asked her if she knitted or anything."

Olivia was as beautiful and fascinating as Lenore had led us to imagine. She was tall, with such gorgeous silver-gray hair falling in drifts about her face that it made me want to stop dyeing my hair instantly. Her eyes looked green, but I later noticed that they changed hue depending on what she wore. I found myself studying her clothes, but they were nothing special: a well-worn turtleneck over a denim skirt, a simple vest, and silver earrings. She made everything she wore seem unique and very wonderful. I made a mental note to get my denim skirt out and see if it still fit, and I wanted a vest exactly like hers. I didn't think she noticed me staring at her, but then she turned and smiled at me.

Olivia didn't say much that first week. I wondered whether Lenore had told her what the knitting group was really about, but she seemed as fascinated as the rest of us with Ruby's excited report of her latest date with the stockbroker who liked to do a strip-tease for her, starting from the full three-piece suit and slowly, excruciatingly, getting down to his leopard bikini skivvies.

"He's so good at it," Ruby squealed. "The way he bumps and grinds. I've never seen a man enjoy his own body so much. It makes me want to touch him, but he won't let me lay a finger on him, not until the end."

They'd both be so hot by the time the leopard undies (or what-ever tiny sexy garb he chose for the night) were revealed that Ruby swore she ripped them off his buns and grabbed his cock, which sprang out fully extended the moment it was released from its spandex leopard bondage.

"Once he's naked, he almost forgets his own body and posi-tively devotes himself to mine. He doesn't even notice that I need to lose fifteen pounds. He oohs and ahs over my fleshy thighs, buries his face in my belly, and oh, how he loves my breasts," she crooned.

I glanced at Olivia, and in the half-smile that flickered across her lips and the fluttering of her long thin fingers as she smoothed an invisible crease in her vest, I saw that she was remembering a man who had loved her breasts like that, too.

Later in the evening, after all of Susie's butterscotch brownies were gone, even the crumbs, Delilah told an unbelievable tale of what happened when the bag boy at the Safeway had helped her load her groceries. Samantha whispered behind her quilt square to Olivia that it was just pretend. We all loved Delilah and in-dulged her stories, but, like Samantha, I didn't want Olivia to think we were overaged teenagers chasing baggers at Safeway. I wanted her to think we were wonderfully sensual, sophisticated, sexy women.

The next week I noticed that both Susie and Ruby were wear-ing vests, and Delilah and Samantha were wearing denim skirts. I was wearing both, with a turtleneck. By then Olivia was wearing a pale blue tunic over black knit pants that made me feel dowdy in my denim skirt. For women the late forties and early fifties are like a second adolescence, with all the awkwardness and uncertainty of being neither young nor old. I could imagine myself being ninety, wrapped in a shawl, very frail and extremely wise, but I was having trouble with being middle-aged. I wasn't ready for the shawl yet, but I had given up short skirts when the blue lines etching my thighs became too obvious, and I stopped wearing anything with a waist when my once slim midline expanded to meet the other excess flesh appearing on my body. Olivia was the first person who had made me think that perhaps my attempts at trying to stay young-looking were not only doomed, but missed the point. Olivia didn't look young; she looked beautiful.

The needles were clicking, but no one was saying much. I think we were all wishing Olivia would speak, but it didn't seem quite right to just say, So, Olivia, tell us about your fabulous sex life. After all, she was a recent widow and probably wasn't even thinking about sex.

"That must have been very difficult for you, caring for Ed," Lenore began.

"Illness is never easy, especially terminal illness, but Ed was such a dear and we had such a sweet relationship that I never minded taking care of him." Olivia spoke with such warmth that I think we all envied her Ed. I know I did.

My last boyfriend had been yet another jerk who'd treated me badly, and he wasn't even very good in bed—too selfish and with about as much sensitivity as an anteater. How I wished that just once I could have a man I would think of categorizing as "such a dear," and I realized that for all the sex I'd had, I knew nothing of what Olivia called a sweet relationship. But I knew it was what I'd yearned for.

"Tell us about Ed," I said, reaching into my bag for a new skein of yarn.

"It's hard to describe someone I've known most of my life," she began. "Do I tell you how he was when he was eighteen and I was not quite fifteen, and already smitten with him? It wasn't that he was particularly handsome, but he had such a way about him, as if he'd just discovered something that was more fun than anyone could imagine and he wanted to share it with me." She paused and took a deep breath. "Or do I tell you how he was when he was old and sick and just holding hands was all he could do?"

No one answered her. The needles *click-clicked* on. Olivia cleared her throat. I felt tears building in my eyes.

"You probably think that sick people don't have sex lives, but it's just like everything else in the face of an onrushing illness: harder to attain and more precious by the day." She paused and reached for a tissue. I could see the long months of caring for Ed, the tiredness, etched on her face, the loss welling up in her eyes.

"Only a short time before he died," Olivia continued, her head held high, "there was one Sunday that I would not trade for being twenty again, even with a dozen suitors."

"Would you tell us about it?" asked Samantha.

"Well, it's not a very sexy story, not what you're used to." We all nodded yes, that we wanted to hear her story. "Because it was Sunday there were no nurses coming, and no home health aides. It was just Ed and me. Even though the aides usually gave him his bath, he asked me if I would for a change. I ran the bathwater, checking the temperature, filling the tub just the way I knew he liked it. I brought him into the bathroom in his wheelchair. As I undressed him, I started to really look at him. Even though he'd lost quite a lot of weight, he was still a good-looking man. Suddenly I wasn't giving an invalid a bath. I was involved in a sensual dance. Steam was rising from the bathwater. Neither one of us said anything, but we seemed to be breathing in unison. I slipped off his shirt and ran my fingers across his chest. He raised his hand to my hair, and I felt such desire rise in me." Her voice wavered, and then she was quiet.

I held my breath, silently urging her on.

"Wheelchairs are very awkward," she continued, her voice stronger again, "and never more so than in a small place like a bathroom. I slid his pants down his thin, thin legs, letting my fingers linger on the soft downy hair on his calves. Ed and I used to dance together, but now the best dance we could manage was getting him into the tub without his falling. He put his arms around my neck. Embracing him around the waist, I lifted him and pushed the wheelchair aside. His breath was hot on my neck. As if we were dancing once again, I turned, still holding him tightly so he faced the tub, then lifted one of his legs into the water, then the other. I always held my breath at that point, for fear his weak legs would give way too soon and he'd slip in too fast. That Sunday he settled into the water perfectly, with a sigh that seemed to come from both of us. I smiled to see his long, naked body stretched out in the tub, his genitals bobbing gently in the warm water. I remembered the first time I'd ever seen Ed naked, more than forty years before, when I'd never seen even a picture of a naked man. I'd seen my little brothers in their bath, but that was all, so seeing Ed the first time was quite a shock."

"Was that on your wedding night?" Susie asked.

"Oh, no. Ed and I used to go for very long walks up into the hills outside town. We knew we would marry and spend our whole lives together, so we didn't wait for the wedding." She blushed, as if we might not approve.

"Please go on about Ed's bath," Emily said. "If you want to," she added hastily.

"Well, I sat down beside the bathtub and began washing Ed. We were both smiling, and Ed was looking right into my eyes. I felt shot through with love and desire and sadness. So many years I'd loved this man, and never more deeply than at that moment.

"My blouse was becoming damp, sticking to my skin, sweat trickling down between my breasts. 'Liv, why don't you take off your blouse?' he suggested, with the most wonderfully lascivious look in his eye. I scooted out of it feeling like an eager schoolgirl with her beau. 'There, that's better,' he said, reaching one hand weakly towards my breasts. I leaned forward and kissed his forehead while he caressed my breast. When he reached the nipple, I felt myself begin to breathe heavily. In recent months we hadn't had any real sex. Affection, yes, but I think we'd both become so consumed with taking care of his body that it had ceased to be personal or pleasurable.

"I resumed washing him, moving down his chest, toying with his nipples, which were very sensitive as always. Even his armpits felt sexual as I slid my soapy fingers up under his. I moved down towards his legs, and he said, 'Don't forget my balls, Liv.' " She had tears in her eyes. Someone handed her a tissue, and we all waited.

"It's so silly, really. Ed and I probably made love thousands and thousands of times over the years, but when I think of him now, what I remember is his balls in my hand that Sunday. The soft, soft skin on his scrotum, the tiny hairs, the always, to me, mysterious feel of his testicles. How fragile they are, and so vulnerable hanging exposed like that. We think of women as being the soft ones, but how delicate the skin of the scrotum is. 'I love your balls,' I said, that was all, but there was nothing else to say. For a long time, I continued to hold his balls in my hand, examining the pink skin, feeling the wonder of this treasure. With my other hand I held his penis, which was the more dear to me in its softness. All the medications Ed had to take . . . it had been a long time since he'd been able to have an erection, but holding Ed's wonderful penis in my hand, I saw its beauty, his beauty really, as I never had before. When a penis is hard and we are awash in seas of hormones, we see only its function and miss its perfection. 'How I love your hands,' he said. And how my hands loved him."

In the sweet glow that fell upon us when Olivia finished her story, I looked into the faces of the women in the circle, and suddenly I thought about my mother and her friends, and her mother and her friends. We had thought we were so modern, my friends and I, and so very wild, as if we were the first women ever to love sex. Maybe we were the first to share our stories, but we probably weren't the first to send the kids off to a mother-in-law so we could enjoy a lusty Sunday afternoon, or to be secretly turned on to repairmen, or to lovingly fondle a sick husband's balls.

Listening to Olivia tell us about Ed's bath, I finally understood that my mother and her mother, and even her mother's mother, had been sexual women, living out their desires and finding perfection as Olivia had in the ordinary moments of loving and caring. What stories they could have told.

Catherine M. Tavel

Letter from New Orleans

Turning up one block and down another, I was surrounded by seductive fragrances. The sugariness of homemade confections emanated from Laura's Original Praline and Fudge Shop on Royal, the sweets themselves staring out from their doily-covered pedestals. The ruby heat of crawfish beckoned from a Decatur Street restaurant window while the essence of spicy red beans simmering nearby invaded the air near the Praline Connection. And I was lost.

As if by magic, I found myself sitting at a table in the Acme Oyster House, the worn white tiles comfortably familiar beneath my feet. Hands folded on the freshly wiped plastic checkered tablecloth, I watched one of the skilled shuckers across the room behind the aluminum-topped oyster bar. The graceful movement of his fingers as they mastered the flat, dull-edged knife, the soft flick of his wrists as he placed each open mollusk on the dented platter, were as soothing as the caress of a long-lost lover.

With the shucker's masterpiece finally set out before me, I lifted the first half-shell to my lips and sucked the meat. It lingered briefly at my teeth, then slid down the back of my throat, cool as a mouthful of jism is hot. One by one, I raised each oyster to my lips. One by one, I swallowed them, engulfed by the clean, chewy taste of the sea. One by one, until the entire dozen was gone. But I needed more. Something different.

A netted basket of crawfish soon took the place of the empty oyster shells. They were boiled to a brilliant red, almost the shade of an engorged cock tip. (Yet nothing is quite that color.) I grabbed one, snapped off the head and squeezed the tail, exposing its delicious chunk of flesh. Gingerly, I grasped the niblet between my teeth. My mouth exploded with the taste.

I was vaguely aware of being watched as I chewed and sucked and licked my meal in sheer delight. A man at a nearby table met my gaze. He said nothing, yet insinuated everything with his penetrating brown eyes. I kept snapping the heads off crawfish as he sank his teeth into a golden, soggy, Po Boy hero. The hot juices from the boiled decapods streamed down my elbows. I wiggled my tongue into their tiny hollow cavities, extracting as much fire as I possibly could. When I finished, my lips and tongue were burning, tingling with Cajun spice. The next time I glanced up, the handsome diner was standing beside my table.

"It's been a pleasure eating alone with you," he said, his intense caramel brown eyes piercing my skin. He moved to leave.

"Wait," I told him.

"No names," he instructed as we walked toward Jackson Square.

"What should we call each other, then?" I ventured.

"You look like a Beth," he said simply.

"And just what does a Beth look like?" I prodded.

He thought for a moment. "Sweet, fragile. That's what I think I'll call you. Beth. You can call me anything you'd like."

I was intrigued; I had grown weary of boring, predictable, buttondown types. But was this man certifiable or safe? I could end it right here or . . . "Peter," I told him. "I'll call you Peter."

Peter and I chose a quiet bench in Jackson Square, past the easels of artists who did charcoal renderings of tourists, past the painters who sold watercolors of local scenes, past the fortunetellers with tarot cards stacked on snack tables. The heat from the bench's wooden slats crept up through my body. I tried my best to mask my arousal.

It turned out that Peter was visiting from New York. A firefighter by trade, his Cuban-Irish heritage explained his exotic good looks and his wicked smile. His body was thick and strong. Staring at his sturdy hands, his solid fingers, I couldn't help but wonder what his cock looked like.

We stopped for reinforcements at the Cafe du Monde: strong chicory-laced coffee and sugar-coated *beignets*. I suppressed a strong urge to lick the sweet powder from Peter's lips. During a stroll along the banks of the Mississippi, we managed to tag along with a walking tour of blue-haired old ladies who welcomed us as if we were grandchildren. An hour into the tour Peter whispered, "I'm hungry."

"But we just ate," I told him.

When the group turned the corner, Peter pressed my back into a wrought-iron fence fashioned of cornstalks and morning glories. The bold outline of his cock etched into my thigh. "Did you ever notice," he said, "that life in New Orleans revolves either around food or fucking?" The crassness of his words sliced right through me, making my pussy throb. I was surprised at myself. How could I be falling for such a ruffian?

"Come on," Peter said, grabbing my hand. "I know the perfect place."

Before I knew it, we were on, of all things, a bus. Not a cab, not a horse and buggy, but a cranking, clanking city bus. We bounced along Canal Street into a residential section that smelled faintly of magnolias. It was a neighborhood of old but well-kept houses with misty front gardens and towering trees whose roots cracked up through the sidewalks. Peter pointed out Mandina's, a simple-looking establishment on the corner.

Across a bare Formica-topped table, Peter and I shared our appetizers: pungent crab cakes for me and spicy gumbo for him. I thought I'd melt when I fed him a forkful of my entrée and caught a glimpse of his tongue running across his lips. My blackened catfish was meaty, juicy and hot. His shrimp *étouffé* was equally delicious. We washed all this down with another cup of robust chicory coffee and a slab of bread pudding. I felt as though my mouth had died and gone to heaven—that is, until Peter kissed me under a moist orange blossom tree outside Mandina's.

As the tip of Peter's tongue gently moved from side to side in my mouth, my knees grew rubbery. He caught me around the waist and held me closer, tugging on my lower lip with his teeth. My nipples sprung erect as I pushed against him. The warm honey began to flow between my thighs as his now-hard prick carved into my belly. He could have taken me right there on Canal Street, but instead he pulled away, looked into my eyes and asked, "How do you feel about Boozoo Chavis?"

Just off Tulane, there's an amazing juke joint called Mid-City Bowling. The locals refer to it as "Rock and Bowl," because that's exactly what you do there. Amid the crashing spares and strikes, you can score some of the hottest music in town. There's a small stage, a dance floor, plus a full-service bowling alley. Culture mixed with crass. Sort of like Peter.

That night, Boozoo Chavis and his zydeco all-stars rocked us with accordions, washboards and spoons. Some people did the two-step and drank themselves into oblivion, while others opted to bowl ten frames. Frosty bottles of Abett's, the regional brew of choice, enhanced the amorousness of the evening. Peter and I clumsily attempted the two-step, but wound up grinding in the crush of bodies, getting lost in a sea of sloppy tongue kisses.

"My hotel's right around here," Peter told me as we stood shakily on Carrollton Avenue. A goodwill store named Thrift City was to our right, industrial buildings and a large looping highway to the left.

"You're kidding," I said.

"I'm staying at the Bayou Plaza," he admitted rather proudly. Beneath the highway was a network of buildings painted a wan, sickly beige. The hotel must have been something in its day, but now the term *fleabag* came to mind.

"I'm staying in the Quarter," I told Peter.

"Why doesn't that surprise me?" He grinned and took me by the arm. "You'll love it."

The pool in the Bayou Plaza's courtyard was unfilled and moldy. The elevator, with its worn carpet, had a distinctly musty smell. Someone had left a crawfish on the emergency call box. Peter laughed and stuck a cigarette butt in its mouth.

Inside Peter's room, both double beds had a distinctly fucked-out look, unmitigated by the chenille bedspreads. As soon as the door slammed shut, Peter pinned me to the faded wallpaper. My mind was pleasantly fuzzy from the Abett's. Peter rubbed against me as his tongue sought to unravel me. My breath came quickly and my clit throbbed without even being touched.

Holding my wrists to the wall, Peter slid my jumper down past my shoulders. My nipples were straining against the lace cups of my bra, itching against the scratchiness. Peter drew them into his mouth one by one, urging them alive. He ground his face from tit to tit, biting softly on my nipples, then yanking them away from the globes with his teeth. He opened my thighs and maneuvered one knee between them. Breathlessly, I rode it.

He pulled away from me and fell to his knees. I noticed that my pussy had left a dark wet spot on the leg of his wrinkled khaki pants—it made me feel that much more decadent. As he unfastened the buttons on my jumper, it fell to the carpet like a discarded flower. Then Peter tore the panties from my hips. Suddenly exposed to the air, my cunt felt both hot and cold at the same time. It was soon covered by his mouth.

Peter parted my pussy with his lips so that my clit stood out proudly, defiantly. He sucked it hard, looking up at me with those wicked candy-coated eyes. I was swooning with the mere thought that I had a big, strong, handsome man I barely knew on his knees in front of me, licking my cunt as though his life depended on it. That alone was enough to send me plunging over the edge, but I held it in. When I could take no more, I pushed him onto his back on the tacky carpet.

My pussy tasted sweet on Peter's kisses. I lapped away the juices, simultaneously unzipping his pants. Tucked into his BVDs was the most perfectly formed cock I'd ever seen. Smooth, slick, bevel-headed. At the base, a hairy, heavy sac with balls ripe as plums. I buried my nose in his honey-colored pubes, and his hips bucked uncontrollably as I slid my mouth up and down along the shaft. I swirled my tongue around the head, flicking the dew of pre-come from the tip. Then I took his balls into my mouth and pursed my lips around them. Every time I felt his body surging, I stopped. When this became too much for him, Peter scooped me into his arms and eased me onto the garish bedspread. It felt rough against my skin. We tore off what remained of our clothing and I lay on my back, legs spread, cunt lips slick with anticipation.

Wordlessly he turned me onto my hands and knees. The fine hairs along my spine sparked with electricity. His balls slapped into my clit with each thrust. I felt myself growing softer, warmer, closer with each movement. Peter kissed my shoulders, my neck, a potent mixture of tongue, teeth and lips.

"I want to fuck you on the balcony," he slurred.

I was shocked. "In public?"

"It's three in the morning. Everyone else is asleep."

"This is New Orleans," I told him. "No one ever sleeps."

Still, the thought of being taken out in the open like that intrigued me. When we reached the sliding glass doors, I noticed that they faced Tulane Avenue, shadowing the Ponchartrain Expressway. Cars and trucks buzzed by in the night.

"Any problem with this?" Peter checked as he bent me over the eighth-story balcony railing.

I smiled over my shoulder. "No problem at all." Rain splashed from the inky sky. The breeze was cool. As Peter rocked from hip to hip, swirling into my pussy, goose bumps covered my flesh. My hungry body clung to every inch of his cock. Lightning flashed in the sky, followed by a distant explosion of thunder.

"Scared?" Peter asked.

"Just cold," I said.

Peter grabbed a handful of my hair. He tugged it so hard that my eyes rolled back in my head. "I think you're lying," he snarled softly into my ear. "I think you're terrified. I can feel it in your body. I can feel it in your cunt."

It was true—I was terrified. I was being fucked on a balcony eighty feet above civilization. The streets below were desolate. If I screamed, no one would hear me. If Peter suddenly decided to slip his fingers around my neck and choke the life out of me, no one would see. He could kill me and easily get away with it. I barely knew this man, didn't even know his real name. He could be a pervert, an ax murderer, a serial killer. This episode could be a pattern for him, his "thing." He could do this with countless other women. I could just be one in a faceless string of others.

Fear crept over my body like a deep chill. I could taste it, like cold, flat metal at the back of my throat, like a gun being held there. Fear oozed down the inside of my thighs.

Fear aroused me: the unanswered questions, the shreds of doubt, the pinpricks of danger. Just the thought that something terrible might happen. It probably wouldn't, but . . . My breath came in ragged chokes. I was helpless. I wasn't responsible for my actions. If we got caught . . .

"Your heart's beating as fast as a sparrow's," Peter whispered, his hand cupped over my breast.

"That's because I'm scared," I moaned weakly.

When Peter bit the back of my neck, I could feel him smiling. "Scared of what? That I'll hurt you? That someone will see?"

"Everything," I said.

"Do you want me to stop?" he asked.

"No," I told him. "I like it."

I grasped the railing with both hands as Peter held onto my ass cheeks and pumped. Mist dampened my face. Thunder boomed, closer this time. Peter wedged his dick deep in my cunt, as far as it could go. One hand pinched my nipples, while the other massaged my swollen clit. Lightning flashed and I started to spasm. Just as I began coming, Peter lifted my feet off the balcony's cement floor. He bent me forward, tipping me further into the abyss. I felt as though I were swirling, falling, floating. "Please don't let go," I begged.

"Of course not. At least," he said wickedly, "not until after *I* come." He, too, was caught up in the moment. "Imagine how you'd look, this bare, broken little body in the alley of this decrepit place," he murmured. "They'd never even know it was me. Could be anyone, anyone."

The railing carved into my stomach. I bowed my head and began to climax strongly, battered by sensations, sounds and emotions. Again, Peter grasped a handful of my hair. Now he was holding me by a mere clump, with just one arm loosely wrapped around my waist. I could fall. I could die.

"Lift your head, Beth," Peter cooed. "I want them to see you. I want them to see me fucking you. I want them to see you come." My legs trembled in midair as my pussy shuddered. I screamed my orgasm into the night. Seconds later, I felt the knob of Peter's cock swelling inside me, spewing ribbons of white froth.

We stood there silent, motionless, for a few moments. Lightning flashed and broke the magic. "I can't believe you made me . . ." I gasped.

"Made you? I thought you wanted to," Peter said.

"Well, I did, but . . ."

We ran inside, giggling to relieve the intensity, dripping with each other's juices. My skin was splotched red from the cold. Stumbling into the bathroom, we turned the jets in the tub until the water gushed steamy hot. We jumped into the shower, rubbing warmth into each other's flesh. It was odd; we didn't speak, really, just smiled and scrubbed. I felt embarrassed, dissected, exposed, vulnerable, extremely naked. In a perverse way, I liked it. Liked being manipulated. Being out of control. It was strangely liberating. But what was Peter thinking? That I was a whore? Was I like all the others, or was I special? Would I ever see him again?

Peter turned off the shower and jostled me out of my mounting hysteria. When we stepped out onto the cold tiles, he grabbed a towel, got down on his knees and dried my legs, my feet. He worked his way up to my spattered ass. Then he looked into my eyes. "Hi," he said.

"Hi," I responded.

"My name is Danny," he smiled.

"And I'm Melissa," I told him.

"Melissa," he repeated. "What a beautiful name."

Felice Newman

❦

Box
A meditation on virtual sex and lesbian cock

My jeans are worn white where my cock fills out the old denim. I've taken off my shoes, my shirt. I don't have the body I wish I had, but I have both more muscle and more flesh than you.

You are naked, stretched out on my white sheets exactly as you described yourself to me: tall and too thin, with lots of dark curly hair falling in your face, and hips that poke out from your body like wings on a starved bird.

I unbuckle my belt and pop the top button of my jeans. I put the head of my cock near your sex, but I do not enter you. This is not what you expect. I am a control freak—just like him—but with a difference: I've got your pleasure in mind. When I don't bang away at your cunt, you don't know whether to be grateful or worried. I laugh.

You are so wet that you slide onto my cock, and I ease inside you just enough so that the muscles ringing the opening of your vagina contract around me. You don't understand how this cock can seem to belong to my body. Your wetness sucks me in, and I whisper in and out of you so softly that I might as well be lips nibbling your flesh, but I'm not.

This you *really* don't understand.

When you want me to fuck you harder, you rock your hips against mine, wrap your legs around my thighs, and tighten your grip.

BOX 19

I know this because you tell me, "I'm holding on so hard that I'm leaving white marks on your upper arms and shoulders." And then you ask me to fuck you harder.

My fiber-optic cock is not what Nicholson Baker had in mind when he normalized phone sex for the HIV-panicked superstore patrons of middle America.

Lesbian cock *is* virtual reality. It is the woman so pleasured who assigns meaning to the act. That thing is real only if she thinks it is.

By phone, that *thing* achieves virtual virtual status.

How much of this affair was about phone sex—and how much about sex with a straight girl; in this case, a *married* straight girl with two children and a big, useless hump of a husband?

I am fascinated by the fascination of straight women for lesbians. I love flirting with them in odd public places, like movie theater restrooms. "Wasn't that a great movie?" I say, rinsing my hands after pissing for at least three minutes upon exiting *Sirens*. These beautiful, anonymous women respond to me in a way I find weirdly delightful. Not sexually, not quite sisterly, certainly not as man and woman, but nothing like the way they respond to each other. Straight women read my difference on such an unconscious level they are unaware they are blushing—or even that they have been flattered.

My latest straight-girl fantasy concerns a woman I happened to pass on a stairway at the gym. It was my first day at my new gym, The Temple of the Body. She was going down and I was going up. I glanced from her face to the surprise of her magnificently developed shoulders and biceps, and she grinned. My friends made much of it and even half-convinced me to question my original assessment of her non-queerness. Since then, I have worn out my own rewind, fast forward, and pause buttons on that moment on the stairs.

And just tonight I found myself salivating over a young woman with pouty red lips. The lovely length of her was squeezed into a tight white knit dress, complete with cleavage and slit up the side. Oh, how I wanted to cover the soft mound of her belly with my warm hand!

But I'm getting ahead of myself. It was a year ago this month, while perusing sound bytes of sex on the telephone, that I stumbled across a woman who said she was looking for conversation with another woman. I liked her voice, which I can hear even now. Dry, a little throaty, soft. No giggles, no silly dime store porn, no *Penthouse Forum* or Hollywood pseudomasochism. Not even *Desert Hearts*.

She quietly stated her business, not affecting a desire for more than she really wanted, which she was willing to state clearly, seeming unaware that most people find it necessary to dress up their desires a bit.

I jumped at the chance to leave all pretense at the cineplex and get down to it with this ostensibly straight woman who had chosen this moment in late winter to own her desire for another woman.

So I had a brief phone sex affair with a woman who was married to a man who raped her when he came home late at night, after closing the gas station where he worked and the bar where he drank. How a sex ad in the local arts and culture weekly was supposed to ameliorate this situation I never got, except maybe that to this woman any small change in routine looked like salvation. When I asked her why she placed an ad in the girl section of the personals, she chalked it up to the lesbian affair she'd had in college years before, an event she reported as being as inevitable as SATs.

Later, she told me she was looking for an all-girl remake of her previous phone sex experience, her only other such experience, she hastened to assure me, a heavy breathing session with her husband's best friend, who answered the only other ad she swore she ever had placed. He said B-movie macho things about big cocks and never recognized her voice.

Lesbian phone sex, she thought, would be just like that.

It's late and cold in my bedroom, a deep blue room with French windows that face a street lamp on the block behind my house. Distant railroad tracks rumble as a train passes. In the front of the house there is a steady stream of traffic until about midnight and then an odd quiet.

"I can usually talk after ten when my kids go to sleep," she says. "He never gets home until late, at least twelve-thirty, sometimes

BOX   21

later. Sometimes he comes home wanting sex. I figure I might as well. He could really hurt me. It's easier this way."

I'm sleepy, only half-listening to her talk of children, husband, children. "It's easier this way," I hear her say, and then my brain works backwards: "He could really hurt me." The blue of my bedroom walls darkens as something passes between my house and the street lamp. For a second I think the shadow is me sitting up in bed.

"He's raping you," I say.

"Well, no. Not really."

I push the comforter from my shoulders and stare down at breasts, abdomen, thighs. My palm rests on my belly, a not-so-small fleshy mound cradling a hard muscle underneath.

You are naked, stretched out on your suburban white sheets. "He never gets home until late, at least twelve-thirty, sometimes later," you say. I picture your small nipples, your long neck, your flat stomach, the little patch of tight black curls between your legs, the bony feet hanging off the end of the bed. I doubt he ever really touches you, and even if he does, you never get his attention.

I draw a nipple into my mouth and suck gently as you speak. "He never gets home until late, at least twelve-thirty, sometimes later. Sometimes he comes home wanting sex."

Nothing he does to you can be called *sex*. This is sex, I say, and I give you my teeth. I hear you suck air, and I bite down harder. This is sex, I say, and I wet my fingers with you.

You laugh. "I figure I might as well."

I close my eyes: now I have you stretched out on my white sheets, your slender wrists pinned under my weight. I'm straddling you, thigh upon thigh, my belt buckle working a dent in your soft white belly. You buck, try to throw me off, and I do slip, only to land knee to cunt, pinning you more resolutely to the bed. You push. I push back. I push back again and again, and you heat up in spite of yourself.

You don't understand how you can be so wet for me. I unbuckle my belt and pop the top button of my jeans. This is not what you expect: I put the head of my cock near your sex, but I do not enter you. I am a control freak—just like him—but with a difference: I don't believe you owe me this sex, which I will now take from you.

I do require a level of response your husband can't be bothered with. When I don't bang away at your cunt, you don't know whether to be grateful or worried. I laugh.

You don't understand how you can be so wet for me, how I can slide into you so easily. When I want to fuck you harder, I rock my hips against yours, entwine my feet with your legs, and tighten my grip. I've got the base of my cock pressing into me, my clit is hard as a rock, and I'm going to fuck you until I come, and you will drown me. This you *really* don't understand.

I know this because you tell me: You don't want this sex. You don't want to hear this wet sucking sound you make. You don't want to feel the muscles deep inside you lock onto my cock. You don't want anything like this at all.

Am I trying to make this "real," or am I trying to make it hot? How much of this story would anyone believe? Did her husband "really" rape her? Did I? Was she "really" married? Did we "really" fuck? Is it "real" if we made it up together? Is it a lie if I make it up now, all by myself?

I think of boy porn: *His cock straining, yearning to be free of his jeans . . .* My cock is an uncomfortable absurdity in my pants. Who taught me to do this? I am straddling my own erection, driving to the bookstore to meet you.

Is anyone born knowing how to have sex? Not me. That's what I'd been thinking as I turned onto the bridge on the way to the bookstore. Such a beautiful early spring day, a drama of clouds, light and dark, moving quickly downriver. How did I know how to strap it on, what to say, how to feel? Where did I learn to move behind this cock?

We meet by the queer porn rack. Two men flip through hunky magazines. They lean back on their heels so that their hips angle forward, accentuating those little bulges in their carefully worn jeans. The room smells like testosterone, leather and new books.

I walk up to the boy porn rack and select a magazine with a brutally stupid name, like *First Hand*. I am wearing this winter's outfit: black boots, jeans, jacket, red hair.

I spot you at the girl porn rack. You are wearing a doe-brown

BOX   23

leather coat with fringes on the arms. You pick up *On Our Backs* and then *Bad Attitude*, pretending to read rather than look at the magazines.

Now I am having trouble remembering this part. I stand next to you, your hips several inches higher than mine. I touch your elbow, my fingers make sparks fly off the soft leather, and you turn to me. Or, I approach you from behind and touch your neck—you get a rush from my chilly fingers—before showing you my face. Which way did it happen? In any case we don't kiss, or talk.

We left the bookstore and beat a path back to my house, where we burrowed into each other in my room, the deep blue room, the French windows, the street lamp, a scene set. My hand curled inside you, the afternoon getting lost as late-winter shadows darkened the room. We had sex standing up by the porn rack, no one came, or we both came very quietly, quickly. Finished, we wiped fingers on jeans, zipped up and said good-bye. We never got to the bookstore at all. We exchanged letters. No letters, but a last phone call. Or not even a phone call. Nothing. You died. I can't imagine how you would have survived. Really, the weekly newspaper is no shelter, the personal ads no savior. What could you have been thinking?

What could I have been thinking?

It's late. I close my eyes and slip two fingers inside myself, which satisfies nothing but certainly heats me up. Here I am in my bedroom, a deep blue room with French windows that face a street lamp behind my house. Railroad tracks several blocks away rumble as a train passes. In the front of the house, there is a steady stream of traffic until about midnight and then an odd quiet. I let the pillow gently cradle the phone receiver against my ear.

"I can't stay on long, somebody's waiting for the phone—"

You tell me you left your useless husband, then moved to Ohio where you hooked up with a lesbian who beat you until you wanted to kill yourself. You call to tell me this and more—how you landed in a psych ward in Tennessee, lost custody of your kids, hit the road with nothing but your stash.

This isn't what I had in mind. I dig my ear deeper into the pillow.

"Then there's my girlfriend in Ohio. She used to come in drunk from work."

I am watching deep blue shadows moving along the ceiling. Somewhere a truck slowly passes by. Then the room is still, empty of sound—except for the wet suction of my fingers pulling in and out of my cunt.

"She gave it to me real bad. They had some mean ladies down in Tennessee. But nobody busted my shit like that girl in Ohio."

I stop breathing for a moment, hold my fingers deep inside.

"Guess she wanted some, like my man. Like you—"

I laugh, turn over onto my back, open up now for my hand. Sing a low moan into the receiver.

"Guess you want some now."

I close my eyes: now I have you on your knees, your ass spread wide. My belt flies through the loops of my jeans. The next beating you get is from me, I tell you, and I can hear your breathing change, know you are waiting for me to hit you, waiting for me to fuck you.

You are naked at the foot of my bed, your knees stretched open, your fists curled around pieces of my white sheets. My belt is an acrobat.

"It's easier this way," you say.

Your thighs are stretched wide, I have fistfuls of your dark curly hair gathered up like horse's reins, and my belt is performing somersaults on its way to meet your skinny ass.

"Do you think I'm crazy?" you say.

I smell your sex. My belt drives a path across your ass cheeks and, hungry girl, you rear back to meet me and open even wider to catch my belt between your damp thighs. The street lamp catches your moisture, the train passes, your skin is so soft, bone so close to the surface. I raise a welt from one blow even as I deliver the next.

Now I want you. I pop the top buttons of my jeans, loop the belt around your shoulders like a harness, and pull tight as I sink my cock between your cheeks, sliding into your cunt which is so wet I fall into you.

BOX   25

I fuck you for every night your husband has left you alone, and I fuck you for every night he hasn't. And when I want to fuck you harder, I rock my hips against your ass, entwine my feet with your legs, and tighten my grip on the belt around your shoulders. I've got the base of my cock pressing into me, my clit is hard as a rock, and I fuck you mercifully, crazily, selfishly, until I come, losing my grip on the reins, until you come—finally, rising up, you grind your ass against me, fistfuls of my sheets in your hands. I sink my teeth into your neck to hold on, and whimpering, finally, you come.

Cecilia Tan

❦

Dragon Cat Flower

The only people who believe in totem animals are those who know their own. Totem animals. A few years ago I wouldn't have believed in them. My Caucasian side would have explained them as genetic memory or some other pseudo-science, and my Chinese side would have taken on faith that we embody inner animal spirits. Either way, it sounds mystical and distant. But really, they're very close—just under the skin. So close you can stumble upon them like a predator in the night.

Like that first time with Jeff. One night we were in bed, making love. We usually made love on Thursdays because he didn't have to teach until the afternoon on Fridays and my weekly department meetings were over with by Thursday. I'd been thinking we'd have a kind of quick one, though, so we could get some rest—boy, was I wrong. I was holding his back against my chest and nuzzling his neck when I had the urge to sink my teeth into his shoulder— and I did. But instead of the usual "ow!" he snarled and arched back against me, a black panther growling and trying to twist out from under me. We wrestled then, a passionate struggle that heated us up like two sticks rubbing together, until he ended up on top of my back, clinging with the claws of his hands and biting me on the back of the neck as his cock nudged at my pubic fur begging entrance. I lay still and let him enter me—he edged his way in while his shoulders and jaw and hands froze rigid like stone. Only his hips moved the first few thrusts. Then I clenched my muscles tight and he mewed, his cock taking control now and moving faster, his hands flying loose and his head thrown back. *Is this what it's like for she-panthers?* I thought as the rhythm built up inside me.

Our lovemaking had been energetic before, but this was an animal passion beyond the neatness of human words like *love* or *sex*. In fact, I stopped intellectualizing after that and melted into the flow of fucking and rhythm and found myself growling and yowling with him as the pressure of his weight on me ground my pubis into the futon and brought me to a shuddering climax, and then another as he doubled his speed and came, too.

Afterward, it took him a few minutes to regain speech, to return to the reality of his graduate student apartment in Evanston, Illinois. He looked around his bedroom as if it were a strange environment, when really it was about the most normal place you can imagine, secondhand furniture, piles of books alternating with piles of laundry. He shook himself and said, "Wow. That was intense."

"You okay?" I rested my head on my arm and stroked his shoulder.

"It was like I went deep into the panther mind, and I saw and smelled and felt everything differently. I could feel the fur and the claws."

So could I, almost. I'd done my master's thesis on mammalian sexual behaviors and knew more about cat sex than anyone should. Having sex like wild animals could certainly be a nice change of pace once in a while, I thought.

"It was fun," I said, thinking it sounded encouraging.

Jeff gave me that little annoying frown of his and said, "It wasn't fun, it was *transcendent*."

We didn't last long after that. He became absorbed by his search to find out more about his panther "self," reading books on shamanism and mysticism, and he kept pushing me to "discover" my own cat.

"My panther wants a mate," he'd whisper through a growl while we fucked, and I did feel rather feline sometimes, but also almost birdlike, like a flying creature brought down by the hunting cat.

Other times I felt so powerful that I could twist him onto his back. All these random things, wings, claws, teeth, a snakelike tail . . . it was fun, but not *transcendent*. I decided he was sex-obsessed and stopped seeing him. Maybe, I thought, I should just look for someone I can have a normal, intellectual conversation with. When an offer from a behavior studies lab in San Francisco came, I took it as a good opportunity to move on. I'd be working with the old standby, white rats. My parents (one an orthopedist and one a general surgeon) were thrilled. I put all the baloney about totem animals in the back of my mind.

I was lonely at first, I'll admit, but I kept to myself until I settled into my routine at the lab. I could manage being alone, I thought. But I would find myself walking down a busy street in the evening, Chinatown, the Haight, wherever, prowling, hunting, hoping to make a catch. I'd go home when I realized it, thinking to myself, who's sex-obsessed now? I missed the intimacy and contact of warm skin. But much as I hoped things would change, I didn't expect it when they did.

I'd spent the weekend moping around the apartment, ordering takeout and not even venturing into the hallway. Sometime Sunday evening, I mustered up the energy to check my mailbox. As I shut my door behind me, I heard the clicking of the locks in the apartment next to mine. Out came a sheaf of jet-black hair, long and straight and slightly damp, and then the head that swung it as a booted foot shooed a cat back into the apartment, and a leather-jacketed, jean-clad body slipped into the hallway, pulling the door shut.

Must be the next-door neighbor, I thought. I'd heard the low hum of music from his apartment, but this was the first time I'd seen him. The jacket was emblazoned with some kind of animal, and I absently wondered if he was part of some rock band or Chinatown gang, or both, or if there even were such things. He was slipping his key into the lock as I went past him to the stairs. Then I heard him curse softly and open the door again. A furry something ran under my uplifted foot and down the stairs. His cat. I ran after the little beast hoping no one would come into the vestibule just then and caught up to him by the mailboxes. My black-booted neighbor came tromping down after. I picked up the cat, a smoke-gray beast who looked like every inch of him had been dipped in ash, but no, he was just that color.

I turned towards my neighbor. "I think this is yours?"

Now I got a look into my neighbor's face, broad and brown, with dark eyes so much like mine, the dark flat lashes of an Asian face. "Thanks," he said as he transferred the cat into the crook of his leather-covered arm. The cat clawed at his sleeve, but he didn't act like he noticed. "I'm Jon."

"Marilee." We were both staring at one another. He was the most attractive man I'd seen since I'd moved out here. And to think he lived right next door.

"Nice to meet you."

"Yeah." We stood there a moment longer, while my pulse rate climbed. Then he hefted the cat and smiled. "Well, gotta put the kid to bed before I can go out." And he turned back up the stairs.

I got my mail and passed him locking his door again as I went back to my place. "See you around," he said as I shut the door.

I read a book for an hour and watched the news before I got into bed with nothing better to do than sleep. I was thinking maybe I'd get up a little earlier, get in to work sooner, but as I lay there I knew I wasn't going to sleep right away. I replayed the exchange by the mailboxes in my mind. Did I imagine that he had a slightly sweet smell? Not the alcohol tang of cologne, but something else. If not for the cat I would have shaken his hand, smooth and brown, but instead I only felt the slightest touch as we handed the cat off, a mere brush that nonetheless felt alive with energy. I wanted to touch his face, and I wanted to feel that black waterfall of hair going down his back.

Sigh. I held my pillow to my chest and my eyes tight and imagined. He was probably hairless or nearly hairless all over, skin smooth and delicious . . . and yet the image that kept popping into my mind was of those catlike eyes. He was sleek, and intelligent, and slightly hungry. I hugged the pillow until my arms started to go to sleep and then I rolled over on my back and the rest of me went to sleep for the night.

In the morning I was still thinking about him, like I'd had a dream that I couldn't quite remember. It seemed to me now that when we had met, his eyes had a slight dark glow, like an old ember. And the sweet smell. Almost like smoke, I thought. I'd never made love to another person of Asian descent before. I'd grown up thinking that my father was just about the only Chinese man in the States, as he was certainly the only one I ever saw much of until I went to college, where I dated bland white middle-class boys like Jeff. It had never occurred to me to think about the ethnic blood of my lovers, it didn't seem important. But right now everything about Jon seemed important to me, every last detail. How his fingernails were slightly overgrown, how his lips looked dark. I preoccupied myself with thoughts of him until I left work early.

He knocked on my door that evening. As I stood in the doorway looking at him, still in the same jeans and boots, a tank top, his jacket gone, I decided the interest-attraction-chemistry that I'd thought I felt last night wasn't just wishful thinking on my part.

He stood there, wordless and calm.

I went with him to his place, where our courtship maneuvers commenced. We learned enough about one another to be polite, and then he put me in his bed to demonstrate some Chinese massage techniques he had mentioned.

He lit incense and candles while I took off my clothes, and then began the massage. His hands seemed cool at first, reminding me of a doctor checking for fever, and maybe I could say I was a bit feverish, melting into his touch. He was saying things but I wasn't really listening, about how ancient Chinese medicine was based solely on touching the outside of the body to fix what was wrong inside. My father was a doctor, and Chinese, I told him, but I didn't think he ever did anything like this.

His laugh was musical and quiet. "What about your mother?"

"American," I answered, and sighed as his fingers reached the knotted muscles in my lower back. I breathed deeply as I sank into the softness of his featherbed and felt the warmth of his breath on my neck. This kind of closeness was what I had missed.

Nimble fingers played over my sides, enticing me to turn over so he could search my stomach and throat and thighs for soft places. And then the kisses began, under my chin, on my forehead, my eyelids, my lips. As he broke away, I looked up into his eyes.

They seemed to glow as the candles flickered around us and
turned his skin gold. I drew in another deep breath of sweet incense and felt myself buoyed up like a cloud of warm air, as if the
futon had become a cloud rising in a golden sunset sky; my hands
fluttered up like birds to dart into his hair and encircle his neck as
I drew myself up to him or him down to me—there was no gravity
in that floating state, no up or down—and we rolled one over the
other. As he wound around me and I around him I breathed
smoke and we spiraled higher. My conscience nagged me once,
"What's happening?" but I was eager to hear his reassurances as
he hushed me with a golden finger, drawing stripes around my
eyes and across my cheeks and telling me not to worry, to relax. I
started tasting him, and my tongue stretched impossibly long as I
searched out his secret places, and he mine.

The first growl came as one of his legs fitted between mine, our
circling of each other drawing in to a tighter and tighter spiral,
and I sank my claws into his back. The motion of his leg pressed
up against my desire. I had a flash of it then, an image I had seen
somewhere before lighting up the inside of my eyelids like a slide,
a sinuous twisting body rising up like a skirl of smoke . . . the
dragon emblem on the back of his leather jacket. Now I saw
it clearly. What had looked like a shadow when I'd hurriedly
glanced at it the night before I now saw was a second dragon, entwined with the first.

One of his fingers slipped into the hollow between his thigh
and mine and over the edge of the wet cleft of my mons. He
nipped at my chin. I pulled on his generous hair and his back
arched away from me and his dark nipples stared at me like icons
from a Taoist temple. I used my extra-long tongue to trace up the
center ridge of his breastbone, up his chin, and again found myself
looking into those eyes, saw myself reflected there and felt the
spinning begin anew. He closed his eyes and kissed me, and I
closed my eyes too as his other leg insinuated itself between mine
and I fell into the tumble and spinning again. I hooked my legs
around him and drew him into me as the spiral grew as tight as it
could, and we were bonded into one animal.

With him inside me now, I thrashed freely, my long spine curving and twisting as we continued through a heavenly sky. Now the

vision expanded, to the black and gold body entwined with mine, to the feeling of the wind lifting us up as we mated, to the sound of our two wordless voices mixing, to the sensation that we were two alike beings, long and curving like wisps of smoke, flying upon the air, dragons. My awareness opened like a bud blooming as he moved in me, and the room fell away to nothing, and the city below was like one giant temple festival, with incense burning and small human voices chanting. And still we rolled on through the sky, trailing thunderclouds, as I rode him and he me, the feeling of his flesh where it went in and out of mine like the point of perfect balance, like the vortex around which the whole universe rotated.

I flexed my claws and held even tighter to him then, feeling my power. When I'd played at being a cat with Jeff I'd been nosing around the edges of a primal energy, tied to the balance of nature by its raw animalism. But now I felt the surge of ancient power, of something so simple that it was science and magic and religion all at once to my ancestors, a people I had never known. They did not divide up the world the same way as the Europeans or the Native Americans, and they assigned the supreme powers of all animals—the flight of birds, the predatory strength of the tiger, the grace of the snake, and a wisdom beyond man—to one creature who was never captured, never seen for more than a glimpse beyond a distant storm cloud.

This is as it should be, came his voice rolling out of the sound of distant thunder, as he breathed sweet smoke from his nostrils into mine and we rocked together like tides cycling on the shore. Like my tongue, his penis seemed to elongate as he stretched away from me and then swooped in a long slow motion, never seeming to come fully out of me, as though separation were not possible now. And again he pulled away and I pulled him in, inch by inch, over and over in a rhythm as slow as the turning of the world, the cycle of ancient seasons.

My orgasm built in intensity, radiating from the point of balance between us, rippling through me, along my skin, through my mind. I could see the clouds but feel the tangled sheets under us, feel my wings stretching into the sky but also the clenching of his buttocks under my spread fingers as I drove him deeper and I pushed myself into the heart of my coming. The vortex seemed to spin faster and I clung to him, my loins on fire and the flickering of starlight and candles in my eyes, the taste of his sweet smoke on his lips as I shuddered and shook and felt myself begin the long fall from the peak of pleasure. I opened my eyes.

He cradled me tight against him with one arm as he propped himself up with the other and breathed another puff of sweet smoke into my nostrils. We rolled to the side, and his finger again found its way between us to the balance point, to begin the rise again. My second orgasm was quick in coming, and I closed my eyes again and pressed my cheek to his chest. With every throb of my clit it seemed we swooped past another cloud. For one moment my brain remembered that I was supposed to be at the lab in the morning, and surely two orgasms was enough? I roared as my body soared on another wave of pleasure.

My plain white rats could wait. I had discovered a whole new animal inside myself. I clamped my mouth to his, ground my hips hard against him, and the pleasure went on.

Christine Solano

Walls of Fire

His tiger eyes invaded the thin layers of my silk blouse as easily as a hot iron. I could feel the glow touching my breasts. He smiled. He could see every part of me the way a blind man sees, by instinct. Our heat was melting the thick glass window that separated us, rendering it almost useless.

I swallowed, pretending all this wasn't happening, that we really were just having a conversation about poetry. "So what have you been working on, Jesse?"

He laughed his big, easy laugh, the laugh that meant: *I know you're trying not to lose your cool, and it's okay. Whenever you're ready, baby.*

"Something special," he said.

"Haikus?"

"Hell, no. Sex poetry!" He laughed again, delighted with himself and with the sight of me fidgeting on the hard plastic chair and swallowing my juices. My cunt was throbbing. But I wasn't ready to give in. I was here on a serious mission, not to get sucked into phone sex, San Quentin–style.

"What happened to the series of haikus you mentioned in your last letter?" I asked sternly.

"I'll send them to you to critique, as soon as I can manage, ma'am," he replied with an ironic smile. "But don't you want to hear my sex poem? I spent the whole morning learning it by heart, so I could recite it to you."

My ear started tingling, so hard was the heavy receiver pressed against it. The phone was old, and the noise of the other visitors around us reverberated in the cold, hard room. Glancing at the guards in their booth, I hesitated. They seemed preoccupied with their coffee and gossip. I never knew how much of our conversations were listened to, or even recorded.

Three times now I had come to visit Jesse in San Quentin, which the inmates call "The Belly."

Each time I came bearing the banner of "literary mentor to the rising young star of prison poetry," determined to insist on sober, earnest conversation.

But he had interspersed all his letters with giddy kisses ever since I'd made the mistake of sending him a photo of me in my most romantic summer dress, and on each visit, he succeeded in manipulating and seducing me, until I practically kissed the imprint of his fingers on the heavy glass that separated us. Still, I hoped to eventually convert this madness into some kind of friendship, and this gorgeous, crazy, sex-starved black hellcat into a responsible and respected poet.

"Go ahead," I said. *Make my day,* I thought. *Titillate me, until you've driven both of us bonkers. As long as you keep writing, keep creating, something, anything, powerful, beautiful, sad or lovely, out of this hell you're living in.*

His pink tongue shot out and licked his lips. I imagined it flicking over my clit, and a quick, hot flash shot up my belly. *Breathe,* I told myself, *breathe and relax.*

"I wrote this poem last week, when the weather was so hot, I couldn't sleep." He half-closed his eyes, groaned, spread his legs and scratched his long, lean thighs in an overt act of exhibitionism. I tried not to look, not to imagine.

"All I could think of was making love to you, baby." That smile again.

He's not going to get to me, I swore to myself.

"Then that freaky thunderstorm hit, and the poem came to me

like . . . lightning!" Jesse giggled, pleased with himself as a kitten on a tree. *All right, all right, get on with it, Jesse.*

"Close your eyes," he whispered. I sighed, but obeyed. It wasn't a bad idea, anyway, listening to him with my eyes shut, avoiding his gaze, his noticing the widening of my pupils and seeing it as an open door. His voice was gentle, soft like the steps of a Siamese cat walking down your spine.

"I haven't come up with a title yet," he said. " 'Sexual Healing' would fit nicely, but I don't want to steal from a brother. Here it goes." His voice became serious, articulate, as he changed from prisoner to poet:

> *Last night, I watched the thunderstorm,*
> *Embraced in heavy, sleepless air—*
> *Lightning struck against the sky*
> *Until it split wide open.*
> *Then came the rain, its smell of earth.*
> *I held my face against it.*
>
> *One night, I saw your eyes in mine;*
> *You smiled behind the looking-glass;*
> *Fingerprints showed on my skin*
> *Like medals won in battle.*
> *Remember what we're fighting for.*
> *I'll see you on the far side.*
>
> *Some night, I'll dance your breath away*
> *Within the echoes of your soul*
> *Recognizing what once was*
> *You might just find the secret door.*
> *For what are we, but dreams of gods*
> *In sleepless, heavy nights.*

I let out my breath. "But that's beautiful, Jesse."

"Yeah? You really like it?"

"It's different from everything you've written so far. But it's really good."

"You've been such an inspiration." His golden-green eyes turned liquid. "I love you, Chrissie."

I bit my lip, trying to suppress the tears that filled my eyes.

"I love you too, Jesse."

He had done it again. He knew how to push my buttons. But I couldn't get mad at him—he was just trying to stay alive, stay sane while knowing that "by the will of the people" he might be executed next year—or next month. Jesse had never killed anybody. His biggest mistake had been to be born in the wrong place, the wrong color.

My thoughts and dreams about Jesse became more and more entangled. In the past, I had forbidden myself to fantasize about him, but at night, I would be overcome by dreams that left me hot and very bothered. So I switched tactics, hoping that with a bit of unrestrained fantasizing and masturbating, his shadow would leave me in peace at night. Instead, visions of his tall, muscular body leaped at me from everywhere—while staring at the screen of my word processor, while talking to a black student, or while looking across the bay toward the harsh lights of San Quentin.

San Francisco is a city filled with exotic odors; now they started to haunt me. Everything took on a smell of sex; over a plate of spicy Thai food I would suddenly imagine fresh, male sweat; walking down Clement Street, the scent from all the ethnic restaurants would mingle in my mouth and leave an aftertaste of semen on my tongue; passing by a bakery, the fragrance of fresh bread would remind me of the aroma of my cunt.

At night I lay awake, my eyes too tired to read. Listening to the forlorn sound of the foghorns in the bay, I would think of Jesse in his cold and comfortless cell.

"Jesse," I whispered, "can you hear me? Can you feel me holding you, keeping you warm and tight?" In the dark, I could almost see his eyes glowing just a few inches away from mine. Sometimes, as I drifted into sleep, I could feel the light touch of his hand on my thighs, his lips on the nape of my neck. Then the dreams would come.

He had talked about his dreams so often that mine began to resemble them. "If we can both dream the same dream, we'll be together," he once said. "No one and nothing can separate us in our dreams."

It was certainly true that my dreams had become more and more realistic, to the point where I dreamt orgasms that shook me into wakefulness. One night, I slipped into the dream he had written after I'd sent him a picture of me steering my dad's sailboat. In Jesse's dream, I would be waiting just outside of San Quentin, down by the beach, the *Santana* gently rocking on the smooth bay water behind me. I would see Jesse stepping through the East Gate and walking down towards me, a big smile splitting his face. He would blink into the sun and put on his cool Malcolm X shades. He would wear the clothes I had sent him: tight denim jeans, a white shirt, a black leather jacket. He would be so beautiful.

"You take my breath away," I whispered in my dream. His arms didn't want to let go of me. "I'll never let you go, never, never."

The boat was anchored a hundred yards away from Angel Island. That's as far as I had been able to steer it, before Jesse had taken off the last of my clothes. The initial hug and kiss lasted forever—or a couple of minutes, I don't think either one of us could have said. His hands and lips hadn't left me for a moment, while I tried hard to keep some measure of concentration on guiding the boat. I wanted to get us to the first cove on the east side of the island, the first place where we would lose sight of San Quentin.

At last, I could drop anchor, and seconds later his fierce tongue in my mouth made me spread my legs, and we both tumbled onto the deck. I was burning brightly from all his touches, from all the hot, wet marks that his lips had left on my body. I needed him with an urgency that left no space for niceties. I pinned his arms down as I mounted him and felt his hot, hard cock slide into me. His eyes rolled up in his head.

"Oh God, no, yes, please, Christ!" he gasped, his fingernails clawing into my thighs, his back arching up. My legs, my cunt, grabbed him tight as he screamed and turned me around to pound his cock into me while holding me with one arm against his smooth, sweat-sprinkled chest. I bit into his shoulder and he exploded, howling, shooting hot come into my cunt and flashes of bright light through my brain. The sky above us was blue, but for a moment, it seemed red with our passion.

He buried his head between my breasts. I kissed his neck, felt a warm tear falling on my skin, laughed out loud, felt the sun on my skin like a blessing. The wind caressed our faces, our bodies. We gazed across the water, at the distant San Francisco skyline pointing its fingers at God. And at that moment the dolphins appeared.

I woke up to a gray and misty morning, the mournful foghorns still echoing in the distance, my bed cold and empty. My body ached and my head was heavy with the wine I had drunk last night. For a whole week, my mailbox had been empty, empty of any news from Jesse, any of the white envelopes with the familiar red postmark of the state prison. Who was Saint Quentin, anyway? What did he do to deserve the dubious honor of having this hell named after him? What a fate for a saint—having his name crown the letterhead of the document that one day would tersely name the date of my lover's death.

Whatever crimes Jesse had committed when he was twenty-one years old, his twelve years in the belly of the beast should have been payment enough. Instead, a barbaric nation felt they needed to kill my gentle, thoughtful poet.

When I came home late that night, after a long and exhausting school board meeting, I did find a message from Jesse in my mailbox. Some time ago, I had sent him a box of postcards. They were full of cheerful, bright images, meant to bring a little sunlight into his airless cell. One of them was a photo of a school of dolphins, sailing through the water, some jumping into the brilliant, sunlit air. He sent that one back to me, with another poem.

Dreaming with Chrissie

Light ripples on the water
Announced their leaps a beat before
They jumped with their
Amazing grace
Into the sky—
Fell back into the sea and
Cleared the shadow of our bow.

Their joy was all around us;
Their bodies like a song the wind
Once whistled in its childhood.

And when they left
They left us,
My lover, in a trail of light,
With ripples on the water.

Jesse and I *had* been dreaming the same dream.

Kelly Conway

Mind Fuck

There is nothing unusual in the still morning air. I hear the same brown wren that I hear every dawn, taunting my little spotted cat, making a mess of birdseed shells on my porch. The same annoying voices assault me from my radio alarm clock, a pair of deejays who find themselves far more amusing than I do. There is nothing different about the emptiness of my king-size bed, sheets rumpled, my blue down comforter thrown to the floor in the middle of the night. There is no reasonable explanation for the uncertainty that shrouds my senses as I open my reluctant eyes.

My coffeepot does its magic. I have the timer set so the coffee's ready by the time I stumble into the kitchen to search blindly for my favorite mug: painted with Van Gogh's orange and purple irises.

I'm not much for routine, but my little cat is. I have to sit with her for at least half an hour to fulfill her snuggle requirement before I can go to work. My office is a mess, but this environment suits me fine. My desk looks exactly like I picture the inside of my head—cluttered, filled with little notes that I can't seem to throw away, stacks of notepads containing information that's no longer useful, crumpled paper littering the floor around the trash can, the aborted poems.

I am a writer. At least, I like to think that I am. I still feel like a fraud when the words "I am a writer" come to my mind—the sentence feels good on my tongue—but I only say it aloud when I am alone.

I smooth out the folded paper that I have been coveting in the back pocket of my overalls. "Writers sought," says the notice, "for an anthology of lesbian short fiction."

As a rule, I don't comprehend the writing of short fiction. I am a novelist. Short story writers amaze me—how can they say so much, with so few words? Maybe they have more control over their characters than I do. Mine defy me, laugh at me when I try to end a chapter, and continue on even after I've turned off the computer. I never know what I'm going to wake up to, who they'll have become in the middle of the night. They don't invite me to the plot parties, or even to the wrap.

My computer blips cheerily when I turn it on. I find WordPerfect and open a new file, determined to write a short story. But the voice of the solitaire game that comes with this Windows program is louder than my own. It screams to me whenever I see an empty screen.

After losing several games, I realize that I can't really write unless a muse is present in the room. Joni Mitchell? Too depressing. Indigo Girls? Too intense. Nanci Griffith? Too distracting. Joan Baez? Works for me. I load "Diamonds and Rust" into my CD player, and return to the dreaded blank screen.

Now seems like an appropriate time to change the marquee on my screen saver. The bookshelf holding my dictionary, thesaurus, essentials of English grammar and poetry handbook is looking mighty dusty. And why haven't I alphabetized them by title yet? Anything to distract myself while an idea takes root. It feels something like prolonging an orgasm—you know how some women, when giving face, will stop just at the crucial moment, and then begin again when they sense that you're ready to kill them? It's kind of like that. I feel an idea taking root, building, my hands tremble, I feel light-headed, then choose that moment to do anything else but write.

Ah! Saved by the doorbell. I am certainly not expecting anyone. I am too lonely for friends. My neighbors see me as the resident queer, and avoid me accordingly. This distraction comes at the perfect time. Solitary masochism wears thin quickly. It's much more fun to be annoyed by a stranger.

When I open the door, the woman on the steps is not the expected Jehovah's Witness, is not selling an all-purpose cleaner, is not a kid pandering candy with a song and dance about staying out of gangs. It is a woman who looks exactly like a bit character from the sci-fi/fantasy novel that I'm in the middle of writing. She's barely more than a sketch, but I have a lot of plans for her.

I drink in her leather jacket, the knife sheath attached to her thick black belt, her steel-toed boots, the silver in her short black hair, her black t-shirt, sleeves rolled up to show arms muscled with experience, the gray eyes that know every embarrassment I suffered in elementary school. Although I am a born-again femme, having recovered from the androgyne ideal bestowed on us in the seventies, I'm not usually inclined to swoon. I swoon. She catches me.

"I'm Lee," she whispers, hot breath striking my neck like fangs. "You wrote me. You've been dreaming that I'll show up on your doorstep one day and fuck the taste out of your mouth. I'm here. Deal with it."

"You're not real," I say, backing up. "I did not write you, you wrote yourself. And besides, I'm perfectly happy with my vibrator." You know you're in trouble when you start taunting your hallucinations.

"See if this is real, sweetmeat," she says, pushing me into my living room, kicking the door closed, undoing the clasps of my overalls, and pulling my shirt over my head.

"Ah, that feels pretty real," I say, trying to sound casual. Her kiss loosens my muscles, and I fall against her hard body. Fuck it. Who cares if it's real, old acid kicking in, or a nervous breakdown? She's packing. This is too good to pass up.

I hear the unmistakable click of her knife snapping open. Before I can scream, gasp or swoon, she slices through the back of my panties like they're whipped cream. How rude. These are my favorite panties, red lace with no elastic around the legs. I thought they were easy access but apparently not easy enough for my impatient apparition. Still, I don't care if they're ruined or not, I just want her to get at what's inside them.

There are few sounds as sexy as the unzipping of a pair of tight black jeans. It rips through the silence of my living room and wetness pours down my leg. By now I'm totally aroused—whatever the hell this is, let it last until I come. Lee grabs me by the nape of my neck, pulling the fragile hair just enough to let me know she's serious, but not hard enough to cause real pain. She bends me over the back of my couch, leaving my ass in the air, the slice in my panties exposing my pussy, my feet off the ground. I assume that she's going to fuck me, but no, she's got to taunt me first.

"You want it, don't you?" she hisses.

I do, but I refuse to answer a figment who speaks to me in that tone of voice. I ignore her, thinking about what it will feel like when she fucks me. She yanks me back to my feet, twisting my hair around her hand.

"I said, you want it, don't you?"

Why the hell do butches always ask this question? I should think it was pretty apparent that I wanted it. I nod yes.

She pushes me to my knees, digging her strong fingers into the back of my neck. I am eye-level with her crotch. I must admit, the view is not bad, but I'm not too crazy about this position. It seems a bit submissive for me. This is not the way I wrote her: she's supposed to be gentle. I haven't written any scenes where she's a top—yet.

Lee reaches inside her unzipped jeans, pulls out her cock, and forces my head back. "I want you to suck me. You can do that, can't you?" she asks. I shake my head no. I'm pretty freaked out. I thought blow jobs were a boy/girl thing.

"Okay, then, I'm gonna tell you what I want you to do. Stick out your tongue," she commands. I comply. She lays her dick on my tongue and holds it there. "Move your tongue a little bit, not too much. Just get it wet." I try to do exactly as she says. "Okay, a little more. No. Don't touch it." She pushes my hand away. "Now, don't move. Wet your lips. There, that's it. Stick out your tongue again."

I feel embarrassed, kneeling before this stunning butch apparition, my overalls around my ankles. I'm used to being somewhat suave in sexual situations, but this creation has me tongue-tied—literally.

She lays her dick across my tongue again, her eyes fixed on

mine. A moan escapes me and I am mortified. I am trying so hard to remain cool.

"Okay, baby, get it wet, then take the head in your mouth, just a little bit."

This is the first time I have heard anything even remotely resembling tenderness in her voice. I do as she tells me, surprised at how much I like the way this feels, wanting to please her. I savor the head of her cock, licking in a circular motion. I hear her breathing become more pronounced, so I draw a little more of her into my mouth. She starts rocking a little, sliding in and out, gently. Why does this turn me on so much? What the hell is going on here? I suck harder, moving my head, trying to get her all the way in. She pulls me away, winding my long brown hair around her hand again.

"Not so fast. I told you just a little. Now lick it."

I move my tongue up and down the shaft of this sweet dick of hers. It's hard to be smooth without using my hands, but I lift her cock with my tongue and move my lips around the head again, keeping my tongue stuck out as far as I can. Holding still, not wanting to make any mistakes, I wait for her direction. None comes, so I just sit there. Finally, she pulls my head towards her and thrusts hard against the back of my throat. I almost gag, but hold it back.

"Suck," she demands.

I want to say, "Okay, baby, I'll do anything you want," but I just keep quiet and do as she tells me.

"Take it easy, not so fast," she cries out, moving faster into me. I tighten my lips around her dick and work my tongue. Her movements become more and more erratic, she moans till she yells, and rips herself away from my lips.

This is all too weird—I mean, I'm on my knees in front of someone who isn't even real, and I'm so turned on that I can't stand up. I think about the outline for an erotic novel lying in my desk drawer. While there is no character sketch that resembles Lee, the femme narrator talks a lot about her butch top who loves to get blow jobs. I have no idea where this outline came from, and no recollection of writing it.

"That was great, baby." Lee's voice interrupts my thoughts. "Just how I like it. You did that really good."

I stare into her eyes and watch her soften. There's something incredible about the way a butch looks when she's just come—that slight hint of vulnerability in her eyes, when for a moment the walls are down. Lee reaches for my hand and pulls me to my feet. I wrap my arms around her neck—the first full body contact we've had—and am startled to find that she feels solid, real, not like a hallucination at all. "I wanna fuck you now, baby," she whispers softly. "Will you let me fuck you?"

I'm not ready for her to go gentle on me just yet. "Have *you* ever done that?" I ask, challenging her butch pride. "Have *you* ever had a woman's cock in your mouth?" I know this will piss her off, but it's worth it to see that dangerous look come back to her eyes. There's a part of me that wants her to make love to me the way I wrote it in the sci-fi piece, slowly and sweetly. But there's another part that wants her to shove that dick through the slice in my panties, to fuck me till it hurts.

"What the hell are you saying?" she snaps. "For that I just might not fuck you at all." She pushes me away from her. "Fuck you! Goddamn smartass femme," she mutters, shaking her head. "Get on the bed, on your hands and knees, and pull your panties halfway down. Wait there for me. Think about how you talk to me. I might come in and beat your ass, I might fuck your undeserving little pussy, or I might just leave you hanging."

I debate with myself; do I want to obey this strange character? My hesitation, however brief, makes her madder. She shoves me to my knees again, roughly. "Pull your panties down, right now." I pull them down a little, look up at her and smile.

"More. Don't make me do it for you."

I push my panties down around my hips and wait.

"Now, crawl," she says. "I want to see your ass moving in the direction of the bedroom."

I move slowly, on my hands and knees, till I reach my room. I hear no movement from the other room as I settle on the bed to wait, my ass high in the air. I close my eyes, listening intently for any indication that she is approaching. None comes. I have never been a patient person, hate waiting for anything. As I lie there in the silence it occurs to me that since I wrote her, she should do whatever I want her to do. I try to draw her to me, creating images of her coming through the door, finding me posed as she told me to be, and stroking my ass gently, kissing the back of my neck. "Come on, Lee," I think as loudly as I can. "Come on in here, I'm ready for you."

Nothing happens. I remember the feel of her cock in my mouth. I loved that. I want to feel it again. But nothing happens. I imagine her pushing the tip of her delicious cock into the wet opening of my pussy, picture her eyes closed in pleasure as she fucks me. Still, nothing happens.

After several eternities Lee appears, looming in front of me, a perfect vision of what a butch top should be. She kneels in front of me on the bed, undoing her belt. It must have worked, I think. She came back for another blow job. But she only removes her belt, and doesn't undo her jeans.

I recoil as the leather lands across my ass for the first time. "Do you like that?" she asks.

I am too shocked to answer. I just shake my head no.

"Do you have any more smartass questions for me?" she asks as the belt slams against my cheeks again.

I cry out, confused. She's my character. I should be able to get her to fuck me the way I wrote it. My ass gets warm and starts to tingle. What really boggles my mind the most is that this feels good.

"Ouch," I yell, to see what will happen.

"Be quiet or you'll get worse than this," she hisses, snapping the belt hard against the top of my thighs. She rotates the places where she strikes—just when I think it hurts too much, she moves to another tender, previously unspanked spot. I moan, unable to stop myself. She pulls out her dick and sticks it in my mouth. "I said, keep quiet."

I suck her as each glorious lash brings me closer to the edge. It's starting to hurt, but in a really good way, and I am grateful for the distraction of her dick. It's impossible to remain quiet; I scream as she expertly flicks my rigid clit with the smooth black leather. She comes before I do, with a long deep sigh.

Lee stands and walks around to the end of the bed. "Your ass looks really sweet in that shade of red," she says, laughter in her voice. Her soft hair rubs across my stinging skin as she covers my ass with light kisses. Her strong tongue probes my asshole and I flinch. No one has ever touched me there, and I haven't written about it, either. She steadies me with a gentle hand as she licks my crack up and down, over and over, until I cry out. She smears a thick lubricant, still cold from the tube, all over my anus. I stiffen, terrified that it will hurt if she fucks me there—yet I want it.

She enters me slowly, with just her finger. I want more. Her dick bumps against my clit as she slides her finger in and out of my ass. This is too good. I am dizzy, think I'm gonna pass out, it's so good. She squeezes more lube onto her cock and gently eases the head into the one place I have never been fucked. I collapse, letting my shoulders take all my weight as she fingers my clit, fucking me harder and harder until the air goes black around me, and I come harder than I've ever come before.

The phone rings. The telephone is the bane of any writer's life—it only rings when you're on a roll. Lee reaches over, switches the ringer off and turns the volume down on the answering machine. She pulls the knife out of its sheath and absently cleans her nails, reading what she thinks she has written. I'm watching her from inside the monitor. I enjoy the look of surprise, then concern that crosses her face as she reads. She's so funny, thinking she can write. I do all the writing. She might wear the strap-on, but I'm the femme who runs the computer—been living in here since she bought it, kind of like a genie, I guess. I laugh as she discovers the story of a bottom, written in first person, on her very own computer.

I want her to submit this somewhere, so I'll let her use a pen name. She won't want her friends to think she's switched. I'll make her use my name. We all know the bottom runs the fuck.

Serena Moloch

❦

Casting Couch

The Job Applicant (Trixie)

I'm so nervous about this interview. I really want this job.

Let me go over it all again. Why I want the job: I'm interested in getting into film and video production and I'd like to learn from the ground up, producer's assistant would be perfect. Why they should hire me: I'm organized, responsible, learn fast, and . . . what was the fourth, oh, right, *responsive*, I'm responsible *and* responsive to my employer. Previous experience, two years as personal assistant to an executive director. Why I left that job: tricky, but stick to the standard answer, no more room for growth. I just hope Gillian wrote me a good reference, like she promised. Typing speed, 80 words per minute . . . I certainly did Gillian enough favors, a good letter is the least she could do for me in return. Oh, I'm tapping again, I have to stop that. Should I go fix my hair? No, better stay here. Do I have copies of my résumé? What time is it? Early still. Ten more minutes to go.

The Boss (Jane)

As soon as I saw her file, I knew she'd be perfect. With its royal blue letters leaping off a mauve page, her résumé was eye-catching in a vulgar way that suggested initiative coupled with inexperience.

She was underqualified for the position I'd advertised, and I'd be sure to let her know that, so she'd be even more grateful to be hired and even more eager to please. Furthermore, some suggestive phrases in her former employer's reference interested me. Trixie was "a model assistant who never hesitated to provide any service asked, even if that meant helping in ways that some might construe as more personal than professional." She was also "devoted and solicitous."

Trixie must have worked pretty hard, I thought. I leaned back and imagined using that wonderfully ridiculous name in a variety of situations. Trixie, come in here, I'd say over the intercom. Trixie, sit down and take a letter. This is my assistant, Trixie, I'd tell people. Trixie, get me a drink. Trixie, lie down . . . Trixie, take off your clothes . . . now mine . . . very good, Trixie.

I sighed and let the chair come forward again. Too many years of reading scripts had fostered a bad habit of associating names to types and spinning off into little fantasies. Sure, I saw Trixie as a ripe peach, with big round eyes and nipples to match, traipsing her luscious ass around the office in a tight skirt, eager to please. But Trixie would probably be more concerned with her paycheck than with me. Or she'd be all too interested in her effect on me, if the past week's interviews were any indication.

The applicants had been very good-looking, and perfectly competent for the job, but they were all actresses eager to break into the business, and it was obvious they had only their interests in mind and not mine. I had certainly been offered a variety of services.

I didn't enjoy remembering what had frankly been a tiring and unpleasant series of encounters. Jill had stared at me oddly until she finally got up the courage to make her move, opening her blouse and fondling her very beautiful breasts while maintaining intense eye contact. "Do you like my titties?" she asked, and I said, "Yes, I like them, Jill, but I don't like you. Thanks for coming in today."

Then there was Pamela, a redhead in spandex. She was quicker than Jill. After two questions about her secretarial skills she walked around my desk to stand directly in front of me, then lifted up her skirt and started to play with herself through some very transparent underwear. "I could really show you a good time," she whispered as she probed her pussy through the silk. "Not now, Pamela," I'd said, "and not ever."

Lenore had a more sophisticated appearance but an even less subtle approach; as soon as the door was closed she came up to me, got down on her knees, and started tugging at my pants zipper. "Tell me what you like," she said, and though I enjoyed imagining what her tongue might do to me, I wasn't interested; I quoted *All About Eve* to let her know why: "I'll tell you what I like, Lenore. I like to go after what I want. I don't want it coming after me."

Maybe Trixie would be better behaved.

The Interview (Trixie)

Oh, no, the receptionist is telling me to go in, and I just slipped my shoe off, okay, got it, here I go, now she's calling me back, oh, great, I left my bag on the chair, good work, Trixie, all right, review the four points, learn fast, organized, responsive, and responsible. No, responsible and responsive.

"Oh, what a nice office," I hear myself saying. Stupid, stupid, not a good way to begin.

"Yes, I like it very much," she says. "Have a seat. No, no, on the chair, not the couch. I save that for more informal occasions. Well, Ms. Davis—or can I call you Trixie? Yes? Good. Trixie. Why don't you tell me what you like about the office. Why do you find it nice?"

This is a funny way to start an interview, but she's the boss. "Well, it's very comfortable." She's staring at me. Maybe she's checking out my analytical skills. "The colors are warm and there's a mix of office furniture, like your desk and all those filing cabinets, and then furniture that's more, um, cozy, like the couch and the bar and the mirrors."

She's smiling, that's good. What's she asking now? Oh, okay, normal questions, typing speed, my qualifications, why I want the job, why I left my last job. I think we're getting along well. She's very attractive—forties, sharp suit, pants, very short hair.

"You know you're not really qualified for this position, don't you, Trixie?"

I blush, but remember to hold my ground. "I may not be right now, but I'll work hard and . . ."

"But I'm going to hire you anyway," she interrupts. "Because I can tell that you'll be amenable to training, and that you have the makings of a truly gifted assistant. You had a very special relationship with your previous employer, didn't you? Gillian Jackson?"

Now I'm blushing even more, because the way she mentions Gillian makes me nervous. "We got along very well and I really enjoyed working with her."

"And she enjoyed you. She speaks highly of you and mentions qualities that I've been seeking as well: your ability to help her relax, to devote yourself personally to her needs, never to fuss at unusual requests. If you can provide me with the same attention and if you don't object to some supplementary training now and then, you'll have no problem with this position."

Why do I feel that she's saying more than she's saying?

"Can you start tomorrow morning? Good. Ten o'clock, we're not early birds in this line of business. Any questions?"

"I was just wondering what your specialty is here. The notice just said Top Productions, film and video."

"That's a very good question, Trixie, and in fact we do have a specialized focus, but why don't you and I discuss that in the morning. And, Trixie, please call me Jane."

The Job (Jane)

Trixie's first day turned out to be a busy one: in the morning, a casting call, and in the afternoon, a wrap. With any luck, the day would reveal some significant gaps in Trixie's knowledge and skills that would require the kind of extra training session to which she had so readily assented during the interview. Ah, but I was letting myself get carried away again. I can't help but experience the world in cinematic terms, and from my first view of her, her voluptuous body straining as she frantically tried to put her shoe on, Trixie struck me as a complete ingenue in whom sweet awkwardness and powerful sensuality existed side by side. In another era she'd have been the script girl in glasses who saves the show by shedding her spectacles and becoming a beauty just in time to replace the ailing star. Perhaps she could replace one of my stars today.

Dreams, idle dreams.

She arrived promptly, wearing a red wool suit.

"Trixie," I said sharply. "You mustn't wear red to the office. It's very becoming on you, and I'm sure someone has told you it's a power color, but it's too loud and doesn't give the right impression."

"I'm sorry." She looked hurt and anxious. I tingled.

"Try black or gray or brown. Not blue, though—too corporate. Now, look. You should keep track of these things on a list. You have paper? Write down, 'I will not wear red to the office.' That's right. And that goes for your nail polish, too. Stick to clear. Now, I know we were going to spend the morning getting an interview, but the day is packed and you're going to have to jump right in. This morning we have a casting call. You'll sort the files and run through the audition scene with the actresses. Okay? Tryouts start in fifteen minutes, so go through those folders. The scene is in that binder over there."

I watched Trixie bustle, gathering her materials, somewhat ill at ease because I'd criticized her outfit. I sat behind my desk and scanned budget sheets, looking up occasionally to enjoy her growing discomfiture as she began to understand just what it was we were doing. She looked so sweet when flustered. Perhaps she *was* the assistant of my dreams.

The Job (Trixie)

I was glad to be involved right away in the details of a casting call, but nervous about running through scenes. Oh, well, I thought, the actresses will probably be more nervous than I am. I opened up the first file, Rochelle King, and looked at her head shot— stern, unsmiling. I flipped to the next shot and nearly yelped, because there was Rochelle in a black leather corset and thigh-high boots and nothing else except for studded bracelets all over her arms and a whip in her hand. Her breasts spilled over her corset and her legs were planted wide apart. Was she trying to show off her body to get the job? I wondered if I should warn Jane. I looked up, but she seemed busy.

I went through Rochelle's résumé next. She'd done a lot of movies, but according to her résumé they were all "pornographic feature films, with female casts with an emphasis on bondage and discipline." I wasn't sure that *Taming Lola, Slut Punishment* and *Put It All in My Pussy, Now!* were the proper qualifications for this role. Maybe some of the other actresses had more appropriate experience. I opened the next file, and the next, and the next, and they were all the same, scary women in leather wearing all kinds of whips and chains. Some of them even had their noses pierced. Three of them stood out, though: Rochelle King, Vampi Calda, and a woman called Mike.

Maybe the scene is some kind of comic sidebar, I thought, with a bit part for a dominatrix. I turned to the scene to check it out before the run-through. But when I started to read it, I couldn't believe it. This was no sidebar, and we weren't casting a bit part. And there was no way, no way I was going to be able to run through this scene.

"Trixie? I'm ready to call in the first actress."

The Run-Through (Jane)

"Trixie," I repeated, "let's get the show on the road. What's the matter?"

"Um, Jane," she stumbled, "could I talk to you before we begin?"

"Sorry, we really don't have time. Later. What's in the files? Who looks good to you?"

"I'm not sure, but I pulled these three."

I looked at the files. For an innocent, she had quite an eye for experience. "Very good, Trixie. Two of these actresses are my top choices for the part, and in fact we're beginning with Mike. If she reads well, we'll just hire her."

Trixie looked even more troubled. "Is that okay? What about the other auditions we have scheduled?"

"Trixie," I said sternly, "we don't have time for questions like that. I've been in this business for ages. If I say we can do something, we can do it. Where's that list of yours? Go get it. Write down, 'I will not waste time contradicting Jane.' Great. Terrific. Now tell Mike to come in."

The Run-Through (Trixie)

How was I going to run through this scene?

I trudged to the waiting room and got Mike, who looked tall in a leather trench coat and high boots.

"Mike, hello," said Jane, shaking her hand. "How've you been? Working hard or hardly working?"

"Working hard, Jane, working hard."

"What do you think of our script?"

"It's nice," Mike said. "I like it."

Nice, I thought, about as nice as being caught in a shark tank. I bustled around while they chatted and ignored me.

"Are you ready to run through the scene with Trixie, Mike?"

"Sure," she said, and took off her coat. I'd expected her to be wearing leather, but she had on a white t-shirt and black jeans. Metal chains dangled from her pockets.

"Trixie," Jane said. Something in her voice reduced my resistance. So I'll look like a fool, I thought. At least the pay's good.

I sat down opposite Mike.

"Okay," said Jane. "Let's review the plot up to this point. Mike's character, Big Red, works as a jail warden in a female prison. We've seen her on the job, restraining and disciplining various prisoners, helping the doctor administer exams, humiliating her favorites by making them do their exercises naked and pee in public. In the scene right before this, we watched her break up a gang bang. The problem is, she got all turned on by the woman she was saving and couldn't do anything about it. So now she's getting a drink at her local bar, which moves into a fantasy sequence about the prisoner she rescued. Okay, let's start reading. Trixie, you're the prisoner, obviously, and Mike's the warden. I'll read the bartender's lines."

I crossed my legs and opened my script. My lines were highlighted in yellow.

"Hey, Big Red, what can I get you tonight?" read Jane.

"Double bourbon on the rocks."

"Coming right up."

"Okay," Jane said, "so now we do some business to indicate fantasy mode, and when the fog clears, Big Red sees the luscious piece who only hours ago was being viciously humped by five bad girls. She walks over to her."

"Hey," Mike said, looking straight at me, "I thought I told you to stay in your cell."

"I didn't feel like it," I said, using my finger to hold my place in the script. "I wanted some air."

"Who cares what you feel like?" Mike's voice was as sculpted as her arms. "You do what you're told. You especially do what you're told when I tell it to you."

"What if I don't want to? It's a free country, even in jail."

"Hah! You've been spending too much time in the library. You're in my jail, and you'll do what I say. Or I'll let everyone else do what they want with you, and believe me, it won't be pleasant. You didn't like those women putting their hands all over you, did you?"

"It wasn't so bad," I read stiffly. The directions said I should be pouting, but the way I saw it, they were lucky I was doing this at all. "At least they're prisoners like me, not some nasty pig guard."

Whack! Jane made a smacking noise by clapping her hands together, hard. "Okay, so in the scene, Big Red slaps the prisoner and then we move into the action. Why don't you two play it out in front of the mirror so I can see more of the angles?"

I stayed glued to my chair. "I thought this was a reading."

Jane smiled. "It's a run-through. I have to see how actresses use their bodies. Don't worry, Trixie. Mike knows what she's doing, and you just have to stand there. After all, she's the one who's auditioning, not you. Unless you'd like a part!"

"No!" I said. "Um, Jane, could I talk to you for a minute?"

"I don't like to break the flow of a scene," she said.

"Only a second?" I wheedled.

"Okay," she sighed. "What is it?"

I looked at Mike. She was smiling pleasantly. I wanted to ask her to leave the room but didn't feel I could. "Is there any way, do you think, that I could just read the lines sitting down?"

"Trixie," Jane snapped, "where's that list we were keeping?"

"On your desk," I said nervously.

"Get it."

I did.

"What does it say?"

"I will not wear red . . ."

"No, not that. The next thing."

"I will not waste time contradicting Jane."

"Right. Now underline that. Twice. Now write down, I will not make Jane repeat herself. Okay. Now get up and do the scene, for God's sake."

I felt totally humiliated. Mike held her cool smile. I heard Jane say, behind me, in a kinder tone, "I know you haven't done this before, and that it may be embarrassing. But it's just a scene, and we're all professionals here. Okay?"

"Okay," I said.

So we continued the run-through. There actually wasn't much for me to do; I guess this movie was a star vehicle, and Mike was the star. After she supposedly slapped me, she pulled my arms behind my back and pushed me up against a wall, telling my character what an ungrateful cunt she was. "I think you'd better show me some gratitude," she said. "I don't think I'm going to give you a choice about it." Then Mike got to show off how quickly she could get me gagged and bound in a bunch of devices. Still holding my arms behind me, she snapped cuffs around my wrists, tied my arms together near the elbow with some ropes, gagged me with a scarf and put a chain around my waist that she connected to the cuffs at my wrists.

I kept telling myself we were all professionals while Mike read her lines and ran through simulated sex movements. At least I still had clothes on.

"Who's the pig now?" she asked, while she stood a couple of inches in front of me and pretended to grind her hips into me. She looked really convincing, her body strong, her movements lustful, her voice charged and powerful. I even felt myself getting caught up in the scene, wondering how I looked.

"Are you my little heifer?" she grunted, and kept up her air-grinding. "Are you my little sow?" She whirled me around and pushed my hands onto the sofa. Now I could see myself in the mirror. I looked like a cross between a prisoner and a trussed-up farm animal. A twinge between my legs took me by surprise, but before I could focus on it a stronger sensation took over. Mike had taken some kind of whip out of her bag and was whacking the seat of my pants. It stung like hell.

Luckily Jane intervened. "Whoa, Mike, hey, it's just a rehearsal." Mike stopped. Thank God.

"Sorry, Jane," she said. "Got a little too into the scene."

Sorry, Jane? I thought. I'm the one getting my ass whacked.

"Why don't we just skip ahead to page forty-five," said Jane.

"Where I take the gag off and force her to go down on me?" Mike asked.

"Right," said Jane.

If you'd asked me twenty minutes before whether I'd even read that scene, never mind act it out, I would have said no. But I'd crossed a line. Maybe it happened when I saw myself in the mirror; I was excited now.

"Have you learned your lesson, you little bitch?" Mike barked. "You ready to show a little gratitude?"

"Yes," I read. "Let me show you. I'll do whatever you say."

According to the script, Mike was supposed to bring me to my knees, force me to open her pants with my mouth, lick her clit, and then, as the script put it, "etc." But Mike was doing something different. She was pushing up her t-shirt on one side, exposing a breast, and pushing my mouth towards her nipple. "Go ahead," she said, "show me what you can do. Suck on that."

Something about the authority of her voice and the authority of that brown, pointed nipple made me forget myself. I leaned down and took it into my mouth. I'd barely closed my lips around it when Mike yelled "Hey!" and shoved me halfway across the room.

"What's the deal, Jane?" she yelled, pulling her shirt down.

I was confused.

The Run-Through (Jane)

"I'm sorry," I laughed. "Trixie's new. She just got a little carried away. She didn't know that it's impolite to touch an actress during a run-through. Did you, Trixie?"

Trixie looked mortified and stared at the ground.

"Say you're sorry, Trixie," I said, more sternly.

"I'm sorry," she mumbled, still looking down.

"Not like that. Like you mean it."

"I'm sorry," she said, only a little more clearly. Mike stood with her arms crossed.

"Trixie, you've offended one of my best actresses. I think you're going to have to show how sorry you are a little better than this."

She looked up, flushed. "What do you want to do? Whip me? Throw me on the floor and teach me a thing or two? Or maybe I should kiss her feet?"

"Those are all fine ideas," I said coolly. "You pick."

She was mad now. "Or maybe I should read my little list while Mike holds me down and you spank me, since I've been *such a bad* girl."

Mike spoke up. "Hey, Jane, I'm out of here. I'll call you later about the contract." Out the door she went. Trixie and I were alone.

The Training (Trixie)

I don't know what made me say all those things, but I meant them. I was quiet with Mike gone, silently daring Jane to make it all a joke now that we were alone.

She sat down behind her desk and said, "Well, Trixie, what will it be?"

I remained silent.

"I think we're both agreed that you're in need of some correction. You've made several mistakes this morning and it's best not to defer our discipline and training session too long. Since you don't seem able to decide on what your punishment should be, I will."

I felt nervous, excited, unreal. The boss and I were about to go over.

"Take your list, Trixie, and put it on the desk."

I did.

"Now pull up your skirt and hold it up."

I did. My body blushed, my pussy contracted, and the blood rushed to my clit.

"Look down at the list and read it out loud, over and over again. Don't stop, and don't look up."

I did. I read, "I will not wear red to the office. I will not waste time contradicting Jane. I will not make Jane repeat herself." While I read and held my skirt up, I heard Jane rustle around in her drawer. What was she doing?

She got up and came around behind me. Her arm snaked around me and removed the list. "I think you have it memorized by now, Trixie. Keep reciting, but put your hands on the table and your ass in the air."

I tried to do it right, but she had to push on my pelvis and spread my legs apart to get me in the position she wanted. Then she grabbed my pantyhose and ripped them apart from the waist down. They floated free of my legs and settled around my ankles.

"Keep reciting," Jane said. "Your punishment will only get worse if you stop. But if you absolutely can't take it anymore, start saying, I will not type letters to my friends on the job. Got that?"

"Yes," I said, and hastily resumed, "I will not waste time contradicting Jane. I will not wear red to the office."

Whack! Her hand landed where my butt cheeks met, and my skin heated up. *Whack!* again! She spanked one cheek, then the other, hard. I almost collapsed onto the table, and I lost track of my place in the list.

"What's the matter, Trixie? Did you forget your orders? Maybe this will help you remember."

A barrage of slaps on my ass, even harder than before, vindictive but controlled. My skin felt crisp and burned. I imagined the marks of her fingers on my butt and my pussy got electric. I felt completely out of control even though I knew I could make her stop. I liked the feeling. She was the boss and I was a bad, bad girl.

"I'm going to spank you ten more times, Trixie. Keep count now. If you mess up we'll have to start all over again."

Whack! "One," I gasped.

She made me wait, then dealt me another enormous slap. "Two," I said, wondering if I could make it through eight more. But after teasing me by making me wait a long time for a few more vicious wallops, she dealt the rest of my punishment out rapidly, then undid my skirt and pulled it down around my ankles.

"Turn around, Trixie," she said. I did, but I was too embarrassed to look at her. "That's right, Trixie, don't look up. I'm the boss. I'll look at you." She put her hand under my chin and raised my face. I made sure to keep my eyes averted. "I'm going to undo your blouse now, Trixie. I want to see what you're hiding from me." Her hands were warm, her fingers deft, and as she exposed my breasts, I worried about my pussy. It was getting so wet I thought my juices might drip down my thighs and onto the floor.

Her hands cupped my breasts and her fingers teased my nipples. "Nice," she said, "very nice." Her voice had gotten sweeter, but it still commanded. She moved over to the couch and lay down. "Come here, Trixie." I went to her, my movements hampered by the skirt around my ankles. "Get up on the couch, between my legs." I did what she said. "Open my pants." I started to, but was alarmed when I felt something big and hard in her pants. "Take it out," she said, and I did—a long, thick, and very lifelike dildo. She reached under the couch and brought up a condom. "Put it on," she said, "with your mouth." I was clumsy, but I did it. The condom was lubricated, so when she told me to start fucking my tits with her dick, the dildo slid right between them. She groaned as if she could really feel every inch of it. "Suck it," she said. "Get it in your mouth." I moved my chest up and down on it, feeling the friction on my breasts and enjoying it when my fingers occasionally rubbed my nipples. I lowered my mouth onto the head. I sucked and licked it enthusiastically. I moaned and sighed. I felt crazy, and for a second panicked, when I realized that anyone could walk into the office and see me there, naked except for the torn hose and disheveled skirt that held my feet together.

"Oh, that's good," Jane said. "That's it, really put your head into it. Show me how sorry you are that you did your job so badly. Show me what a good slut you can be." She fucked my breasts and mouth some more, then pulled away from me. She got up and rearranged me so that my skirt was completely off and I was kneeling on the couch and looking straight into the mirror. She got behind me.

"I want you to see what you look like when you get fucked," she murmured in my ear. "That way you'll learn your lesson even better." She explored the entrance to my pussy with her dick. "Spread your legs, you bad thing." I moved them. "That's right," she said, "show me your pussy." She edged the dildo in more. "The boss is going to fuck you now," she warned, and pushed it in hard and deep. My pussy swallowed it up and I started moving against it.

She moved with me, working it in and out, watching my face in the mirror. She grabbed my hair and pulled my head up and back. "Watch yourself get fucked," she hissed. I saw her, still perfectly dressed in her executive clothes, knowing that her dick was lodged inside me. I saw my face, tense with arousal, my flushed neck, and my heavy breasts. I felt something change and realized that Jane had put her fingers between the dildo and her skin and was stroking her clit. "You're going to make me come," she told me. "Do you want to come, too?"

I nodded. In the mirror, I saw her stare at me.

"Please," I said.

"The boss comes," she smiled. "The assistant doesn't."

"Please," I begged. I pushed my pussy onto her dick even harder, but I needed my clit touched.

"Why should I?" she asked, stroking herself more and more.

"I'll be good," I promised, "so good. I'll make you come all the time. I'll fuck you whenever you want, and your clients too. I'll give you blow jobs at lunch and a hand job with your morning coffee. Just please, please let me come now."

"All right," she said. "Touch yourself."

And I did, digging my fingers into my clit, hard, thrusting myself onto her dick. In seconds I was coming so much that I didn't even realize until after that she was coming at the same time. I sank into the couch and she collapsed on top of me.

When our breathing and heartbeats got back to normal I realized how awkward the situation was. She was mostly dressed, but I felt ashamed of my partial nudity and my exposed, reddened ass. If I can't see her, I thought, maybe she can't see me, and so I stayed face down even when I felt her get up.

"Trixie," I heard. I turned my head. "Trixie! Sit up!"

I sat up. Jane looked perfectly composed. Her pants were closed up.

"Button your blouse. Put on your skirt. What kind of a spectacle are you making of yourself?" She smiled as she spoke.

"I don't know what we're going to do with you." She took her wallet out of her pants. "Here's some money," she said, and as I struggled into my skirt, I saw that she was giving me $200. "Get yourself some new stockings. And keep the change. Consider it a disability payment—I'm assuming you might have some trouble sitting down for the next two days."

I took the money and smiled back. My first day at work was certainly turning out nicely.

"I hope to see you again after lunch," Jane said. "I think we could work very well together."

"I'd like to come back," I said. "And I'm sure you'll do everything you can to see that I do."

Jane looked puzzled at first, then cleared her throat. "Hm, well, yes, certainly, of course. It's clear that we should be paying you far more than the initial salary we settled on. You're so much more qualified than your résumé suggested. I'll have the new contract drawn up and you can sign it when you get back. How does that sound?"

"Beautiful," I said.

And then I took a very, very long lunch.

Jolie Graham

❧

Drowsy Maggie

It was an unusually warm spring day, the day before St. Patrick's. Music rippled through the pavilion—the Irish Festival was under way. Maggie, who had no idea if she had any Irish ancestors or not, drifted through the crowd, seemingly carried forward by the swirl of music. Booths bedecked in green offered a tantalizing array of handicrafts, most not even remotely connected to anything Irish. *What's Irish about Southwestern jewelry?* Maggie wondered, as she paused by a display of earrings, bracelets and necklaces studded with sky-blue turquoise. The ear cuffs were interesting, though, and one caught her eye—a gray metallic figure of a tiny nude man with a full erection.

He was perfectly proportioned, perfectly shaped. She turned him over in the palm of her hand. There was the delicate hint of musculature along the legs, back and buttocks. One leg was drawn up and one stretched down. His hands were positioned to clasp the earlobe. She tried it on and peered down at the little mirror. It looked like he was either climbing the edge of her ear or trying to fuck it. Either way, the ear cuff was very comfortable; he fit her body perfectly, and Maggie was acutely aware of his penis pressed against her skin.

The girl at the booth sold it to her cheaply, advising her that it would need no polishing if she wore it regularly. "I used to wear one all the time, but when I took it off, it got all tarnished," she said, handing Maggie the change.

Maggie thanked her and went looking for a beer. It really was unseasonably warm for March. Ah, Guinness on tap—she sipped the creamy stout and looked about for a place to sit. The chairs in front of the bandstand were taken, as well as all the cafe tables, so she sat down on a concrete ledge under a tree.

She closed her eyes, feeling a familiar tingling in her body, thinking about a man—not any specific lover from her past—but some vague male figure pressed close to her, breathing in her ear all sorts of deliciously carnal things he wanted to do with her body. After a few moments, she opened her eyes, squinting at the brightness, half surprised to find herself alone under the tree. *Boy, the beer really went to my head fast,* she thought, smiling foolishly.

The music reeled through her body. She unfastened the top two buttons of her blouse, pulled her shirttail out and tied it up like a halter so she could feel the breeze wind around her belly. I *really* should get something to eat, she thought. A hot dog. Very Irish. She felt giddy and strangely self-conscious eating it.

Maggie absently reached up and fingered the buttocks of the ear cuff, sliding it up slightly higher on her ear, then back down into its original position. The penis felt hot against her ear, and for a moment all Maggie could see was a thick hot cock rubbing between her legs. She shook her head, then brushed the crumbs of the hot dog bun off her blouse. Her palms swept across her breasts, noting how tight and hard her nipples were. She was glad she hadn't worn a bra.

When he slipped into bed with her that night she wasn't surprised to feel the growing warmth, the heat of his body. She rolled over on her back. In the darkness she could see his face, illuminated by moonlight from the window. High, delicate cheekbones and an aristocratic nose were combined with a strong jawline and cleft chin. Shiny black hair tumbled down to his shoulders. He wasn't at all like the boyish, blond-haired, blue-eyed Adonises who usually populated her dreams.

She could feel his hot erection pressed against her. She slid her

hands around his narrow waist. Maggie liked the way his hip-
bones felt in the palms of her hands. Gray eyes, soft and open, not
dark and distant, looked her full in the face. Then he leaned down
and his lips brushed her neck. A hand burned on her stomach,
then between her legs.

She spread her legs and gave herself over to him. His mouth
sucked deeply and continuously on her breasts. But at the same
time she could feel his head between her legs. She writhed, sweating, beneath the covers, lifting her pelvis. Gently, softly, his tongue
probed the folds of sensitive skin, stroking her clit. His breath was
like steam against her vaginal lips.

Then he was kissing her. She held his beautiful, distinctive face
between her hands. His hands were large; they cupped her shoulder blades as his penis moved within her. She was still kissing
him, opening her mouth, her whole body tightening.

Maggie cried out and awoke. Her body shook as waves of warmth
rushed over her in quick succession. The sheets were tangled and
soaked with sweat—just as if it had all been real. She fell back on
the pillow, breathing hard. The moonlight illuminated the room.
She was alone. As she slowly sank back into sleep, she thought she
heard a voice, low and warm, whispering endearments. Then,
quite distinctly, she heard "I love you" breathed softly into her ear.

On St. Patrick's Day Maggie awoke feeling great. She showered
and dressed in shorts and a halter. The little naked man still clung
to her ear. He was not dislodged by sleep or shower and still
gleamed dully despite the soaping.

The festival was already in full swing when Maggie arrived, the
crowd even larger than the day before. There was *ceili* dancing on
the center stage and storytelling on the corner. The ground beneath her feet seemed to vibrate with the energy of the music.

It was a couple of hours before Maggie realized that she was
looking for *him*. She caught herself watching the crowd, looking
quickly from face to face. She got a lot of smiles, but none of the
men were him.

Somehow she managed to snag a small table near the bandstand, where she drank her beer and ate a tiny cup of Irish stew.
She sipped the Guinness slowly, closed her eyes and slid down

in the chair, her legs slightly apart beneath the table. The sun warmed her upturned face, but her body was already warm from some other, closer fire. Her shorts were damp and she felt sticky all over as if she had been smeared with semen. That was what Maggie thought about as she listened to the music and her beer grew hot. Smeared with semen. Her body pulsed.

Before long her dreams carried her away. He was there, beside her. In the murmur of voices she could hear him speaking, but could not quite make him out. Unconsciously, she touched the tiny nude man who clung to her ear and caressed her so persistently with his cock. She felt a large warm hand trail down from her ear, across her neck to her breasts. Hands massaged her breasts, first outside the halter, then underneath. Rough palms flat against her swelling breasts, her nipples like two pearls in his hands.

The band was playing "Drowsy Maggie," a tune she recognized from the day before. It started off slowly, then got faster and faster . . . a sticky penis in her hands, between her legs. The table and the crowd had melted away. She opened her mouth to receive either his tongue or his prick. She was thirsty and sweating. Faster. More. All over me.

The song ended with a crash, leaving her feeling naked, dripping, aching for some cataclysmic release. Maggie opened her eyes, her mind reeling more from desire than from the half-finished cup of beer.

He stood about ten feet away, his hands thrust deep inside his jeans pockets, his erection following the line of his zipper. As soon as her eyes met his he walked over and pulled a chair up close to hers.

"My name's Nick," he said, leaning towards her. As his two palms moved up her damp thighs, Maggie stared. A figure of a woman was wrapped around the outer edge of his ear, of the same style and color as her ear cuff.

His hands pressed the seam of her shorts against her clit. It was obvious that his fingers would have been more comfortable inside the shorts. Inside her. It was all Maggie could do not to rip her halter off and screw him right there on the chair while the beer flowed and the band played merrily from another time zone.

Unsteadily, Maggie stood, clasping his hand. Nick was tall and
broad-shouldered, with tousled black hair and intent gray eyes.
Without a word, they strolled languidly hand in hand through the
pavilion, out the west gate, across the parking lot, and across a
small street into the cool deep green shade of the park.

Kneeling in a thick patch of clover, she unzipped his jeans and
tugged them over his ass, her hands trembling so badly that she
was grateful not to have to deal with his underwear as well. Nick
stretched and pulled off his shirt with one motion, sinking into
the lush green bed. Maggie's halter and shorts, along with her
drenched and twisted pair of panties, made a small pile of abandoned clothing next to his.

As she sank into the green beside him, the music rang in her
ears. Silently, they removed the matching ear cuffs from each other's
ears. As Maggie examined the female figure, she wondered, *Is this
me?* The woman's legs were spread, knees bent, and her feet as
well as her hands had clasped the edge of Nick's ear. She was
slightly bent at the waist so that her ass stuck out noticeably. Her
hands were positioned much lower down than were the male figure's. Turning the figurine over in her palm, it struck Maggie that
the woman looked like she was reaching down, as if she had been
frozen before her hands quite made it between her legs. Her
rounded breasts had snuggled around Nick's ear. She looked like a
woman caught at the peak of arousal, her whole body wild with
unreleased sexual tension.

Nick was far less interested in the nude male figure. If he recognized himself in the design, he gave no sign of it. Wordlessly, he
handed it back to Maggie.

Dropped into her open hand, the little man suddenly gave a
start, then leaped onto the female figure, violently taking her from
behind. Maggie and Nick gaped in amazement.

"They're magnets!" he exclaimed. The little man's outstretched
hands, which had clasped Maggie's ear, now grasped the female's
nipples. His penis was up between her legs, and her hands, which
had been reaching achingly for herself, now grasped his cock. One
of his legs was locked over hers.

Maggie tentatively tried to separate the figures, but when she could not, she laid them aside on the pile of clothes. They were bound together by the primal force of magnetism; they were one.

Maggie reached out and stroked Nick's hairy balls. His hands covered her breasts as she slid her fingers around his penis. *Smeared with semen,* she thought as she stroked him. He pushed his tongue into her mouth. They thrashed around in the clover, groping and mouthing each other until he sprayed her belly with come. As if reading her mind, Nick smeared the liquid all over her breasts, rubbing his thumbs slowly over her nipples until Maggie cried out, gasping, her body stretched tight with desire. The music swirled faster through her mind.

As her clit began to throb, Nick—erect again—thrust into her from behind. He rubbed his hands over her breasts, then between her legs as he pushed deeper into her. Maggie came, legs trembling. She raised her buttocks to meet his hips once more before finally sinking, exhausted and spent, into the clover. He had fucked her flat into the ground. The image of the two figurines locked together forever in an eternal fuck drifted through Maggie's drowsing mind.

Winn Gilmore

Celia and the Bed

Celia snaked the black 450SLC into the tight parking space and, with one long, black-gloved hand, switched off the ignition. She checked her electric black mane in the rearview mirror, then smiled. Perfect. As always. She caressed the door handle, opened the door, then slid her long legs out of the car. She smiled again as her tight black leather skirt slid up her naked thigh. Suddenly she shivered, both from the promise of what lay ahead and from the excitement of her thighs sliding together. She was wet already.

"Buenas tardes, señora," the salesman crooned as she entered the bedding shop. He bowed not out of professional courtesy, but to better guide his greedy eyes up the leather-clad woman's long legs.

She lifted the razor-sharp toe of her left shoe toward the bowing man's face. *"Señorita,"* she hissed between clenched teeth.

The man jerked up. Celia slipped off her gloves with the sweet grace of a lover's licking tongue, her eyes darting hungrily around the store.

"Ah, yes." A tough *mujer*, he assessed. He shifted into a tone of frigid professionalism. "How may I help the *señorita*?"

"I am in search of the bed," Celia replied in English.

The salesman smiled condescendingly. His bedding shop was a favorite of teeming Americans leaving the rigid United States in search of the "exotic, magical Mexico" promised by the tourist packages, so he had a reasonable command of English, though his intelligence prohibited him from letting them know that. They preferred his faked attempts at English that limped along like a bumpkin trying to stroll in Givenchy shoes.

But this woman was surely no North American. She was as dark as he. No, darker. Her ancestry burst through her honey-brown skin and radiated a simple, honest beauty that the exotic-seeking North Americans could never achieve, no matter how many days they basked piglike in Mexico's sun, drinking margaritas and sloshing on expensive tanning oils.

She's no better than me, he thought angrily. Then, with a curt nod, he corrected her. "You don't mean you are searching for *the* bed, *señorita*, but for *a* bed."

"*¿Perdone?*" she asked. Her yearning eyes had already swept over the gaudy, more popular beds. She was about to give up when, like a wet tongue, her eyes flicked over a deceptively humble bed tucked around a corner. Celia could only make out one curved, dark wooden leg peeking out enticingly from beneath a silk cover, but a fine sheen broke out on her upper lip. She licked the sweat. "*Repite, por favor,*" she begged, placing her right hand over her thudding heart. "What did you say?"

The salesman drew himself up taller and repeated, "You mean that you are looking for *a* bed, not *the* bed."

Celia dismissed him with a flip of her wrist, eyes stripping the partially hidden bed of its simple, yet ample covering. "No, I know exactly what I mean, *hombre. Yo quiero* the bed. I will know her when I see her." *This must be her*, she prayed, as her nipples tightened and pushed out against her scarlet silk shirt. It called like a demanding lover, long lost but never forgotten.

The man shook his head despairingly. *¡Qué pendeja!* Some people! Try and teach them something, and what *gracias* did you get? The doorbell chimed "La Cucaracha" as other customers, Americans, entered the shop.

"Go ahead," he mumbled to Celia. "Look around. My assistant will be with you *en un minuto.*"

His tightly bound buttocks rushed up to the Americans. "Good afternoons, sir and ladies," he fumbled falsely.

The foremost Americana glowed with anticipation and nobility. Nodding appreciatively at the salesman's attempted English, she sighed, "Ah, Mexico!" She clasped her abundant arms around her peeling breasts and smiled. "Where else can you get such good service? And such goods?" she asked, looking knowingly at her friends.

The salesman hid his grimace, then continued with his sales pitch. They were, after all, *gringos*. "Should you like to see my most popular bedding pieces?" he asked, showing all of his well-formed teeth. "Adapted from the ancient Mayan culture which was ruling the country centuries ago." The Americans' eyes lit up. Fawning, they followed the salesman.

The conversation drifted to Celia like underwater murmurs in a bad dream. Mesmerized, she meandered through the bedding shop, drifting through the maze of unclaimed beds towards her bed, *the* bed. It was partitioned off by fabric-covered particle board and it begged—no, demanded—that she share herself with it. The engrossed salesman didn't cast so much as a glance her way.

She took each step slowly, trying desperately to ward off the hunger propelling her towards the yawning bed. It sprawled before her like an insatiable lover who'd strap her in a deceptively soft grip and love her till she screamed. It was her bed, all right. With neither headboard nor footboard, it called as had no other in a long, long time.

But she had to resist for as long as she could. She stopped at a gaudy bed fringed in red velveteen, with mirrors stationed above that watched down like a god's huge eye. She inhaled deeply and closed her eyes. The smell of fresh cloth, unhampered by that unmistakable odor of love, filled her quivering nostrils. She pulled in deeply, the silk shirt softly caressing her tender, hard nipples.

Her breath came in ragged gasps as her flesh strained against the top button, and her long nails scratched and dug into the top of the mattress. She squeezed her thighs together to lock in the delicious ache demanding that she go to her bed.

Celia stole a glance at the salesman, who was still trying to coax his Americans into a sale. She clamped her teeth over her lower lip and bit down. Hard. She pinched her right nipple. *Apúrate*. I can't wait much longer. Her pussy gave a responding twinge.

More Americans entered the store, and she overheard the salesman apologize, "I'll be with you in some seconds, please. I am sorry, but my help is not in yet. She will soon be here." To underscore his apology, he popped in a Flora Purim tape. Americans loved her, he'd learned, and many thought she was Mexican. Weren't they all the same?

As the music pulsed against the store's walls and bounced back into the room, Celia smiled. Reverently, she placed a hand on one bed and gasped when she felt the music's vibrations running legato through the fabric. She walked on, putting one foot carefully ahead of the other, sliding her hips in sync with the music to intensify her pussy movements.

Breathing heavily, she turned the corner behind which lay her bed. Still trembling, Celia moved tentatively towards it. Finally, it lay a mere three feet from her, begging her to jump on top, to bury her screams and juices in its fresh, virginal self.

Feigning indifference, she turned from her bed and leaned over the more flamboyant bed beside it. Her leg brushed against her bed as she bent over the other, and she buried her face in the covers. *I can wait no longer,* her brain and pussy screamed. But she held on as she ran both hands over the bed's every inch. Flora shouted and murmured wordless fucking noises from the cassette.

Her breasts echoed the desire rising from her pussy and her very center like the heat from her own Pelenque earth. Celia sat and turned slowly on the bed. The music cascaded over her like a mountain stream gone mad, coming over the ground and flooding the parched earth, intensifying until there was only herself, sound and the bed.

Oblivious to the salesman and his customers, Celia kicked off her shoes, wriggled the tight black skirt over her full hips like a gorged boa climbing out of its skin, and stood naked before the bed, *her* bed. The ache consumed her, and her entire body was ashiver. She offered herself to the bed like a virgin to the gods: naked, hungry and trusting. She squeezed her eyes tight as she mounted the simple yet voluptuous bed.

With her long fingers she caressed her tongue, then painted hieroglyphics on her taut breasts. She squeezed her nipples and moaned, her smooth brown skin sinking into the silk covers and soft mattress. She snatched off the top cover, then found her slick pussy. She sighed as she pulled the silk sheet between her wide-spread, kneeling thighs as Purim's voice and Airto's drums dragged her back to the forest. Spreading her thighs and pussy juices over the titillating covers, she growled. Her ass waved high above the bed, and Celia ripped off the remaining sheets. She sat up and yanked off her shirt. Then she sank her nose, teeth and body into the body of the bed. She rolled over and sucked in the smell of her hair and the naked bed.

"*Buenas tardes, señorita,*" a contralto whispered, seemingly part of the music.

Celia's eyes shot open. Before her was a widespread pair of dark, beautifully curved, strong legs. Her eyes traveled up to rest on a tight red skirt barely revealing a pulsing Mound of Venus. Her eyes darted up to the interloper's face, which sneered down, disdainful yet understanding.

"*Qué en el mundo* can I do for you?" the voice asked. She smiled, and Celia's brown face turned darker as blood rushed up from her pussy. She clasped her sweaty, juice-soaked legs together and pulled the sheets over her naked body. Struggling for some tidbit of control, she looked imperiously at the woman standing before her. "Are you the help?" she asked.

Slowly, the woman pulled the fingers of her right hand through her short, curly black hair, refusing to be intimidated. "I guess you could call me that. *O lo que tu quieras,*" she said. Her long face murmured of Dahomey and Maya, and she flashed her impossibly white teeth at the woman on the bed. "Can I help *you?*"

"No," Celia said, despite the tremor which ran through her body. "You cannot help me, *hermana.*"

Oblivious to anything but the Americans, the salesman's voice boomed from the rear of the store. "*¡Marta! Ven para aca y ayúdame. Hay americanos aquí, y esa mujer,*" he said, indicating Celia, "*no tiene nada para nosotros. ¡Ven aca ahora!*"

"*Ayy,*" Marta groaned as she headed for the front of the store. But she does have something for me, *hombre.* For you, *no.* But for me, *sí.* Still, she waited on the Americans.

Celia quickly forgot about the simpering salesman, his delight-fully arrogant helper, Marta, and even the Americans as she re-sumed making love to her bed. She didn't overhear the man's joy when the Americans left him with a traveler's check to cover the inflated price of the bed they'd bought. She didn't hear the sales-woman's sarcastic contralto faking happiness for him. Didn't hear the salesman leave the shop in the assistant's hands, promising to return after *siesta*. Didn't hear the woman lock the door behind him. Didn't hear her crank up the music; didn't hear her stride to where she, Celia, was. But she did hear her say,

"*Now* I can help you, *señorita*." Marta gazed hungrily down at Celia writhing on the bed. She shucked off her clothes and Celia moaned, between gasps, "*No! No es posible. No te quiero! Solo yo! The bed es mia.*"

"But who do you think brought it here for you?" Marta asked gently, and, despite her passion, Celia found herself rolling onto her back, legs and pussy open wide for the stranger.

"*Sí, es la cama*"—Marta put a foot on the bed—"*y yo soy la camarera*" and slid a hand down her now-naked torso. Then she lay atop Celia and kissed her deeply.

Rivers opened in their veins; oceans flowed between them. They streamed together, Ochun finding Yemaya.

"*Ayy, cielo*," Celia cried as Marta flowed down to her thighs. She grabbed the woman, whose wide, wide mouth and sinuous tongue danced around Celia's clit. Marta moaned delectably and rotated her supple body so that her sex was an irresistible oyster taunting Celia's hunger. Celia wrapped her arms around Marta's thighs and ass, pulling herself up to her pussy. Starving, she buried her face in the woman's sex.

But the searing passion was too much for Celia. She rolled over to present her small, puckering anus. Marta sniffed, then licked the opening. Celia moaned, screamed and buckled as one slim fin-ger slid inside. "*¡Ayyy! ¡Mi cama! ¡Mi cámarera!*" she yelled, com-ing all over her bed and her woman.

Dressing shakily, Celia smiled lazily at the woman sprawled on the bed. "And when can I see you again?" she asked, trying to sound casual.

Marta grinned omnisciently, then licked her fingers.

"You never know," she said. "*Quizás mañana.* Or maybe never again."

Celia looked at her, already wistful. She smeared the love juices across her face and through her wild hair. Then she picked up her things and headed for the door.

In her Benz, she started the engine and headed home. The next bedding shop could wait. At least until tomorrow.

Michele Serchuk

❦

Leash

Amanda and I were sitting in my living room after karate one morning, reading erotica, feeling each other out. Not literally. We were talking about bondage, the excitement of the forbidden. Fine in theory, but when she asked me if I liked being dominant or submissive, I froze. Couldn't say the words, didn't know her well enough, choked on shame and pride. I got out some words about power play, the erotic tension built in switching roles and the transfer and exchange of power. All true, but I didn't own anything directly. We went on to safer topics.

Sunday afternoon, a few weeks later. Amanda sashays up the stairs, her libido reaching the fifth floor while her feet are still on three. She wanders about, losing clothing matter-of-factly. Well, yeah, it's not like we've never changed together before. Forbidden fruit, dancing sprite turns naked around the room. Shows dark against white walls, cocoa-sleek, fuzzy and wild. She's happier without clothing, wants you to see her body. I know the feeling.

"Look what I brought," she says. Amanda brings toys. A leash and collar, black leather strip twirling out of her woven pouch. She stands sassy in the middle of the white floor, showing me what she's brought to play with. "I have another one at home with spikes, but I didn't want to get too intense, you know?"

"Oh, yeah, right. Cool. A leash." And what the hell am I going to do with a leash? What's proper leash protocol? I don't want to say this is new to me, appear unsure of myself. Death before embarrassment, you know. My first impulse is always to act cool, a bad habit I'm trying to break. From inside my cool I'm trying to think, to gather myself. I'm more than a little intrigued, but something about this still makes me squirm.

So, what is it about this leash thing? It's this object-thing and I want to conceal it, deny it. I don't want to deal with its existence. More than any silk scarf or bathrobe sash tied tightly around my wrists, this object embodies my fascination and lust for power play, those words, dominance and submission. Object of ridicule, subject of snickering jokes at pathetic degenerates, shame I didn't think I owned. Vestiges of someone else's puritan values lurk, and I feel a flash of political indignation. Scarves are garments until the moment they become bondage; that leash and collar has no other purpose. I want to touch it. I want to hide inside.

That object in Amanda's hands is confession and I am remembering my grade school jump rope made of stretchy, orange rubber tubing with white handles. I am remembering the thrill I got tying my ankles together in my dark bedroom at night when no one was watching. I was too young to know that heat flash as sex, only old enough to know it was "bad," to know better than to tell anyone, ever. I'm thinking of all those spankings my Barbie dolls got. I'm thinking I don't want to think about this now. I just want her to kiss me.

I move into her arms. We begin exploring each other, steamy and soft. Who is she, I wonder, and how can I please her? I've forgotten the collar, lost in her skin, in her curves. Something in her lies sleeping and I want to wake it up, see her on fire, feel her passion. I glide over her, inhale sweet spice, taste salt.

Amanda makes whimpering, cooing noises as I slip fingers into her. Her inner walls suck me inside. My fingers explore, touch the hard dimple of her womb as I push in deeper. I feel her slick and warm against my thigh as she rides me, fingers between my legs, stroking me. I float, riding lazy waves of sex-thrill.

I have forgotten her toy. She hasn't. It's in her hands again and I refuse to say hey, wait, I'm a leash-virgin. She gives it to me. What the hell do I do with this? Nice girls don't play with leashes and feminists don't tie people, other women, up. Funny, I don't recall these thoughts being quite so loud when I played this way with a man. I don't know if it's the leash/scarf thing or a gender thing; my hormones are racing and I'm not certain why I'm doing this, but I can't back down, and, truthfully, I can't resist the challenge.

I hold her down and slip the collar around her neck, moving her body forcefully, feeling her size and my strength. My robe is by the bed and I slip the sash out of the loops, grab her hands and bind her wrists. Her pleasure is obvious, incites me to give her more, her movements and noises showing me the way to be this person, to dominate her. She squirms as I run the leash down between her breasts, between her legs and yank it hard, up her back. Pinning her to the futon, I pull the leather tight. I wonder how the sharp tugs on the collar must feel and imagine the deliciousness of being trapped. Her ass twitches back and forth as she rubs herself against the leash and I tentatively spank her a few times with the looped handle. It makes loud, satisfying, slapping noises. I do it again, more forcefully this time, and watch, fascinated, as she twitches harder.

I am whispering to her, nibbling on her, watching her get hotter and hotter. My hands run over her body, moving her as it pleases me, catching her head, pulling her in to kiss her, spreading her thighs to expose her clit. I want to make her come. Remembering how she liked being penetrated, I fuck her, not exploring like before but pushing, thrusting, filling her. Her response is immediate and fierce. She cries out and gives herself to me, wet and open. I have four fingers in her, see her juices shiny on my knuckles. Her moans come wilder and louder and she rubs herself back and forth over the black leather leash, swallowing half my hand, as she comes.

We sit up laughing and I untie her hands. I'm beginning to surface, not sure where I've been, not even sure if I'm back yet. But she's not done, she remembers my words about role reversal and power play needing to go both ways. The leash and collar are in her hands again and her impish eyes are fixed on me. "Your turn," she says.

Amanda is reaching for my neck. Politics and pride scream in

my stomach as a heat wave engulfs my cunt. I can't move. No,
I don't *want* to move. I want to struggle; I feel our near-equal
strength as we wrestle, knowing she has to win. She has me, slips
the collar around my throat, jerking my head back by my hair. It
feels dangerous and forbidden. She tightens the collar almost past
the point of comfort; blood pulses at my temples from the rough
pressure at my throat. I move over to give myself air, relaxing my
guard; she has me, pulls me where she wants me, flat on my back.
She wants my hands, I see the sash and hold out my wrists even
as I pretend to be able to fight. She ties them so tightly that the
only way to make it not hurt is to bend my elbows with my arms
stretched out and over my head. I have never felt so helpless.
Slowly I recognize that there is nothing I can do, that she has to
please me now. I lie there, wrists aching, and luxuriate in the real-
ization that I am hers and the pleasure now is mine. She has a
dildo in her hand as she moves in over me. I'm your captive, I
think, do me.

Amanda's eyes sparkle. Her hand twists in my hair as her gaze
travels over my body. My breathing sounds ragged in my ears; I
am waiting for what comes next. Her body pins me down and her
thigh is hot against my crotch. Nothing comes next. I am waiting.
Amanda is staring at me.

"You like this, don't you?" she asks. Her voice is soft, low and in
complete control. I buck upwards and grind against her hip.

"That's not an answer. Tell me. I'm waiting."

I can't speak. I am choking from deep inside. The words are
stuck in my chest somewhere and I cannot say anything. I wonder
what I had been thinking when I started flirting with her that
morning on my sofa. I remember feeling so daring; I don't think I
had believed this would actually happen.

Amanda tugs on the leash and my mind bounces back to the
present. There is no place to hide. I can't move my head to escape
her hot brown stare, so I close my eyes. I am conscious of myself
inside my body and of each passing second. The moment becomes
very long and I silently beg her to resolve it for me.

"I won't be the fall guy for you, girl. You'll say it. Watch."
Amanda gets up and leads me to the window, keeping the leash

short and tight. We look out over the rooftops, onto streets bustling with Sunday Chinatown commerce.

"Who are you afraid of? Them? You afraid of what they'd say? Or is it your friends, hmm? Afraid they wouldn't approve of your politics?" Amanda is stroking my hair, her warm breath in my ear. She hasn't let go of the leash. It's beginning to get dark and lights go on in the building across the alley. I can see my neighbors watching TV and preparing dinner. I stand naked, collared, peering through the thin curtains.

"Amanda, the neighbors ... they'll see." I sound ridiculous. Amanda laughs, delighted. She swings me around to face her; the look on her face is pure evil. She reaches over, flicks on a lamp and yanks on the curtain. The flimsy rod falls easily out of the brackets. We stand framed in a pool of light over Canal Street. Amanda holds the leash and collar tight in one hand as the other snakes around and strokes my clit. Her teeth tease at my ear. My knees get weak and suddenly I don't care about my goddamned neighbors, the women at the karate school, or anyone else for that matter. I want her to fuck me and I don't care if the whole damned world knows or what anyone thinks about the way that I want to be fucked.

"Make me come. I want you to. Please." I'm having trouble with words but I am speaking, after a fashion. She's laughing, loving this. Her hands are getting rougher, her teeth biting down on my neck, leaving red marks on my skin. I can see our reflection in the window; I imagine the shoppers glancing up and noticing the glint of light off the thick, shiny collar, suddenly realizing what they are seeing. I imagine them going home hot and bothered, thinking about us later with husbands or girlfriends or maybe jerking off in the dark, alone.

"I want them to see you fuck me. Fuck me." I am screaming it to her. At this rate they won't have to look up; they'll hear me.

"Stay here. Touch yourself. And don't turn around." Amanda unties my hands and kisses me, practically sucking the breath out of my mouth before she leaves. Her footsteps pad across the floor and I hear her rustling around in that bag of hers. I lean against the window frame, put one foot up on the sill and stroke myself.

The leash is hanging down my back, gently swaying. It brushes over my ass and I rub harder as I look out the window.

Amanda is suddenly back at my side grabbing the leash and twisting my nipples. Something hard and rubbery is pushing at my ass—she has fastened the dildo on with a harness. A harness. Oh God, do women really use those things? I've seen one before, but it was hanging on the wall at Ye Olde Local Sex Shoppe, not on a lover. I want to see it but she won't let me turn around. She has one hand on the leash and the other across my chest as she forces me back against her. Her hips are powerful and thrust the rubber cock deep inside me. I scream as I ram into her. She staggers backwards, regains her balance, then pushes me up against the window. I lean forward, holding tight to the frame. The glass is cold against my breasts, her breasts soft against my shoulder blades as she fucks me with deep, hard strokes. The sensation is deliciously perverse. Her long, sensitive fingers stroke my clit and my legs begin to shake. Heat spreads out from my belly and I can no longer stand. Her strong arms hold me up as I scream and tremble in front of the window. We fall to the floor and lie in a sweating, quivering heap. I put my head on her shoulder and let her soothe me to sleep.

It's early evening and she has left hours earlier; I am out walking in the world. Her spicy aroma is still rising off my body. The breeze blowing my hair across my face carries the perfume of her sweat, unchecked by Secret for Women. Her smells are so loud in my nostrils, I can't imagine that anyone who sees me doesn't notice. They don't. Each waft of scent triggers a visceral memory. People see and hear me from so far away, I feel like I'm in a bubble waiting to land. My smile is full of secrets as I turn the corner for home.

In the Mood

Allison sat cross-legged on the bed, coffee cup in hand, wearing one of the white terry cloth robes provided by the hotel, watching Grant dress for his business meeting. He looked bright and shiny from his morning shower. "Downright perky," she told him, smiling fondly. The morning newspaper lay strewn about, mostly read by now.

"What are you going to do with yourself today?" Grant asked.

"I don't know. I feel deliciously irresponsible. I think I'll hang out at the pool. How late is your meeting supposed to go?"

"I should be back around three o'clock. Why don't we meet at the pool bar then?"

"Okay," she responded, standing and kissing him, remembering with pleasure their lovemaking that morning and the night before. "Have a good meeting. I'll be thinking nice thoughts."

"Stay out of jail," he said, smiling as he left her.

She took a leisurely shower, carefully shaved her legs, and trimmed her pubic hair. She slathered suntan lotion over her body instead of moisturizer, paying special attention to those parts of her that rarely saw the sun. She dried her hair and put on makeup.

She was amused at herself, so carefully preparing for a lazy day sweating in the sun. It reminded her of the time that a friend,

watching her in the office ladies' room, had said, "I don't understand why you put on lipstick before lunch. You just eat off your
lipstick anyway." To which another, more astute friend responded
in her sexiest Southern drawl, "But you never know—she might
meet somebody she likes along the way."

Perhaps she would meet somebody she liked today. She was
certainly in the mood.

Allison's attention turned to the weighty consideration of
whether to wear her black bikini with the gold trim or her coral
tank suit with the iridescent sparkles and the high-cut legs. She
tried both on, considering her reflection carefully and assessing
her comfort level in each.

She looked out the window at the pool below to check out the
early crowd—mostly young families, who she knew wouldn't even
notice her as they fussed over their small children. There were
also some single women, dedicated sunbathers who were in no
worse or better shape than she. "What the hell," she thought, opt-
ing for the bikini. She pulled her black beach shift over her head,
shrugging it over her suit, slipped into her sandals, grabbed her
book, sunglasses and other essentials and headed down to the pool.

Allison pulled up a chair at the far end, giving her a view of the
doorway from the hotel where she could monitor everyone's com-
ings and goings. She put down her bag, stood by her chair and
lifted her dress over her head, remembering the lover who had
told her that he could tell a lot about a woman's sexuality when he
watched her strip down to her bathing suit. Some sat down first,
effectively hiding while they stripped off their coverups. Others
stood proudly. The same man put a lot of faith in the theory that
women who wore ankle bracelets were hot, and Allison still wore
the one he'd given her. She hadn't needed him to tell her to stand
tall while she stripped, though. She liked showing off.

An attractive young couple were just arriving at the pool. The
only unattached men were two young pool attendants whose
cocoa brown skin contrasted sharply with their hotel-issue polo
shirts—cute, but too young. She scanned the windows and balconies across the way. A young girl leaned on a railing on the
second floor, wiggling with childish excitement as she called to
someone inside. A kissing couple was visible a floor above and

several rooms down. Great day, she thought, smiling, breathing in the fresh air and congratulating herself on having taken this beautiful sunny day off. She sat down on the chair, leaned back with her hands clasped behind her head, elbows out, and stretched with pleasure.

Before too long, Allison was fully engrossed in the most recent addition to her library of women's erotica. The quality of the writing pleased her. The stories were rich with imagery, emotion and imagination, as well as sex. The specific fantasies of the writers did not all appeal to her, but there were many that did, and the dampness between her thighs was not all sweat from the sun. "Allison, you're a horny bitch," she thought.

A shadow fell over her, and she looked up to see one of the handsome young pool attendants standing at the foot of her chair, checkpad in hand. His eyes took in her body from toes to face with bold appreciation. "May I get you anything?" he asked politely.

She considered him lazily for a moment and then verbalized her request for spring water, please. Allison watched his cute buns as he walked away to fill her order, thinking, "Maybe he's not too young." She laughed out loud at herself.

Distracted, she set down her book and scanned the scene again. Some families were packing up, getting ready to leave the pool and go to lunch. On the balconies now, close to where their room must be, a single man surveyed the pool. A nicely shaped black man, she noticed. Tall and muscular-looking in shorts and t-shirt. Fantasy material. She paused, wondering idly if he was alone and what he looked like closer up.

A few minutes later, the hotel door opened and a tall, handsome, very virile-looking black man stepped through. "Be still my heart," thought Allison as she recognized him as the man she'd noticed on the balcony. He looked back at her, deliberately smiled and slowly walked around the pool, maintaining eye contact with her as he made his way around chairs and other sunbathers.

Finally he stopped in front of her, inclined his head politely and asked, "Is this chair free? May I join you?" Allison smiled her "yes," invited him to sit down, offered her name. His was Warren, he told her, and stripped off his t-shirt. She watched with appreciation— strong muscular chest and belly, broad shoulders, slim waist and smooth, hairless brown skin. He watched her closely as he stripped off his shorts. Flash of white underneath, oh my God, he's wearing a small white bikini.

As her visitor lowered his body into the lounge chair beside her, he turned towards her and began to talk. Rich, deep voice; easy grace. Her body responded deliciously as she talked and flirted with ease.

She's here on pure pleasure, she tells him, with a friend who is working but will return later. Engrossed in their conversation, they are startled by the return of the pool attendant with the spring water she's ordered. Warren takes in the look she and the waiter exchange, the way the young man touches her hand as he delivers the drink. He chuckles knowingly and reaches over for his wallet. He hands a tip to the attendant, effectively dismissing him while claiming possession of her. To Allison, he says simply, "You're dangerous, lady."

As the afternoon wears on, talk becomes more intimate. "Have you ever made love to a black man?" Warren asks.

"Yes," she answers, then hesitates. Should she continue? She's had two black lovers. One, half Italian, had delicious dark honey skin and a football player's body; another was black as licorice and smaller, with an exquisitely sculpted body. Both were quite beautiful; both provided her with long-lasting erotic memories. The first one taught her about her submissive side, simply and definitely. All it took was this—he held her arms loosely but authoritatively away so that she could not touch him while he made love to her. She remembers being helpless to do anything but receive pleasure. The thought of his teasing still excites her.

The second lover was the first man ever to masturbate for her— to stand hot and naked before her, stroking his hard cock while she watched. It was her first real experience with voyeurism, and she felt scared of his quiet smoldering challenge for her to reveal more of herself.

These lovers left her with sensual memories of black skin on white, black cock entering pink pussy. She recalls these images and feels a stirring as she tells Warren about these men. He listens quietly, then rolls to his side and reaches over to stroke her hip in a move that seems involuntary and at the same time deliberately erotic. Her nipples harden and she finds herself moving her arm to lightly stroke this man's face and neck just once. He is closely shaved, his skin warm and smooth as fine leather. She feels a catch of pure lust in her throat and chest. He takes her hand and brings it to his lips. "What are we going to do about this?" he asks.

Allison considers the question, maintaining direct eye contact. There is serious heat going on here. "What time is it?"

"Two."

"Let me change clothes and let's meet in the bar in twenty minutes. We'll talk more about it there."

Warren is waiting at the bar when she arrives. She buys him a drink and begins to tell him, simply and directly, what she would like. She blushes slightly as she risks his rejection while inviting his participation in her fantasy. She tells Warren in a multitude of ways that she desires him. She leans towards him, her voice lowered, her eyes teasing, and she touches him lightly. He looks at her steadily as she speaks. He does not interrupt. She wonders what he is thinking and how he'll respond.

When Allison has finished her proposition, Warren stands, reaches out, pulls her to her feet. He lifts her to him, his strong hands on her ass. She is pressed against him, stretching to reach his mouth for his slow, deep kiss. Out of the corner of her eye she sees that Grant has entered the bar and is watching. He smiles, a little nervously she thinks, as he takes a seat further down the bar, behind Warren. She signals to him with a quick wave, pulls back to look into Warren's face and asks, "Am I right to take your response as a yes?" He sits down on the barstool, looks into her eyes and takes both of her hands in his, pulling them to his chest. He reaches out and lightly caresses her breasts. Then he grins and gives her nipple an insolent pinch. He pulls her hand to his mouth and moves it deliberately down to press against his crotch. He says yes.

Heat floods her face. "We'd better get out of here before we disgrace ourselves," she says, then tells him to wait just one minute.

She approaches Grant, who watches her intently. They read devilishness in each other as he pulls her to him for a kiss. He looks at Warren, who is watching them. "Do you want to fuck him?" Grant asks. She says yes loud enough so both men can hear.

Out in the lobby, she stops and introduces the men. "Grant, this is Warren, Warren, Grant." Grant suggests that all three go up to their room.

Allison undresses Warren as Grant watches, casually leaning against the wall. She's swept up in touching this beautiful man's body. As she unbuttons his shirt, she moves her hands over his chest, drawing feathery-light circles on his buttery-soft leather skin. She brings her mouth and fingers to his nipples as she draws his shirt off his back and pulls it from his arms. Her hands move down to caress his belly. Warren arches his back and moves against her hand, urging it lower.

Allison's attention is on Warren's eyes—she watches his response as she reaches into his shorts to fondle him. She releases his cock and gives it several upward strokes, feels it hardening, watches the lust grow in his eyes. She takes the weight of his testicles in her hands and squeezes gently. His pubic hair is thick and wiry; his cock thrusts hard against his shorts as he moans.

Pressing his shoulders against the wall, she kisses him, then lowers her hands to his waist. She unbuttons, unzips and lowers his shorts, stroking his buttocks and genitals. Allison drops to her knees in front of him, and takes his cock in her mouth. She draws him deeply into her mouth with slow easy movements, one arm stroking his ass and thighs, her other hand holding the base of his hot black cock.

Grant is watching; Allison deliberately does not look at him, though she can see him in the mirror where she watches herself sucking Warren. She uses her hands and mouth together, moving more urgently. Warren leans back and lets her take him.

She senses Grant moving behind her but does not stop her attention to Warren's body. She is sucking deeply now, hands on each of his muscular thighs, thumbs stroking his testicles as she moves her mouth up and down his shaft. Her body is tense with excitement, her ass sways involuntarily. She feels her sundress being lifted from behind, a soft breeze of air playing across her naked ass and wet pussy. She moans in response to the strong hands kneading her ass, spreading her open, touching her asshole and vagina with teasing fingers.

Grant lowers his mouth to her spread pussy, eating her and rubbing her juices over her ass with his fingers. She wriggles against
him in pleasure. Warren watches the three of them in the mirror
with obvious enjoyment. He strokes her face possessively, sensu-
ally, then wraps his large hands around her head and thrusts his
cock into her throat. They move in hot rhythm together, Warren's
hands pulling her forward when he thrusts, Grant's mouth luring
her backward when Warren withdraws.

Warren suddenly pulls completely out of her, and simultaneously Grant stands up, touching her naked shoulders as he rises.
She sits back on her heels, looking only at Warren, deliberately
teasing Grant. But there is more to this, she knows: She has always wanted to give Grant the pleasure of watching her make love
to another man with full abandon. She is not asking for permission
this time. She is hot, very hot, and does not know what will come
next, but whatever it is, she wants it. Looking at Grant might
break the spell, might prevent her from giving herself freely.

Warren reaches down and swoops her up onto her feet. Two
hands move in front of her and two behind her as both men coop-
erate in undressing her. Grant bends to unfasten the ankle straps
on her sandals, his fingers caressing her instep. Warren unbuckles
her belt and throws it aside. She is wearing nothing now but
the sundress, and her nipples are almost painfully sensitive, their
hardness jutting against the thin fabric. Warren reaches under her
dress and smoothes his hands up her thighs as Grant lifts her dress
from behind and runs his hands up her ass. Together the men lift
her sundress over her head. Warren drinks in her body with his
eyes and his hands. He bends his head to her breast, suckling
greedily, setting her on fire.

As he'd done in the bar earlier, Warren presses her body hard
against his. This time, free of clothing and in private, she responds
as she was tempted to do in public—her arms around his neck,
she raises herself, wraps her legs around his waist and slides her
sopping wet pussy down onto his big shaft. Leaning back, her
arms extended, she rides him hard. He lifts her up and down on
him with ease; her swollen clit rubs against him with every movement. Her orgasm begins to swell, heat rising from her groin to

her belly, her chest and then flooding her face as she screams her pleasure.

Warren moves, with her still clinging limply to him, and falls towards the bed. She sprawls on her back as he leans over and kisses her deeply. She catches a glimpse of Grant watching—his pants now off, shirt unbuttoned and hard cock in his hand. Warren moves down between her legs and toys with her pussy. He strokes her wetness, spreads her wide with both hands and watches with enjoyment as she squirms. She wants more. He bends his head to her pussy and tastes. She lifts his face, forcing him to look at her. "Fuck me," she moans. "I want to be fucked again. I want to be fucked hard."

"You do, do you?" Warren asks, but ignores her pleading. He moves up alongside her, leaning on one elbow as he looks down at her face and toys with her clit and her open pussy with his free hand. Smoothly he thrusts three fingers into her; she responds by bucking against them, low growls emerging from her throat. "Look at this," he says, kneeling beside her. "This pretty pink pussy wants cock, doesn't it? You like to fuck, don't you, Allison?"

He has her at his mercy. He is purposely teasing and she is embarrassingly out of her mind with lust. When he finally begins to fuck her again, he does so deliberately and slowly, lifting her ass in the air and drawing her to him. She cannot bear it, he is controlling her movement, the angle at which he holds her keeps her clit out of contact as he pumps slowly in and out. She writhes in his hands as she desperately tries to grind against him to satisfy her want. Warren stiffens; she sees in his face and hears in his sounds that he is going to come without her. Hot, wet come fills her, drips out of her throbbing pussy, spilling down the crack of her ass as he withdraws.

Warren chuckles. "I think it's your turn now, Davis," he says. "I think the lady is ready for you. Would you like me to hold her for you?" And there is Grant, standing at the end of the bed, his eyes hot for her, stroking his cock. "Do you want to be fucked, Allison?" he asks. "Has your black lover made you hot for me?"

Through the haze of her passion, she thinks, "But I never told Warren that Grant's last name is Davis." And suddenly she knows she's been set up. This "chance meeting" by the pool had been prearranged. She likes this—somehow it sets her free. A small explosion goes off in her head. She reaches for Grant, pulling him close, whispering hotly, "Beast—I've been had, haven't I?" He grins in acknowledgment. Warren also grins, in collusion with Grant.

Heat, even more intense than before, floods her body. Warren moves quickly behind her, kneeling and lifting her up so that her head and shoulders are propped against his chest and belly. He takes each of her breasts in his hands, kneading them, pinching her nipples.

"God, I'm hot," she moans. "I need you in me, Grant. Take me. Fuck me hard while Warren holds me."

Grant kneels between her wide-spread legs, and she catches his hard cock in her hand. She guides it towards her and rubs him up and down against her wetness, her juices mixed with those of another man. Grant thrusts hard into her and lowers himself to bring his mouth down on hers, crushing her with a deep passionate kiss, devouring her tongue and her mouth at the same time. Drawing back, he looks at her and says, his face and voice hot, "Tell me that you love me, Allison."

That little explosion goes off in her head again—surrender. Her arms and legs wrapped tightly around him, she bucks wildly, gripping his cock with her cunt, feeling Warren's heat behind her as she and Grant move together against him. "I love you, Grant. Oh, God, yes, I love you." Drowning in emotion and lust, moving hot and hard with him, she comes in long shattering spasms. She holds on, continuing to fuck him, determined to take him with her. Finally, his cries mingle with hers as he shoots into her.

"Beast!" Allison says, smiling at Grant fondly and with no small wonder as he collapses warm and solid against her.

Karen A. Selz

❧❦❧

The Hobby Horse

A fragment of passing street conversation had haunted Becky all the way home. A man and a woman were arguing but not angry. "It just won't work," the woman had said. It was the voice of fact, allowing no dispute. Was it always so clear when something was over, Becky wondered as she unlocked her apartment door.

Shaft, Becky's aging tomcat, sauntered out of sleep on the couch as she turned into the entrance hall. He was talking to her in cat: "Glad to see you. I love it when you smell like outside. Did you know that I'm out of canned food?" He trotted off to demonstrate the last point. Would she follow, please?

The kitchen was lit by the few broad threads of late-afternoon sun that wound through the partially closed Venetian blinds. Becky put out more food for Shaft and decided to let the morning dishes wait a little longer. She checked her answering machine while she crunched on a carrot; there were only two messages. A computerized voice reminded her about a NOW fund-raiser at five dollars for potluck and a discussion of reproductive rights in Pennsylvania, and there was a "just saying hi" message from her friend George. David hadn't called.

So that's how it was. She couldn't feel too hurt. After all, she was the one who had suggested the separation. Living together just hadn't worked.

Kicking off her shoes, tying back her hair, Becky was glad to be alone. Maybe when you got past thirty your habits were just too set, too hard to overcome. What got in the way of love then seemed not so much the improbability of finding someone to love, which would be enough of an obstacle, but more the unwilling-ness to accommodate another object in your life.

The escape from her stockings felt good; so did the cold water on her face. Shaft had eaten his fill and joined her, sitting in at-tendance on the bathroom counter, watching her with seasoned disinterest. He was a good companion—thick, languorous and swaggering in the way of male cats. Soundly convinced of his many perfections, he was a braggart and a bully, but always happy at her coming home, always in her bed when she woke up.

It had been a rough day at work, leaving her tired and unful-filled. The week was only half over. And she *had* really expected David to return her call. Altogether a good day for a ride on her horse.

She fell easily into the ritual. Rose oil rubbed hard into her skin. Sitting on the edge of the old porcelain tub, she let her hands work smoothly down the length of her legs, her fingers finally in-terlacing with her toes. Next the arms, circling each elbow care-fully with the thumb of the opposite hand. She pressed with slicked knuckles down her abdomen, her hands splitting before her mons and then lifting to her breasts. Round, happy breasts, she thought. Nipples large and pointed upward. She felt the weight of each breast and thoughtfully rolled each nipple between her fingers. They really were very nice.

Standing again, she oiled the small of her back, arching her spine and planting her feet against the force of her own hands. Her buttocks, slightly upraised, were next to receive her atten-tion. Then, bending at the waist, she slipped her hands down her legs a second time. Exhaling, she stood up.

But what to wear? To look inconspicuous, to make it to the roof without arousing the curiosity that might produce spectators. She put on her old terry cloth robe and, to feed her developing excite-ment, nipple clamps and a g-string. But then flats, not heels. Drop-ping her keys into one of the robe's deep pockets, she headed for the roof.

Just as she was opening the door of the stairs that led to the roof, Mrs. Eisley from 4B looked out through the chain. "Damn," Becky whispered to herself.

"Oh, it's you, Becky. I heard some noise."

"Yes, Mrs. Eisley. I'm sorry to bother you. I have to get a few things out of my storage area. I'll be quieter on the way down."

Mrs. Eisley paused to consider the explanation, and then, with a nod so slight it might have been Becky's imagination, the door closed, followed by the sounds of three locks being secured in sequence.

Up one flight of stairs she stood on the tar paper and gravel of the flat roof terrace. It was almost evening. The light that still fell was soft, and the slow whir of the domed roof fans lingered in the humid air. Becky turned left from the stairs and walked past four stalls in the concrete block storage structure. At the fifth she stopped, fished the keys out of her pocket, and struggled with the partially rusted padlock.

The cinderblock storage space was small and damp and usually ten degrees cooler than the outside air on these summer nights, a rooftop haven that felt subterranean. A single naked lightbulb hung from the ceiling, dim, forty watts. Becky had wired a plug off the line that fed the light. A cord dropped from the side of the bulb to the middle of the room, then snaked under an opaque plastic sheet.

The tarp hid her secret machine, her conduit to peace, her horse. Nobody else knew about it. When she had given David the keys to her apartment, she had neglected to provide the extra storage room key.

The idea of the horse had been with Becky since she was fourteen or so, but she had had to wait until she had graduated from college, until she had an apartment to herself, to build and keep her beast in private.

The horse was, in fact, her greatest yield from high school industrial drafting class. She was proud of the design. Sturdy, electronically and mechanically simple, and tailored to a specific purpose. She could build a better one now, a more efficient horse with more flexibility, a more sophisticated machine. But that would take time and money, and this one had become an old friend. It would be unkind to replace it. Becky smiled at the ease with which she could project feelings onto machines, especially the ones she made, and the relative difficulty she had empathizing with most human beings. Some people might be forever outside of her understanding.

Becky closed the plywood door and untied her robe. For a second or two she worried about being interrupted. She always had this moment of concern, but in the five years she had lived here no one had bothered her. There had not been even a close call. No one who didn't have building keys could even get onto the roof. Only seven of the twelve apartments were occupied this time of year, and nobody was going to come through a closed door looking into her storage bin at six-thirty on a Wednesday night. She removed her open robe and hung it over a bronze hat rack just inside the door.

Becky took a step into the room and in doing so crossed almost half of it. She pulled up the plastic and folded it neatly along its creases, then laid it on top of a liquor box full of once-read books.

The horse's anatomy had three main parts. An old, now quite stained Western saddle, with an eight-by-fourteen-inch rectangle cut through its concave seat, was bolted onto a perforated metal frame that resembled a hobby horse except for its dual top bars and a shelf that sat twelve inches from the underside of the saddle's seat. The shelf contained the horse's innards, its working parts, two small electric motors. Each, through a nest of gears, drove a single piston up and down through a rectangular housing set into the horse's back. Attached to the front piston was a dildo, straight, stocky and friendly. The back piston drove a silicon butt plug. A newer model might have pitch and yaw, might have joysticks instead of the side-by-side rheostatic throttle levers that were attached where the saddle horn had once been.

Becky checked the throttles to zero and flipped the toggle switch on the shelf. The little engines hummed like a hundred bees. Becky mounted the horse. She had built it so that her feet rested flat on the ground, even when in a full gallop.

The throttle levers, similar to but smaller than those used to control boat engines, fit nicely in the curl of her right hand. Her right arm, crossing in front of her, put a slight tugging pressure on her chained nipple clips. She eased the left lever up slightly, then down again quickly. As she did, the rear piston slid up three inches and stopped. There was no hurry. Pushing her g-string aside, she repositioned herself, letting the plug slide smoothly into her oiled anus. Then she held back, like she always did when everything was in place. With the humming vibration of the desperate little disengaged engines, with the heat in her spine, with the ticklish pushing of the plug spreading into her consciousness, wiping it clean of other thoughts, of thought generally, she counted to fifty, curling her bare toes against the cool concrete with each number she pronounced.

At the count of fifty she pushed the right lever forward slightly. The dildo peeked up through the saddle back. As it entered her she tensed, trying to hold it in. It was a rigged game. Playing against herself, teasing herself, withholding from herself and then delivering richly and abundantly unto herself.

She let the dildo work slowly, methodically. Rubbing back and forth at the pace of her pulse. Filling her with tentative strokes against the plug that already filled her. She pushed the right lever forward again. The rate of successive penetrations increased, forcing the beating of her heart. Becky tensed against the worn sides of the saddle. The horse was driving her in a cold fire.

When the static charge was sharp and spreading, when orgasm hovered, she pulled back on the right lever, stopping the horse in its tracks. Becky held her breath, lingering at the edge of the chasm. Counting again. When the first wave had passed, she tweaked the left throttle with such a practiced hand that she extended the butt plug to its maximum height inside her.

A shiver ran through her. Now for the finale, she thought. She took the chain between her nipple clamps in her teeth and threw both throttles forward. The horse shook slightly, coughed and stopped. The overhead bulb flickered and died. But while the light recovered almost immediately, the horse did not.

"Shit! Shit! Shit!" Mechanical failure. Her machine had never left her in the lurch. Well, once, years ago, but she had fixed that. She sighed and dismounted gingerly, with a gurgle and a pop.

On first inspection the machine looked fine except for the fact that neither engine was running. A power surge? A short? Maybe a problem with the line. Circuit design and repair had never been her best subjects. For all her hard work she had gotten a B in Introductory Electronics.

The electrical connection to the horse seemed intact. Tracing the line up to the ceiling, she could see no breaks nor feel any hot spots. A more thorough examination would have to wait until tomorrow, when she could bring more light and the proper tools.

Becky climbed onto another box of books to unplug her miscreant beast. The lace g-string stretched grudgingly against her swollen vulva, igniting tiny sparks in her back and neck. She would take care of that in a few minutes, downstairs, with one of her conventional battery-operated devices.

Straining, she could just reach the ceiling. It took no small effort to pull the plug, and it wasn't until the moment it came free from the socket that she registered the breeze. It was slight but noticeable against her bare bottom, hot and soft like a breath. And she could feel someone there, behind her, in the doorway.

She turned before she had time to consider the possibilities, and there, not three feet from her, was David. His face had taken on a most unusual expression, one she had never seen before. He looked baffled, maybe upset, certainly surprised.

Becky looked down at her manacled breasts and soaked g-string, her pedestal of books. She looked at the horse, unplugged and uncovered. And somehow she didn't feel ashamed of these disclosures.

"I'm sorry," David stammered. "I came by and Mrs. Eisley said you might be up here. I mean, I didn't mean to . . ." He made some vague and abrupt hand motions. An erection was obvious under his thin summer slacks, his body bold where his speech was faltering.

"Come in. Close the door." Becky's voice was steady despite her excitement. She stepped down from her box, meeting him halfway. "You're the only other person ever to see my machine," she said.

He didn't reply but reached out a hand, tracing her stomach and breasts in the air an inch or two from her skin. His eyes followed his hand in a kind of worship. He kneeled in front of her and in the same motion clasped his arms around her hips, pushing his face onto the flat space below her navel and above the g-string. His hold was tight, compressing. He mouthed inaudible words.

The heat and pressure melted Becky at the knees. Flowing through David's arms, she joined him on the cool concrete floor. His eyes were open but unseeing as he buried his face in her neck, then pushed his nose and chin along her shoulders and under her right arm. Becky whimpered, tugging on David's clothes, covering his face and neck in a cascade of kisses. They were new together, honest and fierce.

Becky made short work of David's clothes. A button tore and flew across the room, unnoticed. She wanted to climb onto him. To be climbed onto. To occupy and be occupied. His erection was large and strong as she closed her mouth over it. He lifted her, turning her gently. Pushing aside the g-string, David immersed his face in her vulva with the almost involuntary rocking of his head. Oscillating up and down along the banks of her labia, his tongue and lips found her clitoris and pulled hard on it. She nursed hungrily on his penis, swirling her tongue along its underside and along the ridge of its head, tugging rhythmically at his buttocks and balls. They were growling and humming and tearing, and just when it was unbearable, impossibly close to orgasm, they disentangled and Becky mounted David.

Above him, facing him, she pinned his arms above his head, her hands locked to his. "Slow," he whispered with each breath, like a prayer. "Slow."

Soaked and stinging with salt and juices, Becky rocked slowly, rolling her abdominal muscles once with each forward thrust of her hips. Lifting David's captured right hand to her mouth, she gnawed on his knuckles as she pulled and pulsed against him. Her rocking was faster, harder, and more tenacious.

David was gasping out almost-words, unrecognizable syllables of their own shared language. Biting and rubbing, body and body and body. Becky's cycles grew still faster and larger until she could press no further. David was pushing up against her onslaught, clenching every muscle, until they both exploded and collapsed, folding into each other.

They stayed like that, he still inside her, as they became slowly aware of the cold, unyielding floor, of the dank air, of muscle cramps and bruises that would no doubt appear in a day or two. Becky laughed a big, deep, open laugh for no particular reason. She swept the matted hair from David's forehead.

David smiled weakly. "Did you know that there's a fuse box outside?"

"No, I can't say that I remembered that. How 'bout we go downstairs and you make me some dinner?"

Marcy Sheiner

❧❀❧

Under His Thumb

It's 1963. My parents and older sister Jackie are in the den of our split-level suburban home watching Ed Sullivan, when suddenly I hear a great commotion. Jackie is squealing like a pig, my father is booming his refrain about "you stupid kids," and my mother is telling both of them to shut up, she can't hear the TV. These precise sound effects have occurred twice before in the history of our family: First when Elvis appeared on Ed Sullivan, and again when the Beatles made their debut. Both times I scurried downstairs to witness history. Tonight I do so again.

Five skinny, scruffy British kids with long greasy-looking hair are banging on instruments and mewling with untrained vocal cords. The lead singer, with his thick snarly lips and defiant fuck-you posture, immediately captures my attention. He is not overtly sexual like Elvis, and he isn't "cute" like the four moptops. But Mick Jagger touches something dark and rebellious in my little teenage soul.

Having recently discovered masturbation, I retire to my room, flop face down on the bed and, bunching the covers between my legs, hump furiously against them while imagining Mick Jagger's thick snarly lips on mine. I come.

* * *

It's 1973. I'm living in Manhattan. My sister calls from her respectable marital abode in Westchester to say that hubby Kevin, who's an ASCAP lawyer, has scored two third-row seats to a Rolling Stones concert at Madison Square Garden. Kevin, a folkie who thinks the Stones are raucous, has volunteered to stay home with baby Joey. Am I available?

The thought of seeing Mick from a distance of merely three rows gets my pussy tingling. But the concert is to take place on the very same evening as a strategy session for a pro-ERA march, of which I am one of the organizers. My feminist comrades, who despise the Rolling Stones for their sexist lyrics and attitudes, know nothing of my fondness for them; I hide their albums, especially the one with the unzipped fly, whenever they come to visit.

A moral crisis is upon me. Jackie calls every day, saying she cannot hold out forever, soon she'll have to ask someone else. She considers me mad with my anti-Stones brand of feminism and reminds me that the band is part of the cultural movement that has led me to seek liberation in the first place.

"Listen to their liberating lyrics!" she sputters.

"Yeah?" I challenge. "Name one."

"Well, there's . . ." I hold the phone patiently and picture Jackie rummaging through her record albums, desperately seeking a feminist message. At last, success: "She comes in colors!" Jackie shouts triumphantly.

Of course, I relent. (Was there ever any question?) The day before the concert I tell my comrades that my sister and her husband have been called out of town on an emergency and I must go to Westchester to babysit my nephew. What could be more sisterly?

From our vantage point, third row center, I can see every gyration of Mick's pelvis, and a definite hard-on bulging beneath the fabric of his torn jeans. He has, of course, matured from the barely restrained bad boy of Ed Sullivan days into the bony steel-eyed fiercely energetic performer he will remain throughout his long career. Some call him androgynous, but when he clasps his hands behind his head, purses his pouty lips and thrusts his pelvis into our faces, I respond to raw animal masculinity. When Mick struts and frets like a peacock, I feel as if he's inviting me to fall before him as before an altar, to unzip his pants and pour all my love and lust upon the center of his manhood. Is he not my idol? Is this not the ultimate meaning of idolatry? I want to be under his gaze, under his cock, under his thumb.

Jackie screams incessantly for the duration of the concert, but I remain silent, mesmerized. My cunt is palpitating. My nipples are so hard I'm afraid they'll push holes through my t-shirt. I wonder if Mick can see them. I hope so.

When I get home there are urgent messages from feminist comrades on my answering machine: There was some sort of ideological split at the meeting, and my presence, according to one caller, could have averted it. Twinges of guilt do not prevent me from flopping face down on my bed and positioning my hand so that my thumb presses against my clit while two fingers snake into my cunt. I imagine Mick's lips exactly where my hand is. I come.

It's 1983. I am living in Woodstock, New York. It is common knowledge that the Rolling Stones are in town recording an album at a nearby sound studio. It's drummer Charlie Watt's birthday, and rumors fly that the Stones have rented out a local nightclub for a celebration.

I go into overdrive: first I call a friend of a friend who waits tables at the club to confirm the rumor. Then I call Jackie, who leaves Joey and his sister Lucy in the care of the ever-patient Kevin and drives up from Westchester. That night we stand freezing in the parking lot along with several other hopeful groupies, watching with dismay as town hotshots, invited by the club's owner, file smugly inside. When the president of the bank enters, Jackie loses it. "The Rolling Stones come from the working class!" she shouts. "*We* should be in there, not the president of the fucking bank!" I am afraid I may have to sedate her.

A limo pulls up and Keith Richards, wearing a silver jumpsuit with the zipper open to the navel, steps out. Five of us immediately surround him. One woman asks how he's enjoying the mountains; another asks if he's dined at our four-star Chinese restaurant. Jackie ignores all sense of propriety: She demands that we, as loyal fans and common folk, be granted entry to the party.

"You want to go to the party, d'you?" Keith asks, seriously considering the request. "Hold on, luvs, and I'll see what I can do." At the door he tosses his head towards us and tells the bouncer to "Let the five chicks in."

We hear murmurs of uncertainty, a consultation with the club's owner, a protest and then, unbelievably, Mick Jagger's authoritative voice: "Keith says to let the five chicks *in!*"

As we file in, Mick, resplendent in black tuxedo, greets each of us with a kiss on the hand. (In retrospect, he was probably bored to death by all the doctors, lawyers and bankers, and thrilled at our arrival.) I am the last one to enter, and after he kisses my hand, I do not let go.

"Thanks for inviting us," I say.

"Would you like to dance?" he asks, looking me up and down.

I am so stunned that I enter what can only be described as an altered state, akin to a drug high. People and objects, especially Mick, become blurred, almost surreal. In a daze I dance to one song after another, sometimes with Mick, sometimes with Jackie, whose envy is assuaged when Keith whirls her onto the dance floor. At some point a cake appears and we sing "Happy Birthday." Slowly the party winds down and the club empties out. Mick and I are among the last to leave.

Soon we are in a cabin, or a country inn, or maybe even a trailer, deep in the woods. An antique dresser topped by a huge round mirror faces a big brass bed. An armchair sits at an angle in the corner. Mick seats me in the chair and pushes buttons on a tape deck, simultaneously ripping off his jacket, tie and shirt.

The slow bluesy sound of "You Got to Move" fills the room as Mick, wearing only his pants and undershirt, faces the mirror. He begins moving to the music, his narrow hips swaying. He rubs his hands along either side of the growing bulge in his pants, up and down from waist to groin. He purses his lips and inhales deeply. His eyes are glued to his own image in the mirror; I wonder if he's even aware of my presence.

He mouths the words to the song, puts a hand behind his head, and struts back and forth between the bed and the dresser. He opens wide his legs, knees bent, and does a few pliés. The bulge in his pants quivers. He unzips his fly and pulls out his long, smooth ivory cock. It's a lovely organ—but more importantly, it's attached to someone about whom I have been fantasizing for two decades. A famous man, a superstar, one of the icons of our time. To be so close makes me dizzy, brings a lump of emotion to my throat.

Mick is oblivious to my reaction. "Ooooh!" he whispers, exhaling sharply and closing his eyes. Lovingly he strokes his erection.

I press my hands between my legs, my cunt aching like a wound. Is Mick planning to fuck me or himself? Will he let me suck his cock? Abandoning all pretext of decorum, I fall out of the chair and crawl on all fours towards him. Mick opens his eyes.

"Just what d'you think you're doin'?" he taunts, his lips curling at the corners.

"I want to suck you," I gasp.

He laughs, or rather, he makes a sound commonly called a laugh but which is too full of cruelty to be categorized as mirthful.

"And just who told you you could do *that*, li'l chippie?"

"Please," I beg. I choke on the lump in my throat and tears threaten to spill from my eyes. "Please let me."

Mick laughs again, waving his cock at me. He stops his dancing to remove his remaining clothes. I am awed by the sight of every rib, every bone, visible beneath his translucent skin. A blue vein zigzags artfully down his right arm. He moves closer and sticks his cock right under my nose. My tongue darts out, but Mick jumps backwards in a hasty two-step.

The song has changed to "Brown Sugar." The pace of his dancing picks up: naked, he gavottes around the small room, clutching his member, ignoring me.

I rip off my clothes, hoping to capture his attention with my naked body. I do. He dances towards me, and when the song ends and the tape player clicks off, he stands still, his hands on his sharp hip bones, his hard cock aimed straight at my mouth.

I reach out and run my forefinger up and down his silky shaft, around the smooth crown. Am I really touching Mick Jagger's naked cock? Curiously I hold it, study it. It could belong to any man. But it doesn't—and that makes all the difference in the world.

Suddenly I am overcome with terror: talk about performance anxiety! He's probably been sucked by the very best in the world. I resolve to give the blow job of my life.

I bend forward and plant kisses all over this prick that millions of men and women have fantasized about. I caress the head with my lips. I take my time licking it from base to crown, pausing to take each of his balls into my mouth and gently suck on them. I return to the head and take him in, relaxing the back of my throat so I can get it all down.

His hands exert pressure on my head, his thumbs pushing hard against my temples. "Atta girl," he whispers hoarsely. "Oooh, you suck it so good. All the girls wanna suck my dick, y'know that, dontcha baby?"

Indeed I do; that's part of what makes this so very thrilling. Cunt juice runs down my inner thighs. I look up, nod emphatically, keep on sucking.

"But only you get to suck it t'night. That's cuz you're such a good li'l cocksucker."

I feel blessed, grateful and powerful all at once. Mick keeps talking for a few more minutes, his voice becoming softer and softer, until at last he is silent. I open my eyes and gaze up.

Mick Jagger's famous lips are hanging loose. All the muscles in his face have slackened. His eyes are covered with a gauzy film. With a rush of pride I realize that I am responsible for reducing this wound-up bundle of raw nerves to a purry little kitten. My cocksucking skills are such that I have tamed the beast. For a moment I'm afraid I'll faint, but it's just a momentary swoon.

Mick falls backwards onto the bed, his skinny legs hanging over the edge. I follow, not missing a beat: If this is what he wants, then this is what he'll get—I'll do anything to keep him interested in me. I lick and sniff his balls. I squeeze his ass. I rub my tits over his cock. A drop of pre-come appears on the head, and I wonder if he'll deign to fuck me or if he wants to come in my mouth. I take the risk and climb up to straddle his thin hips. He does not move.

I gaze down and see the pretty girl in him. I recognize her easily—I've seen her on Mick's face countless times, when he's singing a tender love song, or caught unawares by some shrewd photographer. She's the girl who saves Mick Jagger from crude macho, the girl who enables my generation, with all our faith in androgyny, to tolerate his excesses of masculinity. I run my hand over her impossibly delicate cheekbones, her vulnerable Adam's apple, her hairless chest. Mick whimpers, sounding for all the world like a woman. I plant tender kisses all over her face, her ears, her erect little nipples. Then I reach down between her legs.

Suddenly Mick's energy switches into high voltage, and he's a man again. His face tightens, his lips purse, his pelvis thrusts and his cock jabs into me. He is all hardness, fury, insistence.

"Yeah, give it to me, girl, gimme your cunt. All of it. Uhh. Uhh."

He's a blind, grunting animal, his hands gouging the flesh on my hips as he moves me this way and that, his cock seeking, searching—for what? The ever-elusive satisfaction?

"I'm gonna come in you, girl. I'm gonna come soon. Are you ready for it? Huh? You ready for my come?"

"Yes," I gasp.

"Yeah, all the girls want my come. They scream for my come, you know that, dontcha? And I'm gonna give it to *you. Now.*" He grunts, and his whole body stiffens as his cock erupts inside me. I press my clit against his prominent pubic bone and I come too, the walls of my cunt contracting around his gushing cock. I come, honest to God, in colors. Trembling, I collapse onto his wiry body, and then I do cry, hot tears all over his neck and chest. All the frustration of so many years watching and wanting Mick Jagger comes pouring out of me. So many years fantasizing about him, feeling teased by him yet never believing I'd really have him, are in my sobs. The orgasm that released my cunt has opened my heart and tear ducts as well.

Mick strokes my hair comfortingly. "There there," he murmurs, "it's all right now, y'know. You're an all-right chick."

Hours later (or is it days?) I find myself back in my own living room. The world is no longer blurry, but my brain is fuzzy. Did it really happen? Did I really make love to Mick Jagger, or was it just another fantasy? A hallucination? I grope inside my panties; they're very wet. *Something* must have happened.

* * *

It's 1993. My boyfriend Jonathan and I have spent the evening watching the Rolling Stones' Steel Wheels Tour on pay TV. Now I'm face down on the bed; Jonathan is fucking me from behind. Despite hours of stimulation in several different positions, I have been unable to reach orgasm. I turn my head and say in my sweetest pretty-please voice, "Sing to me, honey."

Jonathan chuckles, clears his throat and sings something to the effect that I can cream all over him.

He's got a velvet voice, not so belligerent as Mick's, but it works. I imagine myself onstage, on my knees, sucking Mick Jagger's cock while he looks down at me and the audience applauds. I come.

Sabrina

Sabrina first caught me eyeing her during English, when we were seniors in Mrs. Cornet's class. Sabrina wore makeup like a mask, and she wore it well. It didn't seem at all insipid that she matched her eye shadow and nail polish to her outfits. With her almond-shaped olive eyes and her tan calves, she struck me as inaccessible and otherworldly. Her ease, her social prowess, her calm floated above me. I slid my eyes—touched with matte-brown powder and black mascara, as usual—guiltily to the floor. She'd noticed. Limply I turned to Mrs. Cornet, cheap red hair dye streaming down her jowls in the late spring's hanging heat. In the temporary buildings we giggled collectively.

Since our last names both began with *C*, we were assigned the same homeroom. Each morning, Sabrina read a new romance or science fiction novel with covers of grossly endowed heroines held at the waist by either an earnest lad clad in white or a cancerously tanned sword-wielding hulk. Like Sabrina herself, these covers drew me inadvertently. They reminded me of dog-eared copies of *Cosmopolitan*—the kind I always flipped through, criticizing the objects of my fascination until I contemptuously abandoned them. But there was something seductive, tempting in those glossy pages: images of worlds far from mine. I considered

my hypocrisy as I continued checking Sabrina out, like the harem
of boys that surrounded her.

She bleached her mousy brown hair white and won Most Beautiful every year. Her two best friends, Nicole and Michelle, were
cruel and stupid, but very pretty. Nicole was sunny, her cropped
hair dyed lemony. Michelle was very tall and wore no cosmetics
but deep red fingernail polish and matching lipstick. Her eyes, like
Sabrina's, were green, but Michelle's hair hung in black spirals
around her bare face. Mostly they fucked college guys, but occasionally a senior would capture one's attention.

All three were in my gym class. Though I tried to impose myself on their tight trinity, I invariably sat on the bleachers alone. I
knew I could never glide through life as inauthentically, but I
wanted to seem like them, to laugh as thoughtlessly. My envy
melted with admiration as I watched them shoot baskets accu-
rately, their teeth white as chalk. When Sabrina occasionally turned
to wave, an effortless throw of her jeweled wrist, Michelle and
Nicole would swivel behind her like the anatomical models in
science lab. Pivoting inward at some invisible joint, they'd smirk.

One week while Nicole and Michelle were out sick—they had
both caught a bronchial infection from some guy they'd gotten
wasted with and fucked—Sabrina came to me during gym as if
we had been friends since kindergarten. Relieved from my soli-
tude, I did not protest. Her unabashed approach seduced me and
soon I considered myself her friend. I began to believe it when
she told me—in confidence, of course—about the time Nicole got
so shit-faced she wet her bed. Our eyes rolled in disdain and met
at mid-arc.

When Sabrina and I became friends I learned that she brought
a different dime-store novel to school each morning not because
she was flaky, but because she went through several a day. She'd
spend every class reading, candy beneath her desk, and then skim
entire texts before finals. Straight A's. After we'd been friends long
enough for me to venture so delicate a question, I turned to
Sabrina and asked, "Why do you read nothing but junk?" She
scrunched her hair and looked away. "Diversion," she answered.

From what, I wondered. Boredom surfaced in her eyes and I

stared, mesmerized. They were as glassy as a pool at dawn. She lowered her lids. We finished our lunch in silence, ruminating. Is she thinking of me? Is she thinking? I wondered if these were her thoughts as well.

For eight months before he left for college, I clung to my boyfriend Victor fiercely and blissfully. During this monogamous recess I introduced Sabrina to Victor's best friend, Jason. Though Jason was one class his junior, he joked with Victor provocatively, as a peer or even a superior would. Sabrina admired Jason's irreverence and soon became his girlfriend. Having more in common and to compare, Sabrina and I were soon as thick as Jason and Victor.

How big is it?

He comes too soon?

Do you swallow?

We'd find nooks in the school theater where we'd meet to eat our lunches (candy, chips and soda), reapply makeup and skewer our boyfriends. Once I asked Sabrina if she supposed they talked about us. She told me that guys didn't talk about sex to other guys unless they were lying. I realized she was probably right and felt simultaneously insulted and relieved. Was Victor ashamed of me? Protecting my reputation?

Often I spent the night at Sabrina's house. After watching *The Shining* while we ate Chinese carry-out and drank Pepsi, I resolved to disclose a secret to impress and shock her. I would see if she'd match me, see just how close we were. I chewed my cashew chicken slowly, pondering my attack.

"Victor ejaculates prematurely," I said in a low voice. Sabrina covered her mouth, her face contorting monstrously, her carefully lined lids wide. I continued for full impact, "He says it's my fault because he was a virgin when we met but I wasn't. For about five months he lied to me about girls he'd fucked." Luxuriantly I twisted my hair, savoring my relentless betrayal. Having already disposed of all boundaries, I finished, "The only way he's ever made me come is by going down on me. But he's very good at it."

I'd revealed gossip that could easily whirl back to Victor via Jason, depending on Sabrina's character. Romantically I imagined

my exchange with her a test, a possibility to either form a water-
tight bond with this veiled and pedestaled idol or to kill my relationship with Victor. I didn't care which.

Sabrina confidentially placed her hand on my lower thigh and
said earnestly, "I've never come." She was eighteen and had already slept with about a dozen guys. "I thought Jason was gonna
make me yesterday, but he came first. Seriously, I knew something was gonna happen—I could tell, you know—but then he just
stopped."

Since she had matched my confidence with an equal one, I
grew bolder. Realizing what my question could lead to, I asked,
"Do you ever masturbate?"

The very word made her giggle wildly, but she answered can-
didly. "I've tried. Do you?"

"I know how," I replied vaguely, my voice softer now. I studied
her slack-jawed profile in the blue television light and admired her.

"Show me," she whispered.

"How to get yourself off?" I reddened inadvertently and hoped
the lights in Sabrina's living room were low enough for her not to
notice. Hadn't I wanted her to watch me for once? Had I not been
maneuvering us to this point? I resisted the urge to claim sudden
illness, walk home, call Victor. I looked at the object of my infatua-
tion, now more vulnerable than I. Never would I have this chance
again. "Do you really want to see?"

"Yeah." She kept her hand on my leg and stroked my hair. I
could smell her, a bouquet of hairspray, soap, lotion and sweat.
Though my panties were wet, I argued that her parents or her little brothers might see. After she assured me that no one would
ever know, I leaned against the sofa's arm and let Sabrina push up
my nightshirt. "Show me," she insisted. Fearful that I'd lose her
camaraderie, I acquiesced.

I said nothing, only did it. Pulling aside my cotton bikini panties,
I watched her face apprehensively as she hunched down on the
sofa, looking frankly at my cunt with the distanced appraisal of a
physician. This remoteness soothed me. It implied that the experience was on a wholly different plane from the one on which
we made out together with our boyfriends in Victor's blue Chevro-
let; it didn't seem like cheating, really. The instant the thought of

Victor occurred to me I felt contemptuous mockery of him, guilt pulsing below.

I dipped my middle and index fingers into my pussy and slid them back to my clitoris. Surely Sabrina must notice I'm already wet, I thought. This probability excited me further, and I began tracing my clit slowly, teasing myself to extend the session for Sabrina. I imagined what Victor's reaction would be if my indiscretion got back to him. Sweet betrayal swept through me, nearly getting me off. I paused, sliding my finger around my ass, tracing the orifice lightly, regaining my bearings.

What if she touches me, I wondered. The prospect simultaneously scared me and fueled my desire to divulge my most secret sexuality to Sabrina, a girl I recognized as ultimately opportunistic and hollow. How far did I want this to escalate? Eventually I felt disappointed that she had no intention of participating—and I dared not ask her to. I began rubbing my clit vigorously, eager to come.

"How will I know when it happens?" Sabrina asked.

"You'll know," I whispered. Conversing with her didn't distract me. The exchange aroused me further and reeled me closer to orgasm.

"Will you tell me?"

"All right," I answered.

Sabrina spread my legs wider and commanded me to "Go ahead."

Her tone stripped me of my defenses. Obligingly I pressed my pelvis into my fingers as I gazed at Sabrina. The last time I had masturbated with a girl I'd been thirteen, nearly six years ago. Memories of Sharon and me hugging pillows between our legs and moaning in her single bed returned to me unbidden, and I spat out "Now" through clenched teeth. Sabrina watched my pussy, and I came longer than I did when Victor licked me, as long as the best times when I'd been alone.

Sabrina sat up. "It doesn't work when I do it like that," she said.

Blissful, I lacked empathy and wanted only to sleep. I'd shown her, hadn't I?

The next morning Sabrina and I awoke vinelike and embryonic. Hastily she withdrew her thigh from between mine and pulled her arm from beneath my head. Masturbating, I listened to her shower. By the time she emerged from the bathroom, fully clothed, I was dressed. We spoke politely about midterms as I gathered my things. At breakfast we chewed our pancakes too cheerfully and bantered with her brothers. When my parents rang the bell and I saw the relief on Sabrina's face, I realized that we'd transgressed some unspoken contract; we'd betrayed our boyfriends and were too ashamed to admit it, even to each other. We'd have laughed for days had we cheated with boys. Loss briefly caressed my heart, but I couldn't muster regret.

I never told Victor about the last night I spent with Sabrina. If she told Jason, either he didn't mention it to Victor or Victor held a good poker face. Nothing ever got back to me, but that could have meant anything.

Because of my own actions I recognized in others the capacity to deceive. I could only speculate as to what Victor and Jason kept between themselves. Whatever it may have been, their friendship eroded after Victor left for Tulane, and then Boston University accepted Jason. I went to Chicago and Sabrina took off for UCSD. Sabrina's and my respective relationships with Jason and Victor hiccupped along until distance and arguments eventually snuffed out the little life that still jerked beneath escalating animosity.

Four years later and two years into my marriage, Sabrina called. "I found your number through Information," she said. "I thought I'd say hi."

"Can you come over?" I asked.

"In a New York minute."

When she rang I was reclining naked on the daybed.

"Come in," I called. She entered and complimented my decor. She smelled slightly of citrus and wore a white silk dress that let the light through. She looked radiant.

"Come here," I implored. I'd been toying with my nipples, thinking how sweet a fuck she'd be, but I was nonetheless taken aback by the depth of my attraction, unfaded by time. My marriage hung in tatters, but this relationship had survived unfrayed.

"How are you, Sabrina?"

"Well. I've progressed to action," she said. Eager to give her the opportunity to demonstrate, I grabbed her hair in my fist and pulled her to me. Her lips parted and she moaned as I traced them with my tongue, tickling her gums and finally invading her mouth. She unpried my hand and ordered me to turn over. Lightly she traced my buttocks, spreading my legs to press my outer labia. My hard clit hung down and she pinched it between my lips and her index and middle fingers. She held my pussy against her palm and her wet finger slid up my ass. After she manipulated me for several minutes, my cunt's spasms drenched her rings.

I rolled over and sighed helplessly as she pinched my nipples. She opened my legs and regarded me as she had in high school. I felt a wave of déjà vu, but it passed.

She lowered her head to my straining pelvis, spread my labia and paralyzed me with her tongue. She licked my asshole and lapped at my inner lips and tongue-fucked my gushing pussy until I begged her to suck my clit. She held my lips apart as I pulled her long tresses back to watch. The sight of her pink tongue leisurely tormenting my clit made me even hotter.

When Christian walked in, he said nothing. He stood and watched, his thick cock seething beneath his trousers. This could have been Victor, I thought. He made no move to interfere. Sabrina ruthlessly flicked my clit, quickly and diligently. She wanted this and so did I. I should have stopped her, but it was too good. Watching Christian made it better.

"Who's your friend?" my husband asked. He showed no agitation, slowly removing his coat as his dick swelled.

I could barely speak, but from his demeanor I sensed a chance for redemption. "Sabrina," I said as clearly as possible. "From high school."

"What are you doing with my wife?" Christian asked, shoving his fingers into my wet, desperately clutching pussy. He began tickling my G spot and I whimpered. He pressed into me until I came so hard I ejected his fingers, ejaculating all over Sabrina's lovely face. Christian stood and licked his agile fingers slowly, staring at me. "She tastes good, doesn't she?" he asked Sabrina. When she didn't answer, he pulled her blond hair back and kissed her slicked face. "Now lick her pussy some more."

Sabrina obliged, lapping softly at my recovering cunt. In one

fluid movement Christian released his prick and pushed up her
dress. He pulled aside her panties and groaned as he penetrated
her. He held very still, reaching around Sabrina's waist to pinch
and massage her clit. Since I knew his touch so well, I could sense
each teasing caress from the changes in her rhythm and the strength
of her breathing. I could see his arm moving, jiggling her clit until
she came. My cunt muffled her cries slightly, but the sound drove
Christian mad. He held her steady between my legs as she continued lapping my entire pussy, from the vulva up to the clitoris, circling it, teasing, then sucking hard. He pulled back a few times
before he came, his chest flushed, his forehead damp. He withdrew from Sabrina and swiftly buttoned his chinos.

I felt a peculiar mixture of jealousy, insult and pride in both my
husband's and my friend's sexual nonchalance. I still couldn't de-
termine Christian's stance. He was unpredictable. That's why I'd
married him.

I broke the silence. "I'm about to come, Christian."

"Don't," he commanded.

"I'm sorry, baby," I moaned as orgasm swept through me like
electricity. I bucked beneath Sabrina and she latched on more
tightly, sucking me to a third and fourth climax. Minutes passed
before I could address Christian.

"Let me suck your cock, baby."

"I'm leaving you," he announced.

"Don't be so sentimental."

After he'd packed for a hotel, Sabrina and I toasted my au-
tonomy. I knew we'd finally resolved our unspoken conflict by
consummating our attraction. Closure settled between us and I
opened another bottle of port.

I didn't see her again for three years. I didn't get her number
and she never called. Our long separation was interrupted last
week when I saw her reading Stephen King at an outdoor cafe.
Her wavy hair had grown to her waist and she'd draped her
breasts with a low-cut jacket. I fought a desire to bolt and calmly
crossed the intersection.

"It's been a long time," I said.

"I'm married," she answered. A diamond teardrop, at least two carats, weighted her left ring finger, a gold band bracing the exhibition. Her fuck-me red lipstick glistened in the sun.

"Of course, I'm divorced," I said.

"Of course. Would you come over for dinner Thursday?"

"I'd love to."

Ginu Kamani

❧

Fish Curry Rice

I can hear my aunt's voice through the wall again, matchmaking. In Bombay, conversations on the telephone are always louder than in person.

"See, this girl is very stubborn. She will never come to your house to meet your boy. But we're going to the club for lunch tomorrow, so why don't you just drop by? That way all of you can take a good look at her. I tell you, she's quite silly. Insists she has a boyfriend in America and is not interested in anyone else. Well, we'll soon take care of all that."

Matchmaking. The favorite hobby of idle adults in India. Sentencing each other's children to a fate worse than . . . .

"How many times have I said to myself, It is an absolute curse having good-looking girls in the family. Better if my niece were an ugly duckling. Then we could take care of her right away without fuss. But once they become aware of their looks, these girls just lose all their sense. Then *we* have to run around trying to fix them up with someone decent! Thankless job, I tell you."

I couldn't move. I was fascinated by the way my aunt was ignoring all my unique qualities and treating me like a commodity. I knew I would go to the club for lunch with her the following day and I could almost predict the fortyish couple who would drop by the table: the man with tired eyes, whitening hair, restless to move

on to his tennis game; the woman plump, with perfectly sprayed
tresses, chiffon sari and diamonds, unwilling to acknowledge my
presence until my aunt introduced us. Then her eyes would turn
on me and her lips would part and she would say with perfectly
rehearsed surprise, "Oh! So *you're* the daughter of Jamini! We've
all heard so much about you. But don't worry, only good things."

She would giggle on cue, pull up a chair and commence an endless session of gossip with my aunt, from which I was pointedly
excluded. The man would look around, spot one of his men friends
and excuse himself in a hurry. I would watch my aunt's friend
glancing at me from the corner of her eye. The bearer would ar-
rive with our lunch and I would grab my usual plate of mutton
samosas and finish them off before my aunt had even started on
her soup and toast. The two older women would watch me eat
with fascination.

"Eating fried food is bad for your figure," my aunt's friend
would admonish sharply. "You should give all this up now, while
you still can."

"Oh, don't worry," I would retort with one of my stock replies.
"I'll go to the ladies' room in a minute and vomit it back out."

"What a sense of humor this one has!" the friend would gasp,
suitably shocked.

"Just wait." My aunt's voice would rise as she adjusted her sari
over her bulk. "After you get married, you'll never be thin again."

"Actually," I would yawn, "I was a lot heavier before I started
having sex. Steady sex in a marriage should do wonders for me."

By this time the friend would be quite insulted and draw my
aunt into another long cycle of gossip. I would close my eyes and
lean back in the rattan armchair, drifting to the hoarse chugging of
a dozen ceiling fans, the clink of glasses and silverware. I'd hear
excited shouts from the cricket field and the sharp crack of the bat.
These were some of the oldest, most familiar sounds embedded
in my consciousness. The effect of hearing them once again was
hypnotic.

"If only your parents would come to their senses, they would
realize how important it is to fix you up with a nice boy. But even
they had their heads turned after living in the States all these

years. Believe you me, one word of encouragement from your mother and I would be dragging you all across this city to meet boys. At this very moment, I have at least thirty boys who would agree to you, sight unseen. What's the harm in at least meeting a few of them? Other girls aren't fortunate to have me for their auntie. You're an attractive girl from a good family with a university degree and a green card. Who knows, you might even decide to move back to Bombay if you meet the right man."

I make a list of questions for my aunt: Will you let us use your house to have sex? Will you introduce me to your gynecologist so she can put me on the Pill? Will you rent us your other apartment so we can live together for a couple of years? Can we borrow your vibrators?

My aunt's cook, Ramesh, was an utter sensualist. His food was so delicious that each mouthful entered my body like some ethereal nectar. I could barely stand to chew it. One night when I was alone in the house, I asked Ramesh if he had ever cooked fish. He said of course, many times, but not in this house. He said he had a special fish curry that he used to make for his previous employer, a Swiss engineer who lived in Bombay for three years. I asked if he could make it for me and he nodded. I was surprised.

"What, here?" I asked, laughing. "In this pure vegetarian household?"

He nodded again, said, "No problem" in English, and left the house. It was dark outside. Where would he find fish at this time of the night?

Ramesh returned in ten minutes with a thick filet of *surmai* in his hand. He had begged it from the Muslim cook on the seventh floor. I stood there with my mouth open, as excited as a little girl. Ramesh was shy, and after a few minutes of pretending that he was alone in the kitchen, he turned to me blushing and asked if I wouldn't prefer to sit in the living room until the curry rice was ready. I said, No, I had to watch him. And, I said to his burning red neck, he had to join me in eating the meal. At that he giggled and stammered: "No, no, *memsahib*, how can I, you are not yet married, it will be a shame on us."

The fish curry was astonishing, its flavors as distinct, yet as blended, as a rainbow. I took two bites of the curry rice and, without realizing, started to cry. Ramesh stood at the far end of the kitchen, watching me eat my first few bites, to be sure I approved. When he saw my tears, he approached me nervously. "It is too much chili, *memsahib*?" he asked anxiously. "Shall I give you a little yogurt?" I took control of myself and wiped away the tears of joy.

The gift of his curry was profound. After years of eating fish fingers in America, my body was overwhelmed by the real taste of fish.

I resumed eating. I inquired whether Ramesh was from Goa. He smiled broadly and said yes. "Don't you drink *feni* with your dinner?" I asked. "Let's have some."

He shook his head sorrowfully. "*Memsahib*, very sorry, but this is not possible. If I drink in this house, I will lose my job."

"I understand," I said. "Where can I get some for myself?"

"No problem," he said in English. He walked into the adjoining servant's room where he unrolled his bed every night, came back with a bottle of clear liquid, plucked a teacup off the drying rack and poured out a small amount. He handed it to me, still grinning. "Very strong, *memsahib*!" he warned. "Only for sipping."

I took the cup from him and drank the liquid in one gulp. The burn down my throat was smooth, and filled my face with heat. Ramesh watched me with open mouth and rapidly shifting eyes.

"It's very good," I acknowledged, and held out my cup. "One for me and one for you," I said, motioning Ramesh to get himself a cup.

Ramesh shook his head. "Sorry, *memsahib*. I am happy for you, but it is not possible for me."

"Call me Renu." I smiled at him. "When you call me *memsahib* it feels like you're talking about someone else."

"Want to come with me and get your hair done? You have very little imagination, I think, always leaving your hair open like that. Just collects dust all day. My Chinese hairdresser is very good. She'll show you some tricks. And while we're there, I'll tell her to fix your blackheads. You really should get them removed before it's too late. And also that hair on your chin looks like a nanny goat. There are only two or three of them, but my god, how vulgar! What will people think?"

"Do Indian men really care about my blackheads?" I teased my aunt. "I think it's just an obsession for Indian women. None of my American boyfriends ever notices such things."

"That's exactly why I'm telling you not to waste yourself on an American boy. Leave them for those girls who aren't so eligible. Americans will marry anyone, you know. Comes from not having a sense of their own history. Mongrels, all of them."

To do or not to do Indians, that was the question. I had more than a month to go in Bombay. Could my aunt really rustle up an interesting man for me? To be or not to be sexual around my relatives, that was the real issue.

"Okay. Find me someone. But no virgins. And no anatomical illiterates. And no chaperones, meddlers or parents, please."

My aunt looked at me in shock—she couldn't believe I'd said yes. She smirked with ill-concealed victory, then broke into a triumphant, generous laugh.

"You naughty girl, there's nothing wrong with virgins! In fact, it's a blessing because you can teach them exactly how you want it. Just don't brag about where you got all your experience."

Ramesh and I began a series of nightly trysts. He cooked me fish—one piece was enough to satiate my craving—and then watched me eat. It took me close to an hour to eat the single piece of fish and the bowlful of rice. The flavors were so intense, so overpowering, that I had to stop after each mouthful and let my quivering taste buds settle into some semblance of calm. If I took two bites in a row, my stomach felt unbearably full, as though I had eaten well beyond my limit and would burst.

After that first night, Ramesh saw that conversation was not the right accompaniment for my meal. Instead, he settled down on his haunches and stared at me with intense fascination as I ate. I might as well have been a child or an animal, given the ease with which this normally deferential, barely literate employee entered into my space. If my aunt had seen the two of us together in the kitchen, sitting so intimately on the bare floor, she would have suspected the worst—that I had lost my mind and become the cook's lover.

Never in my life in Bombay had I been able to look a male servant in the eye without overtones of power, dominance, cruelty,

indifference. But every mouthful of Ramesh's fish became a whirl-
pool flooding my entire being with ecstasy. I was too dazed to be
bothered with the codes of domestic hierarchy. With great difficulty I softened my moans of pleasure into mewing sounds, which
Ramesh took as a signal to bring out the *feni*, surreptitiously pre-
sented in a teacup.

"Haven't you found someone yet?" I asked my aunt impatiently.
She looked at me with tired eyes. She'd been on the phone non-
stop for the past few days. Quite a few of the thirty "sight unseen"
prospects had moved to the United States for postgraduate studies. Several others were engaged to be married, or close to it. Two
families with Gandhian roots were morally and ethically opposed
to green card marriages. And word had gotten around that my sister had divorced her Bombay–born-and-bred husband. His un-
happy family had put out the word that the girls in our family
were fickle and bossy.

Ramesh's fish was having an explosive impact on me. The curry
rice seemed to wander off the normal digestive route and lodge
instead in my groin, creating a slow burn. I hungered for contact.
Bombay was unexplored sexual territory for me, still connected in
my mind to the trusting dependencies of childhood.

I asked Ramesh about the men in the apartment building. He
was incredulous that I wanted information on servants, drivers,
watchmen and janitors, as those were the only men he knew. But
he answered my questions with great gusto. Who were the most
handsome? Who bragged about being the most virile? Which of
them were married, which had girlfriends, who visited prosti-
tutes? Ramesh had an astonishing range of information about most
of the domestics—apparently these men let their guard down
around the sweet-natured cook. Ramesh related these stories to
me with the childlike trust I associated with a prepubescent boy. I
was surprised to discover that he was married and had three children in his village, whom he saw perhaps once or twice in a year.

One night after an exquisite meal of several kinds of spiced roe,
I told Ramesh that Big Memsahib was searching out a husband for
me. The cook's eyes lit up and he broke into a grin. In a rush of

sentences he congratulated me, blessed me with good luck and fertility and shared his conviction that I would be matched to a very good man. Seeing my skepticism, he stopped smiling. "Bad thoughts will hinder the process," he gently scolded.

I looked hard at Ramesh, wondering whether I could trust him with my deepest desires. His youthful face stared back at me, still glowing with the news of my impending matrimony.

I put his hand on my forehead and told him to feel the heat. He admitted that my skin felt feverish. I nodded slowly and added that I felt the same fever burning in my groin and placed my hand meaningfully over my pubis. Ramesh did not understand at first, but then his mouth fell open. He lost his balance and fell forward, almost landing in the remains of the food. He sprang up and brushed himself off.

"You think only men feel a burning between their legs?" I asked sharply.

Ramesh coughed nervously, then began laughing with his hand clamped over his mouth. "*Memsahib*," he said, smiling, "the truth is that if you take a lover from among us poor servants, we will definitely lose our jobs. But if you don't care whether we work or starve, then surely someone among the servants is senseless enough to say yes. Do you want me to ask around?"

Ramesh's words were like a slap in the face; I felt the sour taste of shame in my mouth. Is that what I had seriously been contemplating? Did I expect reciprocation of my sexual urge from men who were in constant fear of being sacked, humiliated, abandoned?

"I didn't make myself clear," I said. "I don't want anyone losing their job, least of all you. So just think very carefully before you do anything. But if there is a *sahib* in the building—unmarried, good-humored, a decent person—who might be alone, just the way I am, then perhaps you could mention to one of his servants that Big Memsahib's foreign-returned niece is in town for a while and likes to have company in the evenings."

Ramesh nodded and cleared the plates. He disappeared into the back room and returned with two teacups of *feni*. Without a word, he placed one cup in front of me and took the other in his own hand.

"*Chin-chin,*" I murmured, and tapped my cup against his in salute.

"You can use my bed," Ramesh offered before draining his cup in one gulp.

"I just don't know why I'm having such bad luck finding someone for you. When you need them, these dashing Romeos disappear into the woodwork like cockroaches."

In a week of hunting, my aunt had found no one. She was beginning to despair. She had lost her appetite. In the past, there had been nothing easier than finding partners for her stable of youngsters.

"I wish your mother had told me openly about your sister's divorce. Honestly, I could have saved face and at least come up with *some* bloody excuse, even if it was a complete lie, who cares, in this city it's all about appearances. It's one thing for you children to have forgotten our Indian customs, but I can't understand what happens to women like your mother when they move abroad. Do they get amnesia or what?"

"My parents supported her divorce. They're quite wonderful that way. If any of us kids are in trouble, they rally around without judgment."

"What a waste, I tell you. Those two were good for each other, really good. The problem was that they waited too long to have children. You have to know how to work a marriage!"

Divorce was a sore topic for matchmakers like my aunt. They took personal offense at the inability of couples to muddle along through life.

"Anyway, Renu darling, there's still hope for you. I've sent your horoscope to be matched through a computer service. Only thing is, the boy may be of a family I don't know. If someone turns up, naturally we will do a full investigation on him. These days you can hire a detective at very decent prices—it's almost become routine, you know, with these caste-no-bar marriages happening all over the place. Personally I can't imagine being married to anyone besides a Gujarati, but youngsters these days seem to have quite the imagination that way, probably comes from reading too many novels. Oh, look, there's someone at the door."

My aunt's bulk blocked the doorway and I couldn't see over her shoulder. There was a brief tussle at the entrance and then she dragged in a protesting young man carrying a ribboned box of sweets. His name was Nemesh Shah, said my aunt, and he was a distant cousin. He looked no older than nineteen or twenty. He shook my hand firmly and introduced himself as Nemo. He said he was just passing through and his mother had sent him with the sweets, and no he really didn't want any tea and he had to get going to the club. I asked Nemo for a ride to the club and he assented.

We drove in silence, Nemo in front with the driver, me in the back. Once at the club, Nemo visibly relaxed. As we signed in, a group of Nemo's friends greeted him with resounding back slaps and cheery hellos. They looked older than Nemo. I studied his face more carefully and saw lines at the corners of his eyes. He was older than I'd thought.

"This is Renu. She lives in my building. She's visiting from the States."

All smiles, the friends began walking toward the tennis courts. I placed my hand on Nemo's arm, signaling him to hang back for a minute.

"I didn't realize we're in the same building! Auntie just said you were a distant relative."

"Oh, that's an old joke, you know, how we're all supposed to be 'related.' Your parents and mine are old friends. We must have met when we were kids."

"So did my aunt call and tell your mother that I was in town?"

"No, no, not at all. The servants were talking, and I overheard them discussing you. Your chap Ramesh is always up there chatting with our cook Hassan."

"You're the ones with the Muslim cook? But . . . but you're Gujaratis!" I sputtered.

Nemesh laughed. "My mother is a Bohra Muslim. Hassan is from her father's village. He's a fantastic cook. Even if the religious fanatics descended on us, the family wouldn't part with Hassan."

Nemesh's laughter brought a mischievous sparkle to his eyes. His smile was brilliant, open, lingering. I looked at him in astonishment, and he stared back. Fast work on the part of Ramesh— here was the *sahib* of his choice. I felt the thrill of the chase engulfing me.

"You . . . you must be circumcised!" I blurted out before I could stop myself. Nemo, who had just turned away to follow his friends, stopped dead in his tracks.

"I've heard about you foreign girls being bold, but honestly, this takes the cake! How would you know?"

"Servants these days know everything." I chuckled. "Isn't Hassan a barber as well as a cook?"

Nemo slapped his forehead in mock distress. His lingering smile proclaimed a sweet challenge.

That night Ramesh and I had an urgent *tête-à-tête*. I congratulated him on his quick work, then interrogated him about Nemo. How old? Not sure, somewhere between twenty-three and twenty-six. Work? Family business, garment manufacturing. Marital status? Single. Series of girlfriends the family had trouble with, and Nemo *sahib* was too obedient to go against his parents' wishes— but too passionate to miss any sexual opportunity. Hassan had often turned over his bed to the *sahib*. Very good lover, according to Hassan, very satisfying to his women. Girls begging not to be sent home in the morning. Some mornings sleepy *sahib* even came to breakfast with the girl's juices on his unwashed face, and mother holding her nose tightly, saying not to eat fish so early in the day. Mother prefers nice Jain Gujarati girl for her son, even though she herself is Muslim. Boy has brought home all kinds—Hindu, Muslim, Parsee, Christian, foreign. All leave Hassan's bed with big-big red bug bites. For the first time I noticed that Ramesh himself had red marks on his arms and neck.

"Who else has been sleeping in Hassan's bed?" I asked, pointing at the bumps. He blushed and turned away but seemed pleased to have been caught. "Hassan is my best friend," he whispered confidentially.

"Darling, I have the most exciting news! Two very nice boys are coming from the suburbs, one for lunch, the other for tea. The lunch-*wallah* is just back from an assignment in Delhi. He's quite shy, so you'll have to do your best to draw him out. Normally, of course, these boys would come with their mother or someone, and are not used to having to speak for themselves, if you know what I

mean. But these two are willing to try. The tea-*wallah* actually
lives in the U.S. and, surprise-surprise! is in town looking for a
wife. He lives in Detroit or Denver or Delaware or something."

My aunt looked quite relaxed as she chatted about the boys
from the suburbs. I knew she felt tremendously relieved at having
drummed up some hopefuls. Ramesh was preparing another one
of his master meals in the kitchen, and the wonderful smells had
us feeling slightly tipsy.

"I'd like to invite Nemo over for the day as well, if you don't
mind," I said. "He's easygoing and comfortable with everyone,
and that way the two guys won't feel like it's us against them,
okay?"

"Hmmm. That's not a bad idea, Renu. Why didn't I think of it?
That Nemo, isn't he darling? He's going to be quite a catch one of
these days when he grows up. They're all so sweet until a certain
age, and then, I don't know exactly what, but something happens."

Lunch-*wallah* turned out to be a fashion photographer, just
as shy as my aunt had warned. The ubiquitous Indian mustache
sat dark and thick over his lips, and his round face was made
even rounder by comically oversized glasses. Mohan photographed
mostly teenage boys from the suburbs who were hoping to make it
big in modeling. He had brought along his portfolio and passed it
to my aunt, who quickly immersed herself in the semi-nude shots
of airbrushed hopefuls. She murmured and clucked over each
provocatively posed boy, and even took down the names of a few
of them.

Mohan asked me a series of questions about life in the States,
but before I could answer he interrupted me.

"You have such a straight nose!" he stated emphatically. "You
should consider modeling."

The doorbell rang and I excused myself to answer. Nemo stood
at the door, his wet hair hanging in a curled bunch across his forehead. I tried to read his face, but like every good Indian, he had
on his social mask. He sensed the impatience in my eyes and pro-
duced a bouquet of flowers from behind his back. He held my
gaze warmly, effortlessly, like an old friend. Ramesh's cot and mattress swam into my mind's eye. Just that morning the cook and I

had fumigated the cotton bedding and set it out in the sun. It would be baked dry and clean, ready for a post-lunch respite.

Nemo's arrival caught Mohan by surprise. He did not like surprises. He thawed a little when I introduced Nemo as my distant cousin, and further relaxed when he saw the flowers were meant for my aunt. Finally he smiled and commented on the family resemblance. Ramesh brought out the food, and my aunt and I attacked it in silence.

As expected, Nemo put Mohan at ease, and the two men chatted up a storm through Ramesh's glorious lunch. As happened after every meal by Ramesh, I sat in stunned silence. Mohan grew more animated, his voice rising higher and higher, making him seem like a twelve-year-old. At one point my aunt looked at me inquiringly, and I shook my head in a definite No. She nodded agreement and winked at me.

Mohan had an appointment right after lunch, so he left in a hurry. As the door shut behind him, my aunt sighed with a mixture of frustration and relief. She declared that she needed a recharge before the next one arrived, and retired to her bedroom for a nap. Ramesh cleared the table and brought out cups of *feni* for Nemo and myself. He announced that he would be gone for many, *many* hours, buying food for the evening. Ramesh was nothing less than a genius.

There is no greater aphrodisiac for me than having a man open himself up to my probing, revealing himself with subtlety, honesty and wit. The *feni* proved to be just the right lubricant to bring out Nemo's eloquence. He was surprised more than once at my questions, but he spoke with ease about his family, his girlfriends, his work, his dreams. I asked questions that I knew would provoke laughter. His response brought the heat to my face and I knew he could see the flush. We reached for each other's hands at the same moment, our fingers greedily entwined on top of the table, our bare feet hotly entangled beneath. I leaned over and fed him *feni* from my mouth. We melted together at the lips, rolling the strong liquor around, allowing it to blister our palates and tongues. Like divine Indra exploding under his mythical burden, I felt a thousand vagina-eyes swelling and surging along the length and breadth of my skin.

*   *   *

Ramesh had left his bed tidy and turned on the fan to keep out flies. There was still much left to be said between Nemo and myself, but the dialogue now would be wordless. He sat on the mattress with his back against the wall and I sat on his lap with his hands under my clothes. With shirts unbuttoned, our erect nipples prodded each other's skin, sizzling like hot coals on ice. Like the slowpoke game of childhood, where each contestant "raced" to be the last one to the finish line, I set the pace for the slowest, most unhurried arousal.

I swept my tongue across his nipples, and they wrinkled and reddened. I struck them again and again until they were purple and bulging. The twin ridges of his ribs rising over his sunken stomach signaled the breath held in anticipation. I bit a nipple. He turned his dilating eyes on me, struggling to focus, pleading, laughing, challenging me to arouse him further.

Nemo's hungry gaze was thrilling. Not since childhood had I felt comfortable enough to drown in the gaze of an Indian man; not since viewing those open-shirted, sardonic actors whose posters used to line my walls. Searing eyes, fleshy pink mouths, chests thrown back with the promise of unending embrace. But this was no movie star in bed with me. I felt more and more like I was making love to a beloved companion. We must have met as children and perhaps even snuck an embrace or two in a dark corridor.

Nemo curled his legs around my back and rolled me over. Finding my armpits unshaven, he rubbed his nose in the soft tangles. The thousand vagina-eyes coalesced into the throbbing recesses under my arms and between my legs, and soon we were wrestling on the bed. The drops of his musk scent spread slickly over me as we stroked together in the hot afternoon breeze. I spread apart his lips to get a look at his tongue. Out it came, dangling over me like the hood of a cobra. I grabbed at it with my teeth, but he moved down, down, winding and coiling his tongue around and between my thighs, the slow full burn of a heated rope climbing inside me, opening me wider and wider. My thighs stretched to their limits, and I tucked my feet under his chest as my legs began to tremble. His tongue braved the currents like a homing salmon climbing the steep rapids of my desire. I felt my breathing begin to stall, felt the rush of blood humming in my ears, heard my mind command, "Inhale!" but the tongue hammering out a Morse code on my aching, stretching skin signaled a different demand, and there was no breath to be had because my nose and lungs and mouth and arms had all rushed down and were pushing up from under his tongue, pushing up a molten iceberg of immense proportions through the tightening mesh of his strokes and like snow yielding to water, his pressing tongue melted into the tunneling wave of my heat, which finally erupted through the roof of his mouth. My screams shot through the ceiling and down the shuddering walls, scattering into the skyscrapers of Bombay.

At five o'clock Ramesh knocked and cracked open the door just enough to announce it would soon be teatime. I was dozing and oozing, too aroused to actually sleep. I sniffed the odor on Nemo's fingers and brushed against his distinctly fishy mouth. Nemo couldn't possibly settle for an arranged marriage either.

I remembered the way the lines around his mouth hardened with anger when he'd told me how he had allowed his mother once, just once, to "bring a girl home." It was maddening. The parents were pigs, disgusting, selling their daughter like the newest gadget from Hong Kong. The girl couldn't even look him in the eye—or anyone else, for that matter. She was a Bohra girl, so beautiful . . . fifteen, maybe sixteen. Nemo was so upset, he took her father by the collar and told him to get out of his house. He was horrified at their expectation that he feel excited by this young chit of a girl. He asked his mother whether she was planning to pimp his younger sister the same way. Nemo had mimed a hard slap across the face, and I'd winced in sympathy.

It didn't end there. Nemo had become "eligible." Complete strangers found some excuse or other to parade their daughters in front of him—at weddings, movies, even right there in the building while he was waiting for the lift; he started taking the stairs because of them. He dreamed of running away to some country like the U.S., where no one would know him, where no girl would be dragged in front of him, where no parents would dare shower their filthy money on him.

*   *   *

Tea-*wallah* introduced himself as Nick. "Short for Nikhil?" I asked blandly, and he smiled sheepishly. He'd been born and raised in the U.S., and every member of his family had a practical Anglo nickname for their traditional Indian appellations: Jay for Jayant, Vicki for Malavika, Candy for Kundanika, Sid for Siddhartha. Nick was a software programmer being actively recruited by a company in Bangalore. He hadn't been back to India since childhood, and was here to check out the scene.

Nemo sat beside me, the fingers of his left hand trailing secretly along the inside of my thighs. He seemed to know a lot about software, and soon Nick and he were heatedly debating the merits of various accounting programs. I let my head rest against the back of the chair and closed my eyes. Nemo's fingers were like tentacles of dry ice, alternately scalding and freezing the surface of my skin. He felt the trembling in my muscles and dug deeper in acknowledgment.

Ramesh brought out the fragrant ginger tea and an assortment of crisp patties and cutlets. Two he placed directly on my plate, and I knew without being told that they were fish patties. I asked Nick whether he was vegetarian, and he said he was. "Too bad," I said, popping one of the patties into Nemo's mouth. An uncertain smile hovered around my aunt's lips as she registered this sudden intimacy. Propelling food into the mouth uninvited was an accepted Indian custom, but generally reserved for relatives and intimates.

It would be just a matter of time before I told my aunt that Nemo and I were lovers. However conservative she appeared on the surface, she cherished her confidential relationships with her nieces and nephews. We all confided in her, and she maintained our trust without exception.

After a while, Nick forgot that he had come to see me, so animated was his conversation with Nemo. My aunt and I excused ourselves from the table and retired to the swing on the balcony.

"The things you don't find out about young men until you have to deal with them alone," sighed my aunt. "Usually, when the boy comes to see the girl, it's us oldies who do all the talking, you know. This rule of yours of not allowing parents to accompany their sons is turning out to be a social disaster!"

My aunt paused. "You really should let me take you to the hair-dresser, Renu. I'm sick of seeing your hair flying in all directions. How many Indian women do you see roaming around with their long hair open?"

"That's the first time you've ever referred to me as a woman. Up to this point I've always been a girl. What happened?"

My aunt looked at me as though I were daft. "Honestly, darling, you find the most unusual ways to torture your old auntie." I took her hand in mine and massaged her fingers. Her eyes took on a faraway look and she sank back against the padded silk of the swing. "Well, if all goes well you'll be married soon. It's hard to remain a girl once you're married."

"You know, Nemo isn't nearly as young as you think."

"Hmmm . . . ." My aunt exhaled pleasurably as I pressed the ball of her thumb. "It's his Muslim blood. Makes him look more childish."

"He's just two years younger than me, you know, twenty-five."

"He's that old?" My aunt looked at me lazily. "I suppose I'm always confusing him with his younger brother."

"How come Nemo didn't make it onto your list?" I whispered. My aunt's arm tensed and she drew away.

"In the old days, we were all families of equal standing. It didn't matter whether we were Muslim or Hindu. Not anymore."

"You know," I said, choosing my words carefully, "I'm not really looking for a man to marry at this point. I love you and was curious to see who you'd pull out of your hat, but I don't think I'm destined to be married anytime soon."

"Hunh!" she snorted. "That's what they all say, until they tie the knot. Then they wonder how they managed to live so long without it!"

"But honestly, Auntie, is it the sex or the marriage that people find so thrilling?"

She rolled her eyes and swatted me on the arm. "You know you can't ask that around here. Most have never had the one without the other."

"But I have, and so have my sisters and most of my cousins. You know that."

My aunt lashed at me with the loose end of her chiffon sari. "You youngsters think you'll end up in fairy-tale marriages because you've slept with a few horny men? You're wrong. Eventually you'll come to see the error of your ways. We're from a different generation— duty first, and all that. We hardly even knew that sex was something separate from marriage. We've all been brought up in terror of it."

She sprang off the ornately decorated metal swing, which jangled with the sudden movement. Her eyes betrayed her hurt.

"You obviously don't understand that an old woman like me would be forgotten like a rusted nail in the wall if I didn't find some way to keep myself in the picture. At least I make the effort to get to know all of you. I do a decent job, all in all."

I took her hand and kissed it. "I understand all that," I said gently. "But I'm talking about me. Things have changed, and you know it." My aunt turned to go, but I held onto her hand. She sighed, and tilted my chin upwards.

"I don't want to know," she whispered. "Do what you must do, but please be discreet. *I don't want to know.* All I can say is, don't ruin your chances for the future. You might just change your mind."

Inside, the two men stood up and walked towards the front door. The visit was over. At the last minute Nick remembered my aunt and me and turned to wave good-bye. Nemo graciously saw him out the front door, then staggered back to the couch and flopped down with a thud.

My aunt whispered to me under her breath, "Isn't he the cutest? You may think it's all your good luck, but it's not. I told his cook Hussan that you were in town and that you needed a little company. You owe me one." She wiggled her bulky hips at me and blew me a wet kiss.

I gasped. My own aunt setting me up for an affair? I felt the knot of anxiety tightening in my stomach. My aunt's eyes darted hungrily over Nemo, taking in his languid limbs and his fatigue-softened lips. She rubbed her abdomen and sighed.

"Ramesh, oh, Ramesh," she called. "Where are you hiding, my love? I wonder if Ramesh has learned anything useful from that boyfriend of his. Don't know what it is, but these days I feel like eating fish."

Susan St. Aubin

Glory

The five months Evelyn spent at cooking school, she never learned a thing she didn't know. Béchamel sauce? White sauce? How to parboil vegetables and cut them up for hors d'oeuvres? She'd learned all this, and more, from *her* mother, who wasn't even a particularly accomplished cook. Where were those guys in her class all those years when her mother showed her how to stir a sauce creamy smooth, or how to boil an egg in salted water so the shell wouldn't crack? Everything seemed new to them, as though they'd never thought about how food got to the table. With each tip from Gregory, the instructor, they smiled at each other, licking their lips and sometimes even stroking each other's backs. Evelyn felt invisible. "They're all gay," whispered Charlotte, the other woman student.

They weren't, of course. Laurent wasn't. Evelyn felt there was something promising in the way he stared right through her rather than around her like the others did. Laurent's reasons for ignoring her had nothing to do with disinterest—he was a serious student. Evelyn admired the way his knife molded radishes into roses or tulips and carrots into birds—unlike the others, he went far beyond Gregory's limited skills. He told Evelyn he'd worked in restaurants in France. She was charmed by his accent and his long brown hair, which he was required to wear in a net just like Charlotte and Evelyn.

She liked to watch his hands as they scraped and sculpted vegetables—sinuous, long-fingered hands that seemed to blend with the paring knife they held. In her head she made a film of those hands all over her—caressing her hair, her shoulders, her ass. She ran it frequently to alleviate the boredom of her days at school. In this private movie, Laurent's fingers noodled her clit and buttered her cunt; then he ate her like a creamy pudding.

Charlotte wrinkled her nose when he walked by, but Evelyn found his scent erotic. She thought of him whenever she picked up a garlic press or sliced a lemon in half with one of the school's cheap, dull knives. A lemon garlic dressing with a hint of fresh pepper, that was Laurent. Her mind wandered to him several times a day, but to Laurent food was just food, and his concentration on that was perfect.

There was only one bathroom upstairs near the experimental kitchens where classes were held, though the restaurant downstairs, where the advanced students practiced their skills on the public, had the usual men's and ladies' rooms.

"We're all boys up here," Gregory told Evelyn and Charlotte on their first day, "or we *were*." He forced a smile at them. "But we *need* more female chefs, and of course we must have them."

"Chefs and chefettes," one of the boys said, wriggling his fingers above his head as he spun around once on his tiptoes, like a self-propelled top.

Charlotte stared at the floor while everyone laughed.

"They're disgusting," she told Evelyn later in the bathroom, where they crowded in front of the small mirror over a rust-stained sink, combing their hair.

In this bathroom were two stalls and a small rusty urinal, which Evelyn thought was a sink until Charlotte, who had three brothers, set her straight. She'd never been in a men's room before, and wondered how men felt about peeing in public like that. How could they stand next to each other, as her boyfriend Hal described it, looking straight ahead, never down or to the side? Since this urinal was for two people only, Evelyn realized the guys must often use the stalls—on their breaks, they went in three and four at a time.

Charlotte wore more makeup than Evelyn had ever seen on a person offstage. Her eyes were outlined in black and circled with shades of silver, blue and green, like a tropical bird's. Charlotte told her the thick eyelashes she applied every day were made of real mink.

"Did you ever think of doing something with your eyes?" Charlotte asked her.

"What do you mean?"

"Makeup," Charlotte answered. "Here—I could lend you this." She handed Evelyn a pot of green gloss. "Put some on your lids. It'll bring out the color of your eyes."

"Not my style," said Evelyn, handing back the gloss. She told Charlotte she was thinking of getting her hair cut short and adding more piercings to her ears—one more in each lobe, and another on the side of her left ear.

Charlotte opened her mouth, speechless. She was easily shocked. Evelyn loved to walk down the street with her after school and pick out some innocuous man feeding quarters into a parking meter, then whisper in Charlotte's ear, "See that guy? He's gonna turn around with his dick out, what do you bet?"

Every time Charlotte would gasp, and then say, "Oh, you!" when Evelyn started to laugh. As they walked back to the kitchen, Evelyn thought she'd get a silver ring through the top of her ear just because it would be such a treat to see Charlotte's reaction.

When they picked up their spoons she said to Charlotte, "I saw a guy last week who had a real demitasse spoon hanging from his ear. I could have one made into an earring."

"You *wouldn't*," gasped Charlotte. "The weight would pull your ear out of shape."

Laurent stood on Evelyn's left side, muttering to himself in French as he scraped the side of the bowl in which he was beating eggs for a practice omelet.

"What?" Evelyn asked, thinking for a minute that he spoke to her, perhaps about spoon earrings; she recognized a French word, coming back to her from high school. *"Cuiller,"* she thought she heard. "Inferior utensils," said Laurent. "Inferior everything in this place. It is impossible."

That afternoon Evelyn left early for her break and found Laurent still at the bathroom mirror combing his long red-brown hair.

"You're here too soon," he said.

"I couldn't wait." She held the door open.

He shrugged. "Come in. I don't mind. Not if you don't. Of course, that Charlotte, she would be shocked if she's right behind you, eh?"

Evelyn smiled and came all the way in, letting the door swing shut behind her.

"Don't worry," he said, "I'm finished. But look." He walked into one of the stalls. "Have you seen this?"

She stuck her head into the stall.

"Go into the next one," he said. When she did, she saw Laurent's finger wiggling through a hole just below her waist. Around and around went the finger, side to side. Laurent bent down and put his eye to it. She watched the brown iris surrounded by viscous white, an eyeball cut off from a human body. She put her finger to the hole, and Laurent's eyeball jerked away.

"Hey," he squawked.

She ran her finger around the edge of the opening, which was neatly cut and filed smooth.

Laurent leaned against the door of her stall. "You know what goes on in there?" he said. "You know what this is for?"

"To watch?" she asked.

"Yes, there's a good view. But there's more."

Laurent came into her stall and stuck two fingers into the hole beside her fingers.

"What is almost this big?" he whispered in her ear. "A cock! He sticks his cock in."

His long vowels and *s*'s lingered in her ears. "You see?" he said. "It's for more than to watch. The glory hole, they call it. Glory!" He laughed through his nose.

Evelyn felt his smooth warm fingers against hers in the hole. She heard the restroom door open; she heard Charlotte suck in her breath as the door closed.

"I was just leaving," Laurent called, withdrawing his hand. When he was gone, Evelyn shut the door to her stall and sat down.

The restroom door swung open again and Charlotte came in, slamming the door to the other stall.

"That guy's got some nerve," she said. "What on earth was he still doing in here?"

Evelyn felt no obligation to answer; stalls were private. Beside her, Charlotte sniffed, flushed, and stood up, snapping the elastic of her underpants and tights as she pulled them up.

At the sink she said, "*I* wouldn't have stayed in here a second with him."

Evelyn tried a Laurent shrug. "He was just combing his hair."

"Hah," said Charlotte. "You can see a lot in this mirror."

"He wasn't looking at the mirror. You saw us. We were looking in the stall." She waited for Charlotte to ask what they were looking at, but she put her comb back in her purse and left Evelyn alone at the mirror.

The next day the hole in the stall seemed larger. Was someone working on it, or was vigorous use eroding the metal? When she ran her fingers around the edges, it felt freshly cut and not quite so smooth. By Friday the hole was even bigger, and edged with slick gray electrical tape. As she sat on the toilet, Evelyn slipped a fist through—a tight but not impossible squeeze. She moved her hand around and stretched her fingers into the next stall, feeling the smooth tape against her wrist.

Charlotte was alone at the mirror, fixing a false eyelash that had almost slipped into her soufflé that morning. Evelyn withdrew her hand, leaving her fingers on the edge. Charlotte rinsed her hands at the sink, then came into the stall. Evelyn heard the lock click and Charlotte's sigh as she sat down, making the toilet seat creak. Her urine hissed into the toilet bowl. Evelyn pulled her fingers out and put her eye to the hole. Charlotte was just standing up; her rump flashed pink and white as she pulled up her lace-trimmed underpants and brown tights. Evelyn watched Charlotte's long skirt roll down over her tights, and watched her smooth herself with her hands, front and back, and slide open the lock on the stall door.

When Evelyn stood up and opened her door, Charlotte was at the mirror combing her hair. "Better hurry," she said. "We've got one minute." Evelyn washed her hands, then ran them wet through her hair and pulled her hairnet back on.

The next morning Evelyn stood beside Laurent at the long counter as Gregory rapped on his lectern with a wooden spoon, calling the class to order.

"Today is soufflé day again," he said.

Laurent muttered to Evelyn, "Every day is soufflé day. These people never learn, so all we do is soufflé, soufflé." He did a shuffling dance in place. Gregory rapped with his spoon again, and began the lesson.

"How you break the eggs does matter," he announced as he hit them sharply against one of the two metal bowls before him, separating whites from yolks with one hand.

Laurent matched his deftness while the others shrieked and laughed, dropping eggs to the floor, smearing their arms with yolk, and getting bits of eggshell stuck to their noses and eyebrows. They beat the yolks first, then the whites, then both together.

"When I have my own restaurant," Laurent told Evelyn, "I'll call it *Chouette*."

"What's *chouette*?" she asked.

"It's a wonder, fine, super," he said, stopping to wave his hand. "It also means 'owl.' Intelligence. An intelligent nightspot. I want the world's most famous night restaurant. I want to be known for that glory."

"Mr. Gagne," Gregory said, "your eggs have fallen. You cannot stop beating a soufflé in the middle like that."

"Do owls lay eggs?" whispered Evelyn. "You could just do omelets and soufflés out of all sorts of unusual eggs, like owl eggs. Or duck eggs. Chinese restaurants use duck eggs."

Laurent snorted. "Oh, I'd do more than eggs," he said. "This would not just be some soufflé cafe." Once their soufflés were in the ovens, the boys left for their break. Laurent stayed behind, as he often did, going into the bathroom between the men's break and the women's.

"Mr. Gagne, Mr. Gagne," Gregory would say, "you'll have no break if you don't leave now," and he would go.

Evelyn began slipping out early, just as the men were coming back. Their instructor glared, but what could he say? She could be ill, she could have her period; blood could be running down her legs. He wouldn't want to ask. She never again caught Laurent in the restroom as she planned. Sometimes he was just on his way out and would hold the door open for her with a smile, but more frequently he was nowhere in sight.

"Do they ever *do* anything in there?" she whispered to Laurent once as they passed each other. He held the restroom door open and leaned his head in after her. "No, mostly looking," he answered. "Giggling. There's no time. What can you do in ten minutes?" He let the door swing shut.

Although Evelyn liked a man who would scorn such a short time frame, she could think of a lot to do with Laurent in ten minutes. Her mind was a projector through which she ran images of herself and Laurent in the restroom stalls.

She imagines that when she sticks her fist through the hole, smooth against the padded sides, it collides with something soft— the flesh of Laurent's ass. She presses further until her hand is out the other side, the sides of the opening slipping against her forearm, the hole itself like a living, breathing beast against her arm. Her fingers search, feeling the smoothness of Laurent and the muscles beneath the soft surface. She's looking for hardness, for a penis, but she doesn't find it; he's standing with his back to the hole. As he bends over, she feels his muscles tighten and stretch.

What do the boys do in ten minutes? This, she thinks. She pulls her arm out of the hole, licks her fingers, puts it back. Her wet blind hand feels the soft hair on his ass, glides down the crack, pushing in, curious as a cock probing, sliding against the skin as her fingers enter him, smooth as a tanned deer hide.

She pushes further—two fingers, three. He moans. She stops. Does he like this? Hate it? Hate her for treating him like a faggot, like a girl? Would he push her hand away, like Hal did once when she reached one hand back there while he was balling her? No hands allowed, he'd whispered. But this time it was all hands.

What would she run into up there? What if she got shit in her fingernails, or even pulled out a turd? She makes herself think of a chocolate soufflé, light, fluffy, creamy sweet. We take it in our mouths and nobody finds that disgusting. We slosh it around our teeth, over and under our tongues; we swallow the glutinous, liquefied mass, we lick our teeth, we take another bite.

She has four fingers and the tip of her thumb up Laurent's smooth hole, the flesh tight yet yielding as she pushes. Imagine each bit of chocolate soufflé as it glides down the esophagus, its coolness passing through the chest and into the stomach where the milk and eggs and nutrition of it are absorbed, leaving behind the unnecessary brown fluff that floats down and is squeezed through the tubular intestines, down and out.

Evelyn thinks of peristalsis as her hand, breaking through a tight ring of muscle, pops into a thick softness. She moves her fist up and down. Laurent bends towards her, moving himself on her hand, until, with a shout, he slides away.

At the sound of the bathroom door swinging open, Evelyn pulled her hand out of the hole.

"Evelyn? You there?" Charlotte came into the next stall, slamming the door.

"Yeah, right here." Evelyn put her hand down to her cunt and twisted her fist around in its wetness. Two fingers up herself, three—she was slick enough to get her whole hand in. It was different from the way she imagined Laurent's ass—moister and more spacious. Half her hand was in, but she couldn't reach all the way up.

She waited for Charlotte to peek through the opening, but she still hadn't noticed it was there. Instead, she chattered about some guy she was going out with who had this tiny tattoo of a rose on his left earlobe that looked just like an earring. "It's the neatest thing you ever saw," said Charlotte.

Evelyn felt like yelling, "Hey, I can't come unless you shut up," but that might push Charlotte beyond the edge of mere shock. Breathing carefully, she moved the four fingers in her cunt around in circles while her thumb kneaded her clit like a small biscuit. She thought of dough rising, mysterious and white inside her, stretching her with the force of its growth until it popped like a pale giant bubble, rippling away from her.

She pulled her fingers out and wiped them off, then flushed so Charlotte wouldn't wonder what she'd been doing in there. At the sink they washed carefully because they were kneading dough for rolls and had been instructed to keep their hands clean and free of oil, or the bread wouldn't rise.

Back in class, Evelyn stood beside Laurent, smiling inwardly at the secret trip up his ass he'd never know about. All he seemed to care about was *Chouette*, and perfectly beaten eggs.

Aurora Light

❦

Playing for the Camera

Suzi kept after me. "Come on, Calla, this is a way to make some money for tuition, food and rent."

We're college seniors. Suzi is my roommate. We were discussing our disastrous financial situation in the tiny kitchen of our studio apartment. The rent was due in four days and we didn't have it. Suzi had a lead on a part-time job posing for amateur photographers, which actually meant horny guys who wanted to take pictures of pretty young gals in sexy outfits and provocative poses.

"It sure beats working at a fast food place. The pay is better, much better. And we'd only have to work three nights a week."

"What if Jeff finds out?"

"So what if he does? He doesn't own you. My boyfriend doesn't mind; actually Tony's the one who told me about the job. I think the idea of me posing for a bunch of other men turns him on. Tony says the man who owns the studio is sixty-five and won't give us any grief. And the men aren't allowed to touch us, only look and take pictures."

Finally I agreed, and the next night we went to the studio. Lorenzo, the owner, showed us to the dressing room and told us to pick out costumes and be ready in half an hour. There wasn't much variety—Victoria's Secret–type lingerie and some swimsuits.

I'm a big girl, five-nine with a forty-two D-cup bosom, flame red hair and sea green eyes. I put on an electric blue swimsuit cut down to my navel and high up the hips. With extra mascara, eyeliner, glossy lipstick and long rhinestone earrings, I looked, Suzi said, trashy but hot.

Suzi, a petite, perfectly proportioned blonde with blue eyes, chose a black string bikini and four-inch stiletto heels. Nervous, but excited at the prospect of being ogled by strangers, all male, we went onstage.

The carpeted stage was brightly lit. The rest of the studio was in semidarkness, so we couldn't see the men clearly, which eased our nervousness—but we could hear some comments: "Check out those tits on the redhead!" and "Oh, Jesus, that blond babe has a dynamite ass!"

Later, after the picture shoot, Lorenzo said we did okay for the first time, but we had to heat it up. The customers liked the models to jiggle, wiggle and look like they were enjoying their work.

The second night Suzi and I really got steaming, giving the customers plenty of boobs and bun shots. At the end of the session Lorenzo was pleased. He had a request—two of the men wanted a private photo session, with us in the nude, and we would be paid double the usual rate. Suzi and I hesitated for a second, then nodded yes.

We had decided to pretend we were posing for a high-class men's magazine, and we'd get naked via a striptease, an old fantasy of mine. We came onstage wearing thigh-length negligees over sheer white teddies, garter belts, lacy stockings and spike heels. Five minutes into the hour, the moment of truth arrived.

When Lorenzo put on a cassette of stripper music, what had been fantasy suddenly became real. I gave myself up to the moment. Erotic images flooded my brain, bringing a tingle to my breasts and a surge of moisture to my pussy.

Concentrating on the insistent beat of the music, I began my strip with some bumps and grinds and a spread-legged squat, wanting the men to see my crotch, more revealed than concealed by the wisp of silk between my legs. A wild wantonness inside me was awakened by calls to "Take it off! Take it all off!"

At first I did everything slowly, unfastening garters, rolling down stockings, twirling them around and pulling them back and forth between my legs, then tossing the stockings out to the men. I took the top of the teddy down one shoulder strap at a time, exposing my breasts, leaning forward to make them jiggle. Increasing the tempo, I pranced around, gyrating, before pushing the teddy down past my hips and stepping out of it. I heard their cameras clicking like mad.

I felt totally vulnerable, and that, in some inexplicable way, increased my excitement. I felt the men's hot eyes devouring me, and I knew their cocks were hard and fiercely aching to penetrate me, to possess me. For an instant I wondered what it would be like to be endowed with that demanding, pleasure-hungry appendage. Suzi was lying onstage naked with her legs up in the air, showing off her dimpled ass and the hairless pink lips of her pussy. I lay down beside her and did some rapid hip thrusts that brought an appreciative "Whoa, babe, you're hot!" from one of the men. The voice sounded oddly familiar.

I whispered to Suzi, "I think Jeff's out there."

"I'm pretty sure the other one is Tony," Suzi whispered back. "Let's pretend we don't know it's them."

A wicked gleam in her eyes, she started caressing her pert breasts and swiveling her trim hips. Slowly, I stroked my pussy, then raised one moist finger to my lips and sucked it. The guys went wild.

"Oh, I'm so hot and wet," I said breathlessly. I wasn't acting. My whole body felt meltingly warm and blushing. "Why don't you boys come up and join us?" I teased.

With embarrassed grins Tony and Jeff came up onstage, major erections bulging in their trousers. Laughing, Suzi and I quickly stripped them of their clothes. I'd never been naked with another couple, but I was so hot and horny that any shyness I might have felt vanished.

"Where's Lorenzo?" Suzi asked.

Tony shrugged. "Maybe he left."

I didn't say anything, but the thought of Lorenzo lurking around somewhere watching us, getting a stiff pecker and jerking off, gave me a wicked thrill.

"Pretty Woman" was playing. We started dirty dancing, which is super-sexy when you're nude and the guy has a hard-on. In an instant my pussy was sopping wet. I felt as though all my senses were exquisitely, almost painfully alive.

Soon Jeff and I were on the carpet giving each other some serious head. Out of the corner of my eye I saw Tony humping Suzi. Watching them, it didn't take long for me to come. Seconds later I heard Suzi cry out in orgasm.

The guys were still hard. Suzi looked at me and I knew what she had in mind. I agreed to switching partners with a nod. The guys were more than willing.

Then Tony confessed that he had a video camera filming everything. A part of me couldn't believe that I was doing, and enjoying, these outrageous acts—but another part of me reveled in the feeling of power and freedom. Knowing the camera was filming us made the sex even more sizzling.

Jeff and Tony switched places. Tony was really hung, with a thick, blue-veined cock and hairy balls. I spread my legs and his impressive prick homed in to my scorching pussy like a heat-seeking missile. I clamped down on his dick with my vaginal muscles squeezing and releasing as he fucked me relentlessly, grunting with each stroke. I came twice before he jetted steamy come.

Suzi and Jeff were doing a sixty-nine, making lewd slurping sounds. I saw her ass jerk as she came. Jeff's cock was halfway down her throat when it erupted. Suddenly things turned into a free-for-all, with lips and tongues, cocks and cunts coming together, parting, forming new, more complicated combinations. My blood and nerves resonated with a wild, electric music.

Watching Tony go down on Jeff, and seeing Jeff's reaction, gave me a rush that almost made me come. When Suzi started eating my pussy I really went nuts. Fiercely she licked and sucked every inch of my slit and clit. "Oh, yeah," I urged. "Right there. Don't, please don't stop." Then a ragged "Uuuuuuhhhhh!" as my cunt spasmed.

Then it was my turn to taste Suzi's cunt. Her pink pussy lips parted under my probing tongue. It was my first time eating a girl. I felt what she was feeling, and my cunt pulsed with shared pleasure.

The guys cheered us on from the sidelines. Suzi grabbed my hair and pulled my face tight against her burning pussy, chanting,

"Oh God, oh God, yes, yes," then coming in convulsive waves, creaming my mouth and chin.

Exposing myself that night to the eyes of the camera and the hot eyes of Jeff, Tony and Suzi was physically and emotionally liberating. Now, whenever I'm making love, playing the goddess, bitch, savage or slut, a part of me is always playing for the camera.

Carol Queen

❦

Marilyn

Kitty and her lover rarely leave the house—they're usually too busy rutting like weasels. When they do go out it's almost always to unusual events of the "urban night creatures" variety, like orgies and SM parties. The way they dress (in black, naturally) frightens tourists. He almost always wears black leather. Kitty can usually be found in rubber or lace, but this time it's black velvet, the tiniest strapless dress with lots of visible flesh, her tattoo hung like a moon (well, it is a moon, with a serpent twined around it) on the upper slope of one breast. And she wears tall high-heeled, thigh-length black suede boots.

Tonight's event is not an orgy. Tonight they're going to an ordinary party, given on behalf of a slightly wild gay organization. Kitty and her lover are there to hand out condoms, and maybe cruise a little.

The place is swarming with drag queens, mostly the thoroughly tasteless, never-mistake-her-for-a-female-in-a-million-years type that Kitty particularly appreciates. How can you possibly worry about what kind of woman you are, surrounded by these fabulous creatures? That one over there is more feminine than Kitty will ever be. This one has hairy legs and a beard. Hanging around with drag queens takes all the angst, Kitty thinks, out of being a girl.

The queens are wearing everything but the kitchen sink. On

them it looks like clothing, even though a lot of it isn't. One of
them wears a slinky dress made of bubble wrap. Another one's
outfit is mostly tinfoil. On them it is amazing, eccentric, gorgeous
couture. If the little old Latina clerks at Thrift Town could see to
what use those nice young men had put their purchases of chiffon
curtains, old lace antimacassars, and size-eleven silver Dream
Step pumps, they'd have a fit. And eyelashes! Pounds and *pounds*
of eyelashes.

Among them Marilyn stands out like a star. Well, because she is.
It's Marilyn Monroe, whom scores of drag queens have courted
and precious few have possessed. She is impeccable: tasteful yet
sexy peach satin gown, that unmistakable face, even—it would
appear—her own hair. She's lost a little weight, but it looks good
on her. Oh, those long satin gloves. Oh, that birthmark. Oh, that
sweet little pout.

She gives a breathy little laugh when she comes close enough
for Kitty and her lover to offer her condoms. She tries to demur.
Kitty's lover pulls out all the stops.

"Oh, but you must," he says. "Such a lovely lady must have so
many opportunities to use them. You know you can't depend on
most *men* to take care of these things. Unless of course there's
someone waiting at home . . . ?"

Marilyn blushes, lowers her (not-too-heavy) eyelashes, shakes
her head. Apparently she's between husbands at the moment. She
opens her clutch and gazes limpidly at Kitty's lover as he murmurs further niceties and stuffs a handful of rubbers inside.

Of course Marilyn falls for him, so tall and handsome, his gen-
tility such a contrast to his scary leathers. She gets flustered and
has to run off and have a couple of drinks before she gets up the
nerve to come back and flirt. When she returns she carries the
peach satin gown gathered up in one hand so Kitty's lover can ad-
mire her legs—which he does.

The devil is cruising Marilyn Monroe! Kitty can do nothing but
stand back and watch, amazed and amused. She's always been hot
for Marilyn Monroe, and this apparition has her salivating. The
knowledge that she could travel up the silken legs and find a cock
curled under the peach satin makes Kitty's clit hard.

Marilyn Monroe's cock! At the thought of her lover making that journey, gently unveiling her, the touch of his hands making Marilyn's cock stiffen against the lace, Kitty rubs her crotch surreptitiously against the back of a chair. Meanwhile she watches the two of them flirt.

Now, Kitty's lover doesn't do men very often. Sometimes he'll play around when he and Kitty are at sex parties or when Kitty occasionally brings another guy home. But his heart isn't really in it—well, maybe it's his dick that balks. Still, he isn't so straight that he won't run with a promising flirt, no matter what the gender.

But Marilyn isn't flirting with Kitty at all—no lesbian blood in this starlet. Kitty's lover is going to be on his own with Marilyn, and Kitty is dying to know how far he'll take it. And licking her chops at the thought. On one of Marilyn's runs to the powder room Kitty puts her lips close to his ear: "Baby, Marilyn wants you." And Kitty wants to watch. Really she wants to turn this femme boy Marilyn into a lesbian, but she knows that's out of the question. A certain kind of gay man could no more imagine having sex with a woman than your average citizen from Dubuque could picture making it with a gibbon, and that's the sort of boy Marilyn is.

It's a shame to be this close to Marilyn Monroe and know she could never in a million years be persuaded to go down on Kitty. Reportedly Marilyn herself (that is, the original) did plenty of that sort of thing with Lily St. Cyr. But Kitty can generate plenty of orgasms on her own just thinking of her lover's strong hands closing around the slender arms in the elegant satin gloves, pulling Marilyn to him . . . those wide eyes and little moans of acquiescence, oh, it just makes Kitty want to squeal.

She draws in a sharp breath of delight when Marilyn returns, a slip of folded paper showing white against her chest where the real Marilyn Monroe would be spilling cleavage and this Marilyn sports, instead, perfectly formed ersatz breasts. Kitty knows what's on that piece of paper, and laughs silently as Marilyn pulls it with a flourish from her bodice, hands it to Kitty's lover, suffers a moment of helpless shyness, and, making a quick excuse, hurries away again. Kitty laughs aloud as her lover unfolds the paper. Of course it's a phone number, and the name written next to it isn't Marilyn, it's Dirk.

Back home Kitty is still laughing, this time because her lover is
flustered and a little abashed. He doesn't know what to do about
Marilyn. No—he knows just what he wants to do about *Marilyn*,
but he's at a loss over how to relate to *Dirk*. Had he led her on? he
asks. He certainly had, Kitty tells him. He wants to respect Marilyn's flirtatiousness, Dirk's courage. Maybe he should send roses
to make it up to her? Not unless there's somewhere specific you
want to lead her, Kitty teases. To bed, for instance.

"On second thought," she says, "why don't you lead her right
over here?" Kitty wants to see it. She wants to see Marilyn's im-
peccably made-up face go soft as her lover clasps the tender neck,
kisses the painted mouth, caresses the peach satin over the faux
breasts. She wants to watch him run his hands up Marilyn's slim
thighs, the dress rustling as it's raised. The hard cock straining under the sexy lingerie, and his hands on it, freeing it to spring up,
ready for the careful tongue of Kitty's lover to tease it delicately
up and down. Would her lover's cock be hard by then, aching for
Marilyn's perfectly painted boy-lips to sink down on it, leaving a
little gleam of lipstick in their wake?

Kitty wants to watch so badly she can taste it, wants to see Marilyn's eyes fill with that yielding, that womanly giving over of resistance that's so precious in the eyes of a man. She wants to see her
lover grinding against Marilyn, rubbing his cock against the satin
of the torn-off dress, wants to see the wet spots of his pre-come on
the shiny peach-colored cloth. Then she'll roll over, ass raised,
hips bucking in desire and thrusting back hard against Kitty's
lover: Marilyn wants to get fucked.

"Give it to her, honey." By now Kitty is saying this out loud,
telling the story in gasps as her lover's cock thrusts into her
deeper and deeper, making her cry out and catch her breath.
"Baby, I want to see you fuck her ass right now!"

She'll reach for condoms and lube, roll the rubber down the
length of her sweetheart's shaft, slick it up so he's ready; she
wants this sight more than anything—his cock opening Marilyn
slowly, sliding in, pumping his hips to get it all in as he holds her
by the shoulders and Marilyn arches back and takes hold of her
own ass cheeks, pulling them apart. Sinking in deep, pulling back
and riding. Her cock's rubbing against the sheets with every

thrust, and Kitty knows that soon her bed will be scented with Marilyn Monroe jism. At that thought, Kitty comes.

Now Kitty and her lover are fucking like the sex pigs they are, in each other's arms writhing and grunting and growling, and the story is over for the moment; talking about Marilyn has gotten them into pure rut again. Kitty's fantasies now are past plot and coherence, and anyway, she couldn't force herself to narrate anything, no matter how sexy, because her lover is fucking her so hard she's almost screaming. She is all breath and cunt and her hands where they touch him. It's too bad Marilyn is missing this, though for the time being they've both forgotten her. She'll come shimmering back into consciousness when the fuck is done. Maybe she'll become a regular fantasy companion, or even . . . .

Who knows? After all, they *have* Marilyn Monroe's phone number.

Blake C. Aarens

❧

Get on Your Bikes and Ride

Friday. The last long, hard day of a long, hard work week. Finally over. Irene lunged off the elevator and practically ran down the corridor to her apartment. She didn't even see the cobwebs in the corners, didn't give a thought to calling maintenance. She wanted in. To her own little sanctuary. She wanted out. Away from the rest of the world.

Keys in her right hand, Irene unlocked her apartment door and tried to keep the mail from falling out of her left. Her briefcase, hanging from a strap on her shoulder, insisted on bumping against her thigh. She nudged the door open and slipped inside. Leaned back and let the sound of the lock clicking shut bring the beginning of a smile to her lips. She let everything drop—everything, that is, except the mail. That she went through one at a time, flinging envelopes across the room when she saw what they were. PG&E bill (fling!). The public television station asking for money again (fling!). A letter from her mother. That one almost landed in the fish tank.

Suddenly she stopped flinging envelopes, because in her hand she held the brand-new Honda motorcycle catalogue. Irene's slight grin became a full, gap-toothed smile. The rest of the mail slipped from her fingers and was left in a pile at the front door.

Catalogue in hand, she made her way to the bedroom. She

stopped to stare at and straighten the Georgia O'Keeffe print on the wall. Between the image of the dark iris—a stylized pussy with charcoal gray lips and a burgundy clit—and the anticipated thrill of the motorcycle catalogue, Irene's cunt was already throbbing. She set the catalogue on her pillow, positioned herself in front of the full-length mirror, and assessed her image.

"Not bad," she said, grinning. "I'm not a teenager anymore. But then again, I wouldn't wanna be."

Licking her lips and blowing a kiss at her image, Irene began to slowly strip. For herself. First she unwound the black silk scarf from her throat and smelled the thick scent of jasmine oil she'd massaged into her skin that morning. She pressed the silk to her face like a veil and breathed deeply, then let go and watched as the scarf drifted slowly to the floor.

She unhooked the black belt from around her waist and pulled it slowly through the loops at the sides of her red blazer. A snake retreating through the grass. She flicked the leather at the catalogue on her pillow, snapping it against the glossy paper. Like a tease. Like a tamer. Irene threw her head back and laughed. She knew exactly where this was going.

Next, she unbuttoned her blazer and shimmied it off her shoulders. She folded it neatly at the foot of her bed. Watching in the mirror as she unbuttoned the shimmery fabric of her white blouse, Irene spread the fabric apart and blew kisses as the caramel-colored curves of her cleavage came into view. She bent her head and kissed the hills of her breasts, leaving burgundy lipstick marks. She stretched her arms to the ceiling and watched her tits rise with the action. Slowly, she unbound the coil of her dreds and shuddered as the springy locks fell to her shoulders. Irene grinned slyly at herself in the mirror and pulled the catalogue to the center of the bed. She opened to the first page.

A Gold Wing SE. The sight of that pearl green touring machine brought back memories. Of big-hearted, broad-shouldered Cody. A big butch of a woman with laughing eyes and the steadiest tongue in the state. Memory was in Irene's fingertips as she wet them and dipped them into the cups of her bra to pinch and pull at her nipples. She squeezed her breasts together, then flattened them close to her body and thought about all those rides when she'd press her tits against the broad expanse of Cody's back. Irene closed her eyes and inhaled, recalling the rich, oily smell of Cody's leather jacket.

Rubbing her thighs and ass through the fabric of her short black skirt, Irene relived the slow rumble of the big bike as it vibrated the cheeks of her ass apart. Straddling that bike on long trips had made her walk bowlegged for days afterward. And easier to get at, Cody used to say. Irene took a wide stance and jiggled her hips to simulate the vibration.

But Cody and that enormous machine of hers were more than Irene was ready for right now. She stopped herself just short of coming and went back to her reflection in the mirror. She peeled her shirt the rest of the way off. Unzipped her skirt and slid it down her legs to the floor. The sound of the wool against her stockings made her purse her lips together and sigh. She held onto the bedpost and stepped daintily out of the circle of fabric. She reached down and turned the page.

Dirt bikes. And memories of Darlene. Her affinity with the machines reflected in her sex—their high-pitched whine like the sound of her coming, her rough-and-tumble fucking like spewing gravel when she'd hit a rough spot. And the coming she'd treated Irene to—like taking flight at the crest of an unexpected hill.

Darlene would come home from the races covered with dust. She'd strip in the hall and drag Irene into the bathroom with her, rolling around in the tub 'til they were both covered with mud and sweat and each other's come. Muddy handprints down her throat and across her breasts. Long, sticky streaks down the inside of her thighs and wedged in the crack of her ass. Irene shuddered with a mixture of lust and joy. She squealed with delight recalling the rough, raunchy times they'd had. But Darlene was long gone, probably at this very moment tumblebugging some sweet young thing who'd never been with another girl before.

Irene turned to the center of the catalogue. Her breath caught in her throat. There it was. A black Honda Shadow. The bike Layla rode. Layla. The woman who currently rode Irene. This was what Irene had been waiting for. She grabbed the black lace hem of her half-slip and pulled it up and over the brown contours of her body.

This picture brought back memories of the past as well as anticipation of times to come. The rubbed leather seat she couldn't wait to be straddled over, again and again. The name "Shadow" on the black fuel tank in deep violet script, Layla's favorite color. And the chrome polished so bright you could see your reflection in it. The sight of the tassels hanging from the handlebars made Irene blush. She remembered the time Layla had pulled them off and whipped her with them.

Trembling with body memories, Irene turned from the image of the pretty black bike to her own image in the mirror. She turned her back to the glass and looked over her shoulder. High-heeled pumps made her calf muscles tense. Black silk stockings covered her legs, the seams in back like the lines of a treasure map. Leading upwards. The tiniest black lace g-string covered little and served only to frame the cheeks of her ass. Twisting at the waist, Irene admired the demi-cup bra that made her breasts stand up and out and barely hid her nipples.

Irene turned to face her reflection again and hunched her shoulders. The bra straps fell. She reached inside the cups and pinched her nipples again, pulling her body away like she sometimes did with Layla. She slid her hands between her legs and encountered the wetness of the world. She was so ready.

Irene unhooked her bra and pulled it off her arms. Ass in the air, she bent and rested her tits on the picture in the catalogue. She rocked and rolled on the image of the Honda, pinching and pulling on her clit with her right hand, burying the fingers of her left deep inside. She came like that, mouth open, cunt open. Heart. Open.

When the spasms finally stopped, she rolled over onto her back. She kicked her heels in the air and laughed out loud. She painted pictures on her thighs with her own juices. Eventually she curled up on her side and fell asleep.

Layla found her just like that. All but naked. Grinning. Dreaming. The motorcycle catalogue still open to the center page. Layla put her helmet on the floor quietly and peeled off her leather jacket. She sat down slowly, taking time to let the mattress adjust to her weight. Her eyes glazed over with fierce love as she watched Irene dream. She moistened a finger between her full lips, then reached out and flicked one of Irene's nipples. She grinned at Irene's moan and sigh and fidget. Suddenly she pinched the nipple hard. Irene's eyes fluttered open with her sharp intake of breath.

"Someone's been looking at the Honda catalogue," Layla teased.

Irene giggled, snatched up the catalogue and tossed it onto the floor.

"Never mind the catalogue," she said. "Why don't you fuck me?"

"Let me smell you," Layla said. Her eyes had that greedy look in them.

Irene rolled over onto her back and spread her legs wide. She grabbed Layla's short afro and held her face just inches from her cunt. Layla made a noisy business of breathing deeply.

"Damn," Layla said, lifting up to look Irene in the eyes. "You're dripping."

"Are you thirsty?"

Layla grinned and nodded.

Irene arched her back; Layla slid her hands beneath Irene's ass. She lingered there to cup the cheeks, to feel the warmth of her lover's flesh, then dove her head between Irene's legs. She traced the contours of Irene's cunt; she ran her tongue between the inner and outer lips, sucked on the hard little clit. She listened with satisfaction as Irene sang sensation to her with sighs and groans and finally, when she could come no more, with tears.

Irene pulled Layla up her body. Buried her face in Layla's neck and licked her there, tasting the salt of Layla's sweat. "I love the way you love me," she whispered.

"I'm not done," Layla said. And she rose up off the bed and began to undress.

Michelle Stevens

❧❧❧

The Appliance

Bonnie's in the bathroom crying again. It's the third time this week. I ask her why. She says because she's sad.

"Mad?" I ask.

"No," she says and slams the door on my nose.

We fought about it again. This time we were in Denny's. She was halfway through her Mexicali Combo when I brought it up. Next thing I knew, we were back in the bedroom, and she was dangling it in front of me like a dirty sock.

The Appliance. Her name for it, not mine. Personally, I think the word *appliance* is a little too literal, too Montgomery Ward. But I can't think of anything better. I mean, how do you describe 900 volts of sheer pleasure?

"It's not what you think," I said to her. "I . . . I was using it for my back."

She looked at me with that sad, sad look. "Why do you lie to me?" she asked. Then she started to cry.

It's been like this since the beginning. Literally, since the first night we met. I was lonely, had just ended a six-year marriage to a man. I'd never been with a woman before, never even kissed one. Everything I knew about lesbians I knew from Katherine Forrest and Rita Mae Brown.

Saturday afternoons, while my husband watched TV in the den,

I'd lie under the comforter in our bed, flipping through the pages of *Curious Wine* while I jacked off with his Radio Shack three-speed massager. I never could handle the highest speed.

When I finally got up the courage to tell him I was gay, he didn't know how to take it. "So you have sex with women?" he asked lasciviously.

"Not yet," I said.

"So how do you know you're gay?"

"I just do," I told him.

In the end, he was pretty good about it. For his anguish, he got the car, the condo and a hot new girlfriend who was willing to do all the wifely stuff I hated—like cook. I got the cat and an old electric back massager he vaguely remembered getting for Christmas.

Months later, lying on the futon in my crappy little apartment, I spent a lot of nights wondering how I could've been so stupid. Telling my well-meaning, well-paid husband I was *gay*? I didn't even *know* any lesbians! What had I been thinking? Why did I have to go and make my life so hard? I mean, sure it was a loveless marriage. Sure I was lonely. But not *this* lonely.

I stared at the ceiling, thinking about what an idiot I was. I'd toss, I'd turn and, finally, I'd pull out my only friend. It lived at the foot of the bed. As I envisioned all those beautiful heroines and perfect lesbian love affairs I had read about in books, the gentle hum had a magical way of keeping me company.

Finally, six months after my divorce, I saw a flyer at the bookstore while I was picking up a copy of *The Well of Loneliness*. The flyer advertised a coming-out group at the Gay and Lesbian Center. I wrote down the information in the sleeve of the book and promised myself I'd go.

The night of the group, it took all my courage and two glasses of wine to walk through the door. When I finally went in, I was relieved that no one seemed to notice me. I found a chair in a corner, sat down and tried my best not to make eye contact.

Then it happened. Across a crowded room, I saw her. And I knew.

She was sitting in a chair in the opposite corner, trying her best not to make eye contact, either. I don't think she saw me at first. She was all alone. This tall, lean, butch, beautiful Molly Bolt, Stephen Gordon, Lane and Diana all rolled into one. Yes, indeed, she was the heroine in every wonderful lesbian story ever written. She was the woman who'd been holding me all those nights while a vibrator buzzed under my sheets.

I don't remember how I got to the other side of the room. I don't remember how we got to my apartment, either. All I know is, pretty soon we were two naked women lying on my living room floor. I'd had no idea that skin could feel so soft, that hands could touch so lightly, that one tongue could be in so many places all at once.

"Maybe we should go to the bedroom," I whispered.

Bonnie chuckled. "Yeah, I guess hardwood floors can get pretty hard."

She got up. She was naked. Standing above me. The street light through the window made her skin glow. She was like an angel. A six-foot large-breasted angel. And she was heading towards my bed.

When she pulled back the comforter, it was lying right there, extension cord trailing to the wall. Long. Plastic. All three speeds. She raised an eyebrow. I blushed.

"It's been a long time, and I . . ."

"It's okay," she grinned. "I understand. Every single girl needs her appliance."

She picked it up and tossed it on the ground, where it landed with a loud thump. She pushed me down on the futon and started doing those amazing things with her tongue again. It felt good, as good as before—but in the back of my mind, I couldn't help wondering if the fall had hurt it.

The next morning I sent Bonnie off to work with a stale french pastry and a long french kiss. Then I called in sick to work and crawled back into bed. Even if Bonnie couldn't be there, I was determined to make the best night of my life last a little longer.

Lying on the threadbare sheets, I thought about her soft skin. The way her back curved. How her hair had tickled my breast.

When I came back to reality, I was comforted by the familiar hum of my Radio Shack massager, singing between my legs as usual. Thank God for nonbreakable plastic.

In the weeks that followed, I spent a lot of time in my bed. And on my floor. And once in the stairwell, when Bonnie couldn't wait for me to open the front door. We did it constantly. We did it every-where. We did it every which way. Her on top. Me on top. Three comforters on top so the neighbors wouldn't hear our screams.

In those rare moments when Bonnie and I weren't together, I found myself thinking about her constantly. Her stomach. Her hands. The weight of her body on top of me. It drove me crazy. All alone, I stayed in the bed, the vibrator humming away, the electric meter spinning.

A few months later, I surfaced for air. I had run out of sick days. My boss wanted to know why I was so lethargic at work. I still loved Bonnie madly. I still wanted her constantly. But I was tired. Some nights, I just wanted to sleep. Bonnie, on the other hand, was a jock. She ate too many Wheaties. She still wanted to do it every night.

"I can't, I'm too tired," I said, as she licked my neck.

"You didn't want to last night, either," she said.

"I'm just not in the mood." I rolled over and put a pillow over my head.

"You were in the mood to use the appliance," Bonnie said.

I sat up. "How did you know that?"

"I just know." Bonnie shrugged.

"Did I tell you?" I was confused. I only used it when she wasn't at home.

"You use it every day," she said matter-of-factly. "Usually more than once."

"How do you know that?" I asked. I was starting to get suspicious.

"The other woman always knows," Bonnie said. Then she rolled away from me.

There was a deadly silence. One of those active silences, where you have to work hard not to say anything, where you can't possi-bly fall asleep.

Finally, I turned to her, spooned her from behind, ran my hand through her hair. "Just because I use the appli . . . the massager, it has nothing to do with you. I'm just tired tonight."

Bonnie just sighed, and we fell asleep.

Three days later, I sat quietly fuming at the kitchen table, star-ing at the front door, waiting for my beloved to come home.

"What did you do with it?" I hissed when she finally walked in.

Bonnie smiled. She found this amusing. "You're addicted. Tough love. I hid it."

"I am not addicted!"

"Ooooh! Denial. Classic, classic, classic," she said as she hung up her coat.

"I'm not denying anything. I'll be the first to admit I like it. Give it back."

She laughed at me. A pitying, condescending laugh. Then she pulled it out of a bag in the hall closet. I was holding it again. It was in my hands. Thank God. Thank God.

A few nights later, no matter what Bonnie did with her magic tongue, I just couldn't come.

"Honey, you must be getting tired," I whispered. Gingerly I suggested we use the massager.

"You like it better than me?" Bonnie asked, defensive.

"No, I like *you*. I like you a lot. I just don't think your neck can hold out much longer."

"It's that damned appliance," she yelled. "It's making you insensitive!" She got up and started to pace. "You're addicted to the vibrator," she said ominously. "This is your first lesbian experience, honey. You don't understand the danger. Lesbians get addicted to an appliance, then they can't have real sex anymore." She took a deep breath for emphasis and warned, "If we stop having real sex, we're eventually doomed. Don't you understand? It's inevitable. If you don't stop using the appliance, *we will break up!*"

The thought of losing Bonnie frightened me. I handed over the massager, begging her to keep it safe.

A few days later, after consulting my old library of lesbian literature, I took Bonnie to dinner. To discuss.

"Joann Loulan says a vibrator can't make you insensitive to human touch," I said between bites of my Dennyburger.

Bonnie put down her fork. She looked me in the eyes. "Are you going to bring that up again?"

"I have to," I said. "It's bothering me."

"It's bothering you because no addict likes having their drug taken away."

"First of all," I countered, "using a vibrator is a perfectly natural form of sexuality. Secondly, my using it has nothing to do with you. And third," I added, "I don't like to be told what to do."

"I didn't tell you what to do."

"You threatened to break up with me if I didn't hand it over," I yelled. "You've been bugging me about it for weeks. You're trying to control my life."

Bonnie looked away, deadly quiet. She was trying hard not to cry.

"Let's go," she whispered.

"The waitress didn't bring the Colossal Fudge Sundae yet."

"I'm not hungry."

The car ride home was like a funeral with no guests. She stared out the window, her face turned away so I couldn't see the tears.

By the time we got home, she wasn't crying anymore. She went straight to her dresser and pulled the appliance out of the bottom drawer.

"Here." She held it out with the tip of her fingers.

"Uh, maybe we should talk about this," I tried to reason.

"I don't want to talk about it anymore."

"But if you're angry . . ."

"I don't want to talk about it. I don't want to see it. The issue is dead," she said flatly. When I didn't grab the massager, she let it drop to the floor. Then she turned on her heels and walked away.

I followed her, almost tripping over the appliance in the process.

"It's not that I need it," I said.

"I don't care."

"I don't even have to use it."

"I don't care."

"It's just an issue of control."

She walked into the bathroom and shut the door on my nose. And that was the end of it.

Until the next day. Saturday. She was out playing softball. I was busy in the bed. Over the hum of the vibrator, I distinctly heard the rustle of keys at the front door. I was able to turn it off, but there was no time to remove the evidence.

"Oh, hey," I mustered brightly as she walked into the room.

"Hey," she said back as she sat down next to me. "What are you still doing in bed?"

"I'm, uh . . ."

"Sick?" she asked. She leaned over and put her hand on my forehead.

"No, just resting. I thought you had a game."

"I couldn't concentrate. I hate it when we fight."

"Me too," I said as I carefully sat up to give her a kiss. I kept one hand on the vibrator, which was dangerously close to her thigh.

"I'm really sorry," she whispered. "I just don't like those things. But, you know, it's your life, and as long as I don't have to see it, well, I guess out of sight, out of mind."

"Great," I mumbled through my plastered smile.

"God," she went on, as she stood up and took off her jeans, "I've really missed you. This whole thing has been really draining."

She crossed over to her side of the bed, pulled back the sheets, and crawled in.

"Oh . . . you're naked," she said.

"Yeah, well, I, uh . . ."

"Hmm." Her hand cupped my breast. "I like this. Easy access."

She moved closer and started to suck my neck. I didn't know what to do, so I just lay there. Enjoying it. Her magic tongue moved from my earlobe to my collarbone. Her magic fingers squeezed my nipple. Before I knew what was happening, she was climbing on top of me.

"Ow!" she screamed, as her weight came down on my body. "What is that?"

Her hand fished underneath the comforter. It resurfaced with an old Radio Shack massager. Three speeds.

Oh, God, I thought, here we go again.

Bonnie just sat there for a while, on top of me, staring at the appliance. She rolled it around in her hands; she moved the switch up and down, testing out the different speeds.

"You do it naked?" she finally asked.

"Sometimes."

"Show me," she said. She rolled back over to her side of the bed, propped her head up with her arm and lay there, waiting.

"Is this some sort of weird reverse-psychology thing?" I asked.

"No. I just want to see what it is you like so much."

She nodded for me to get on with it, so I lay back down, fluffed the pillows for a while, checked to see if she was still watching. She was. I'd never done it with someone looking at me before. I didn't know if I could.

I closed my eyes. I turned on the vibrator. Low speed. There was that familiar hum.

"This is no fun," she said. "I want to *see*." She flung back the covers, so I was just lying there naked, holding a big plastic appliance to my private parts.

"I don't know if I can do it like this," I whined.

"Oh, please! You do it seven times a day! Go on."

So I did. I closed my eyes and tried to concentrate. It was disconcerting but kind of exciting, knowing that she was right there. Watching. The vibrator started to feel good. I started to rock back and forth. Next thing I knew, there was a hand on my neck, stroking my hair. Then a magic tongue on my nipple, licking, licking.

I grabbed the back of her hair and pushed her face into my breasts. Her breath, her cheeks felt good on my skin. I took her hand, the one stroking my hair, and brushed it across my face. I took her middle finger and licked it. Slowly. Up, down. Feeling the wet, the warmth. I put it in my mouth and sucked hard.

Suddenly, she was covering me. Her face to my face. Her breasts to my breasts. We were sharing the vibrator. Me underneath. Bonnie on top. We were in rhythm, she and I. Rocking, sucking, back and forth to the hum. Then the familiar wash came over us. We screamed at the same time.

When I came back to reality, when sound and sense and the world came back, I realized she was giggling. Her brown eyes peered at me over my breast.

"What's so funny?" I asked.

"You never told me we could do a threesome!"

Julia Rader

Thirst

What is it about him that I'm sitting here inches from the telephone, forehead cradled in my palm, praying it won't and craving for the ring? The heat of the summer night carries the smell of salt through the open windows. It's been a whole year, but memories flash like last night's movie. More than anything, it has to do with the way he taught me how to suck cock. (Not technique. They taught me that a long time ago.)

I see myself in the bedroom where we lived together near the foothills of the Rockies, in a suburb outside Denver. In a dark basement I make out the vague shape of his body. I'm wearing a stiff corset—it squishes my breasts together and pushes them up with underwires. I don't have any panties on and his hand is making slow circles on the cheeks of my ass.

Inside his briefs, his cock bulges. I can see it perfectly even in this dim light. In his other hand is a glass of ice water. He shakes the glass close to my ear. He wants me to listen to the sound of the tinkling ice cubes.

"Are you thirsty, baby?" It isn't like he wants to know. He's suggesting thirst, creating and building it—like going for an afternoon hike in the woods, the way the waterfall sounds in the distance when you've been walking upstream to find it, and you first hear the crashing water. Even if you've walked a long way, you're suddenly not tired anymore. The sound itself charges you with energy, beckons you on.

He moves the glass of water down to his crotch and rubs himself there. His hand on my ass moves up to my head. He pulls my face down to his still-hidden cock.

"Umm . . . can you smell that . . . are you thirsty, baby?" I let out a small moan, and he quickly pulls my head away, giving my ass a sharp slap.

"I didn't say you could drink yet. I might spank you if you suck it."

I get confused. I don't know what he wants. I look at him. He pulls my head back down and resumes the slow circles on the cheeks of my ass, the sound of tinkling ice cubes close to my ear.

"Can you smell it? What does it smell like?" I moan again, and this time I open my mouth and make contact, soaking through the fabric with my tongue.

"That's right, I know you're thirsty. But if you don't stop I might have to spank you."

I continue to lick him, until he slaps my ass, harder this time, and the harder he slaps me the more I want him to keep on doing it. When he stops spanking I stop sucking. He still has the glass of water in his hand and rubs it against my face, close to my mouth, then down to his cock, rubbing it all over.

"Are you thirsty?" he asks again.

"Yes," I say.

"Don't you want to take these off me so you can drink? Don't you need to suck?"

My hand reaches out to pull off his briefs, but he pulls away and I get confused again. He continues to back up, several feet away. The tinkle of ice turns mean. Suddenly I'm scared.

When our sex transcends playacting, time and space converge into a laser-beam focus of the immediate. Now, abandoned near the foot of the bed, I see childhood monsters baring ugly fangs. My lover is the devil, and physical union is a sick joke intended to own and pervert me.

I can't help it, I break down and cry, I'm the stupid, trapped baby and I can't help it, please don't hurt me leave me alone I'm scared.

He puts the glass down and comes close to comfort me. He unhooks my corset so that I'm naked, strokes my belly and face, and lifts my breasts up one at a time to kiss the soft skin underneath the folds.

I'm happy again, allowed to touch and please him, and I reach down to pull off his briefs. He puts his hand on my cunt, makes soft, slow circles on my clitoris so that when I finally get to see his naked cock I'm all the more aroused.

"Maybe you want to drink cock water. Do you want some cock water?"

"Yes." His cock brushes my throat. My nipples have gone hard and tingle. He gets up onto his knees and hands me the glass of ice water. He dips his cock all the way in and leaves it there for a minute. Seen through glass, his erection looks bigger. He takes it out and tells me to drink.

"But you know what happens when you drink cock water, don't you? You go crazy and you have to suck."

I'm drinking now, icy liquid and the knowledge of his secretions.

"Drink more . . . drink it all up. There you go, that's a good girl . . . and now you're crazy. You *have* to suck."

He pulls my face down to his cock again. "Can you smell it, baby? How does it smell now that you've drunk the cock water? Suck."

He chants the word, putting me inside of the craving to suck him; my throat opens wider than I thought possible. He thrusts deep inside and I want it. Want this getting fucked all the way down the back of my throat.

"Suck, suck, suck." I'm being force-fed as he guides my head up and down.

And then he begins to spank me, hard. His flat hand stings the surface of my bottom, hard and fast. The blows keep rhythm with my head bobbing up and down. Inside my throat his cock keeps on pushing, deeper and faster. I smell and taste his dripping semen, and feel the electricity shoot between my legs. My bottom's burning and the whole world is on fire and I've learned to love the devil, and surrendering to my destiny is all the safety I'll ever need and the flames shoot up, hot liquid down my throat and I'm coming and I'm drinking, I'm gratefully coming and drinking.

When the phone rings and I hear his voice, I know it's starting all over again.

⚜

Tame

I opened the door of a moving car. There was no choice. The windows were glossy with spit, a man was barking at the wheel, sputtering, brutish. I remember the high pitch, the jerky driving, my silence like gasoline to his flame, the thought that I could die because lovers kill lovers in scenes like this. There was no choice. His words clattered like castanets: He said I was pathetic, I heard "prophetic," and then I heard nothing but my lungs, my chain necklace sliding up and down my belt buckle, the shriek of a branch-snapping wind in the woozy black night. I opened the door. I hissed, Stop the car, Steven. And Steven, Mr. Hyde, put on the brakes.

He said, You get out of this car and it's fucking over.

He said, Jude, get back in the car.

He said, Nobody's going to want you like I do. I'm sorry I said some mean things, you're not sociopathic, now come back in the car.

Please, he said, with a broken sound in his throat.

But I cut loose anyway. I knew that trick.

So it's midnight in the Kwik-Mart, my shimmery stockings are wild with runs, thin ladders threading up my calves, my eyes are dry and dusty with mascara flakes, and I am reading dog-eared pop mags like all the other midnight waifs. The man behind the counter—bald, porky, and oddly moist—watches me as if I will slip candy into my purse. When he's not staring at me directly he is watching the silver ball in the corner, then he glances at *Saturday Night Live* on the little Goldstar TV on top of the popcorn machine. I want to go up to him and say, You've got the wrong girl, Mister. I'm a fucking secretary to the CEO of a Fortune 500 food brokerage firm. I could buy you. But I'm frightened by this, I'm frightened that I really am a fucking secretary, not a euphemistic "assistant," let's get real. Every day I take a memo it hurts my pride; when I try to appease Nick Martinetti's temper it's like swallowing his come, it's so vile, my sweet good-bye is me wiping my lips, murmuring, Delicious.

My heart shudders, then beats like a gerbil's; I lose the rhythm, tense up, then find it again. I am aware that I started out beautiful and became hideous at some point this evening, at some point things snapped, my creamy skin cracked, my teal silk dress started smelling sour, like old milk.

Tonight something scratched my brain, ripping zipper-swift to my heart. Steven sneered, You are Teflon Woman, everything rolls off your back—would you just be fucking honest for once. I said, I am sick of your verbal abuse, feeling certain of the definition for the first time. And he retorted, You don't have a clue what abuse is, Jude. Have you ever been shoved down the stairs by your drunk 200-pound father? Don't talk to me about abuse—you had the safe childhood, I didn't.

At the stoplight I was going to sock him. But I couldn't. I can't hurt people, everything drives inward, caustic, searing. It stays in my gut and burns through my pupils. There are so many things I've never done. I ache, flimsy.

When the man seems transfixed by a car commercial I tuck a small pack of Tic-Tacs into my I. Magnin wool coat. To assure him of my integrity, I go up to the counter and ask for Virginia Slims, though I don't smoke. He smiles at me, sweating. He asks me where my boyfriend is. I tell him he's in the parking lot waiting for me to decide how I'll break my twenty, knowing that Steven is long gone.

On the TV there is a skit about a chubby, flannel-wearing androgyne named Pat whose questionable sex is the source of endless jokes and futile attempts to crack the mystery. The man behind the counter is interested in this, and watches it while he makes change.

He says, You just know that's a lady. But they keep on going. Ha ha—it's still funny. The fanny pack, stuff like that. I mean, on TV it's funny, but in real life you like to know what side of the toast the butter's on.

He trusts me now because I bought something. I am shocked that deceit is so easy. It makes me sad.

Take you, for example, he says. You got the dress, the high heels. I can tell what you are.

Thank you, I say, with a miserable smile, putting the cigarettes in my purse with the Tic-Tacs.

Have a good night, hon, he says.

Tonight I am a runaway, a pissed secretary, a thief. He cannot tell what I am. These high heels are scuffed and my wrist is still pink from Steven's grip.

Understand this was not the first time Steven erupted, but it was the last time I could take it. As Dr. Jekyll he was sweet, humble, and brilliant. He wanted to call me "muffin," he was full of cringe-provoking terms of endearment and sappy sentiments; this made him happy. He liked the brat in me. He was intimidated by my cleverness. He liked my skinny ankles and fluffy red hair and the tricks I would use to get him hot. And I liked his fucked-up childhood, academic musketeering, Buddhism, and the way he would whisper what he wanted to do to me as we'd walk down the sidewalk past all the corporate shitheads and how, as we stood against a stone wall by a Dumpster, he would delicately lift my skirt, watching me closely, reading me, our lovemaking a muffled quake, opening and closing, little breathy wings, the only time I could let myself trust him.

He would break things. He would never touch me that way. I got a call from my brother, he thought it was an ex-lover, he punched a hole in my wall. You'd think a bright woman like me would get a clue. You'd also think an assistant professor of philosophy at a famous private college would be more emotionally refined. Because he was smart, wrote lovely letters, and atoned for his tantrums, I let it all slide for three months. Until tonight: the wrist burn, prisoner in his car, suicide drive. If he hadn't braked, I would have jumped.

I'm getting ideas as the coffee hits me like shock therapy, and they have to do with Frankenstein. I want to be the doctor *and* the monster. I want to take parts of myself—my skeleton, my musky voice, these dimples—and create an alter ego. Tonight I believe I could do anything because as of this moment, I am abandoning my former life of the 5:30 alarm, Martinetti's scowl, StairMaster, Crystal Pepsi, and Steven's insanity.

The radio in this all-night diner is playing Muzak of Billy Idol's "White Wedding," which I find sinister. Hey little sister, what have you done?

I am attempting to smoke. As soon as the barbershop opens this morning I'm going to be sitting in that chair, hair's going to fall, I want a fuzzy scalp and stunningly groomed eyebrows, 'cause if you saw me you'd know something was beating inside, gerbil-time, and things aren't always what they seem.

Where did I come from? Let me describe it in objects: a mansion, two parents; a trailer house, one bitter mother. A stepfather, a TV that grew larger with more channels every Christmas, a secret canister of pot in my pink bedroom, a scholarship to a famous college. A palpitating heart, eager thighs, a cruel streak. A fishbowl of dollar bills, bartending tips, my only savings account.

But this is the new Jude, ready or not, and where I come from is just a stack of singed newspaper clippings.

Oh this city, my reeking hutch, creepy-crawly and deafening. I see everything at night. The turkey bone, gristled and chomped, lying mid-sidewalk as a cannibalistic threat. The disease slathered bumpy and red over some faces, the saggy butts, the mildewed sleeping bags. Voices skittering down slimy alleys. Men who speculate at the cost of my cunt, then turn outraged when I give them the glassy eye. I hate this city, there are no lovers, only stern, squalid fuckers.

The barber didn't want to cut my hair. Too pretty, he said, but money is money, and now I am a duckling in need of a beret.

I dip into a boutique, startling the gentle proprietress, all of my secretary charm chucked out the window. I manhandle the wool suits, seeking the strongest fabric, the sharpest style. There is a rich burgundy suit with black velvet retro buttons and cuffs, it looks killer-chic on my petite, wiry body, it is mine with the flick of a credit card. Black beret, leather gloves: I am evil, evil.

Noon at the Greek Cafe, a collective Sunday morning listlessness: solitary youth and sexed-out, latte-slurping couples with the classifieds. It may be the worst time in the world to pick someone up, but there appears to be one person who wants to go against the grain.

To my right at the window seat there is a woman who has just borrowed the sugar from my table. It was not so much the reaching over, the polite murmured rhetorical question (May I borrow this?), but the grin that followed, a grin that showed her cards then snatched them up again, a grin that wagged, I know your type. And I felt a surge, a sudden panic—she knows my type?— and a gratitude so fierce I almost lunged forward.

She is a silky-haired, kohl-rimmed Cleopatra in white, black fringe brushing her eyebrows, bronze lips in motion, following her mind as she sips and speculates. She looks like she is used to controlling people and having them adore her; she looks bored but satisfied with that role. She may be someone avoiding fame.

We are trying to photograph each other in a series of quick, furtive glances. Or perhaps I am the furtive one: Whenever I look over she has those dark, knowledgeable eyes on me, and I flutter, turn away. It occurs to me that this is the first time in my life I have felt desired by a woman, and the first time since I lost my virginity that I have felt so humble, incredulous, and glaringly naive.

Panic rolls in like an unwelcome guest on my driveway, cranking up the terror-rhythm: evacuated brain, blood loss, the grip, the release, the dizzy lurch. I'm thinking, What if, what if. What if I pass out right now. No one knows me. What if something bad happens. I am not so brave.

Cleopatra leans over and says, You're white as a ghost—what's wrong?

Suddenly I am girl to her woman, abandoned kid, not what I wanted, but right now all I want to say is this: I fled, my hair is gone, please take me home.

I tell her that I'm having second thoughts about my new look.

She studies me. But it's gorgeous, she says. Your high cheek-bones lend themselves well to that pared-down, glam look. The only thing missing is your skin color. Can I buy you some hot tea? Chamomile?

I let her buy me some tea, and as she wends her way to the counter I begin to place her age, her story. Late thirties, forever bisexual, artistic, solitary, beach cabin, bare feet, purples, whites, deep blues, graceful hips, gemstones, rings, no wedding ring, and now she has moved into the seat next to me, and I thank her very much.

I'm a little disoriented, I explain. Within twelve hours I have wiped out everything—the lover, the job, the look—and now I'm just sitting here contemplating my next move.

Have you changed your name?

I could, but I won't. It's still Jude.

Jude. It makes me think of Judas. But I am always looking for dark connotations, that's what I do. My name's Corinne.

A pretty, hardly threatening name, I conclude, feeling my color return.

She asks me where I come from and I give her the list. I do not mention being a secretary because I want her to think I am a drifter, an adventuress. But she guesses that I worked in an office and seems attracted to that fact, if only for the irony.

She murmurs, It all makes sense. She says, Jude, you're in shock.

Yes, I say, feeling my nerves rustle again, ready to freak.

She stares at me.

I think I've met you before, she says. Or you remind me of someone. I used to dance. My stage name was Cassandra. At Monique's? That classy joint? You remind me of this woman who used to come every Friday and watch me critically, solemn in the corner, always wearing this equestrian get-up.

It wasn't me, I say, But I like the thought.

My eyes surf from shoulder to shoulder, calculating curves,

imagining her jiggling and not liking that image, then replacing it with her winding slowly and sensuously around a pole.

Why do I remind you of her? I ask, adjusting my chair closer.

Corinne lets a smile glide across her face. Because you're a self-conscious watcher on the verge of implosion, she says. And I mean that compassionately.

So it's compassion, then, that leads me to her house in the hills. I am mild as a calf, following her upstairs, mute, warm, touching smooth stained oak, peacock feathers, cream-colored membranal leaves. She knows I haven't slept and advises me to take a bath and crawl into bed. She says she will either be gardening or reading in the living room.

It is as though a fire has been snuffed.

Her towels are velvety crimson; essential oils in blue glass vials line the windowsill. I am afraid that if I climb into this black tub of steaming lilac water I will melt to my marrow, or sleep until I have absorbed the bath like a plump golden raisin. I am only half-conscious; stranger things have happened.

In my dreams there is violence. I am in the car with Steven, his nostrils are flaring, he is wearing a man's version of my burgundy suit, I am screaming, Stop the car, stop the car! as we thunder down a graveled hill and then I realize there are no brakes. We smash into a tree, unhurt. He begins to cry. I urge him not to cry because it scares me. I start to cry, too, and then he turns indignant and says, You're not supposed to!

You don't have to wake up, a voice says.

I'm in a dark room under heavy blankets, naked. I move my sleepy body toward the voice. She says, I'm here if you need me, Jude.

I need you, I mumble.

What?

I want you.

There is a pause and then I hear the bed creak and her breathing beside me.

I wonder if you know what you mean by that, little girl, she says, stroking my fuzzy scalp.

What do you think I mean? I ask quietly, tingling.

You are so pretty you make me sad, she whispers, her hand suddenly tightening at my nape. And I want to kiss you, but there's something wrong, I don't want to steal anything, it's like I could just reach through your skin and pull out your heart.

I don't care, I say. Corinne, you brought me here.

Don't trust so easily, she says in a voice that tells me it has started.

Shadows and slithering drapes, two female bodies confined within four sweating walls. I can smell her aroma—spicy, acidic—and it stirs me. I am spacy from desire, where is she?

Put your hands above your head, she says.

Like angel wings they rise up, only to be bound swiftly with a sash. No childish knot, it is tight, hard-core.

You're going to get what you asked for, my Cleopatra leers. I saw it in you, I knew what you wanted.

But my heart, my lungs—they are frantic, shallow, frenzied. They don't match the beat between my legs, the liquid pulse. I would beg her to tame me if I didn't think she knew that already.

Hands on my legs rubbing circles on my skin, around my belly, across my collarbone. Fingernails suddenly grind into my arms. She has me high-strung, soprano-sexed. Just as I begin to melt she tightens her grip, bruising me. She murmurs words that make me yield: open, beautiful, good.

I want to tell her something, I want to warn her that I am a hard come, to not work on me as if I required work—Corinne, I want to say, I'm the impossible knot, a sexual glutton, I could be wound up forever and still crave more.

Don't even try, she says, smearing me, teasing.

A heavy wave inside glides downward, pooling at the base of my spine.

She says, You are a child, you are unformed, you are my creation, follow this rhythm.

She kneads a pulse into me, her palm is warm, she breathes into my ear, and we begin to merge, it is so dark in here, my hands are bound, my blood is rushing, she is so strong, overwhelming, hot

cloves, vapors, breasts kissing breasts, what else is there, where
else should I be except underneath this woman, echoing, undulat-
ing, my edge sanded smooth, gerbil-heart put to sleep.

It is like waking up from a bad dream and realizing conscious
life is no better.

In the morning I prowl through her house looking for explana-
tions, reasons why it had to be her, the one who opened me. Her
books are all philosophy, Eastern religion, Renaissance art. There
is no junk food in her kitchen, nothing harmful except red wine.
Her apparent sincerity frightens me. Where is the danger, I want
to demand. I am cranky. I am tired of being such a pussy, suc-
cumbing to other people's wills. I want my hair back. I want my
virginity back. Corinne made me come; I want that back, too.

Time is running out and there are always tricks. In any enclosed
space I risk imprisonment. Hey, I know the power trip of the
driver, the knot-tier, the one who nurtures.

I count to ten. I walk backwards, erasing the night.

She had wiped my melt on my cheek like a gash, triumphant
when it was over. You're exorcised, she declared.

What I'm saying with my fleeing is: Not even close.

karen marie christa minns

Sauce

When I heard the sobs outside the stall door, I knew I was trapped. Shit! I flushed again, hoping she'd get the message—like, split already; maybe somebody's sick.

I come from a long line of mannered people. We don't ignore children, sick animals or crying women. I cleared my throat, giving her a last chance to save face and escape into the lobby. The ladies room at the Port Theatre is way too cramped to pretend one hasn't noticed the kind of tears this woman was manufacturing. I kept my head down, washed my hands, cursing under my breath at the lack of soap and the shred of towel. Still, our eyes connected. A millisecond of light and shadow, but it was enough. She gulped, swiped at her puffy eyes, then spoke.

"I feel so foolish, but I just can't bear the death scene."

"Excuse me?" I turned in resignation, my fingers still dripping from the sink.

"When Ruth dies." She gulped back more sobs. "I know this is ridiculous, believe me, I don't usually do this sort of thing, crying in public rest rooms, speaking to strangers out of the blue."

I handed her some sheets of toilet paper, peeling them off my fingers as carefully as I could, given the circumstances.

"It's just that I'm new here and this film . . . I grew up in Georgia . . . and today, with the rain, God, you must think I'm crazy!"

The woman attempted a smile. It came out crooked, and just a wee bit snaggle-toothed.

I think it was the snaggle-tooth that got me. Or maybe it was the gray rain drumming over our heads. Maybe it was my own embarrassment at seeing this film again, for the third time—a matinee, no less, during the week, sneaking off work. I'm not the sentimental type. I didn't want this woman to get the wrong idea about my own misty-eyed wanderings in the bathroom.

I took a good, long look at her, feeling invited, sort of. She was five-nine at least, in plain leather pumps. Her hair was pulled back into a French knot. Dull-gold ear posts and a plain gold band on her left pinky were the only jewelry I could see. A tan trench coat swathed her down to her slim ankles. A touch of makeup; some eyeliner, smudgy now and rose lipstick. Maybe no lipstick. She looked as if she'd been chewing her lips, instead of popcorn, in the dark. Her hands were long, thin, the nails trimmed and un-bitten. Maybe this crying jag wasn't in character. She smiled again. Her teeth were very white and only a little snaggly in front—that sexy country look, not enough for braces, but enough to let you know she hadn't had them capped. She held out one of her long hands.

"My name is Veronica. Thank you for not calling an usher." Her accent betrayed her Georgia roots. She'd been working on losing it, though. "I work at the university. I'm a translator."

"Oh." I blushed, caught cruising. The pause implied I should supply my own name. "I'm Emily. Emily Maple." I took her soft palm.

"You write! I've seen some of your work. I like your column in *Coast Tide*. Actually, it's the only part of the paper I read. How did you convince that paper to let you do a liberal column?" Veronica dabbed at her reddened nose. The shift in focus gave her more steam but knocked the wind right out of me.

I wasn't exactly a closet case, not by a long shot, especially these days with my new haircut and leather jacket. Still, it *was* a conservative town. The local paper was trying to live down accusations from mostly university people that it was racist and sexist, and I was the token tidbit thrown in the direction of the school. She was right, I was an anomaly and I walked a careful line. Showing up at a semi-queer (albeit whitewashed) film in the middle of the day wasn't exactly living safely. Another good reason to hightail it out of the theatre before the credits rolled.

I stuck my hands in my jacket pockets, not knowing where else to put them.

"Emily, look, I feel like I owe you . . . I mean, this is so awkward. Could I buy you a cup of coffee? Parting in the ladies' room seems kind of abrupt."

The door opened. A stream of gray-haired women filtered in, some of them, too, dabbing at runny noses.

Suddenly Veronica took my arm and more or less guided me into the lobby. The final strains of the soundtrack flowed around us. We rode the edge of the sound outside, into the rainy afternoon.

I took her to my truck, running ahead to gallantly open the passenger's side. It was pouring now and the cold fingers of rain assaulted us, collars to coattails. Still, I kept my smile clamped on. Veronica, with the grace of a dancer, skirted the wider puddles, unfazed by the downpour. She climbed gingerly into the Toyota, pulling her skirt down carefully and smoothing the raincoat over it as she sat.

I let the engine heat up for a few moments. The rain on the roof sounded tinny and sad. Outside, everything was dove gray, that particular soft color that seaside towns are swathed in during storms. We were fogging the windows with our breath.

The air between us seemed colored by pearls, softened somehow. I began to relax. Veronica unbuttoned the top of her coat. She smiled, noticing the color in my face rise again. I could smell the clean, pure scent of lavender as it escaped from her clothes.

The pulse in my neck, then lower, began to change. A quick hot drum between my legs; a recognized, memorized beat. It was both embarrassing and exciting. Shit, for all I knew she was some married lady with a cop husband and two kids at home. For all I knew she was a sociopath who picked up dykes all across the country at matinees just like this one. What better trap than the PG-13 version of a queer novel? The thump in my lap calmed down. I felt sweat mix with cold rain against my back.

"Emily," her voice cut across the sudden glacier forming between us, "am I making you uncomfortable?"

"What?" I looked ahead at the fogged-in windshield, not wanting to meet her eyes.

"My apartment is right down the beach. I make terrific espresso. Look, I don't know how to say this without it sounding exactly like a line, but I can't face a loud coffee shop right now, and I really don't want to walk alone into a cold apartment. This is not the right thing to do, especially in California, but, well, how about if I show you some ID or something?" Veronica flashed the snaggletooth.

I tried my ultra-butch cool. "Maybe you're the one who should be worried." Had absolutely no effect. The woman sat back, comfortably laughing.

"Turn left at the light, Emily."

I did.

Veronica took my jacket, hanging it up to dry. I sank into an overstuffed chair by the bay window. She flipped on a CD of Bach, filling the space between us. My writer's eye pulled all the details into focus. I forgave her the fake southwest-by-the-sea furniture after catching the row of diplomas on the wall—either extremely convincing forgeries or she was who she'd claimed. I preferred to believe the latter, especially after she emerged from a back room. She stood in the living room doorway, her hair down, a full wave of gold around her shoulders. The skirt and blouse had been replaced by a shell-colored camisole and very faded Levi's.

"You look striking, sitting there in that light," she said. "I love rain in the late afternoon, it's like an early twilight."

That familiar cousin, "the thump," began somewhere in my lower belly and moved south fast. This was going much faster than a first date. Maybe the critics had truly underestimated the effects of that film.

I ran my fingers self-consciously through my rain-slickened hair, ruing the day I'd decided to be daring and have it boy-cut. Veronica came over to the chair, sitting on the arm, looking long and slow, watching me from above. Reading my mind or my bemused expression, she said, "Don't you realize how much I like the way you look?"

Shitfire! This woman was nothing if not direct. Maybe it had something to do with being a translator. She reached down, taking both of my hands. I just knew there was no coffee involved. She led me towards the back room. Behind us, Bach dimmed and was finally lost amid the rain sounds. We came to an open room. Her room. Her bedroom.

Candles. Many candles. The scent of melting beeswax and her perfume filled the air. It wasn't cloying, though, only clean and warm, breathable but somehow denser than regular beach air—like ether, maybe. Amber and gold suffused everything. Even our skin seemed burnished. The silver-blue day had been bathed in gold dust. Warm. Suddenly all of the cold, wet melancholy of the cinema and our first hour together dissolved. It was as if we'd entered a different time.

The furniture added to the atmosphere—an antique four-poster bed and a dressing table with a huge oval mirror attached. The coverlet on the bed had been pulled back. Fresh pillows primped and plumped crested the puff of mattress. I knew if I sat I'd sink—but sitting wasn't really on her mind.

And then I saw it. A mason jar, covered with a muslin cozy on the lid, filled with the oozing comb of a beehive. It was just a wee bit creepy, too planned for my taste, but I had to admit the cool shiver it elicited was kind of delicious in its own way. I half-expected river sounds, lightning bugs, cool bluesy spirituals to emerge from the closet.

"A gift, honestly, from an old, very sentimental friend back home," Veronica said. "Come on, Emily, could you resist?" She slid behind me, leaning slightly into my butt and the small of my back. Her breasts brushed against the thin chambray of my shirt. I felt the hard tips of her nipples rise at the touch, and my own responded. Corny or not, contrived or not, all of this was having the desired effect. I was on sensory overload; Veronica was terminally homesick; it was a gray, cold evening, rainy and sad, both of us alone; and she was beautiful.

"I've been reading your columns in the paper for months. Always figured we'd meet someday ... this is such a small town, really. Never expected it would be like this," Veronica breathed into my ear.

"Did you know I was a dyke?" I could scarcely breathe. Every muscle in my body ached. I wanted to turn, jump her bones, ravish her on that pristine, ruffly candy box of a bed, pour honey in all the crevices of her luscious body, hear her talk about my column through all of that. But my mind . . . she was snagging at my mind. Oh, she *was* a Southern woman, in the best sense—slow, so slow. Play all the nuances, taste every subtle flavor, savor the textures. So I held steady while Veronica crept over me like a big voluptuous cat, rubbing and almost purring into my ear, teasing me, easing me to her magic bed.

Still behind me, her vulva now rubbing against my ass, her hands circling my shoulders, pinning my arms to my sides, more of an insinuation than a hold, she cupped my breasts but didn't let go, only stood, behind, still moving, and judging the weight of each breast as if this was the most important thing in the world. Her tongue traced the inside of my ear, hot and almost as wet as she was making me in other places.

"Haven't you always wondered," she breathed jasmine, she breathed fire into my head, "haven't you wondered what it must have been like, I mean, for Idgie and Ruth? That first night in Idgie's parents' house, after she'd rescued Ruth from her terrible husband? Everyone home, all asleep somewhere in that great southern gothic, and knowing exactly what was happening down the hall? And they finally together after years apart, the door closed and locked and safe, the world outside and only them inside?" Veronica raised her long, slim leg and gracefully brought it up between mine.

The wet fire drove like a hammer into my clit. I was hard and melting and I could not speak. She was going to kill me with her voice, her touch, her smell.

"Emily," she continued, caressing my neck with her lips, "their first night together, their wedding night, the way it should have been from the beginning. Idgie would have to somehow explain how she'd come to so much knowledge about making love . . . and then, Ruth, the only sex she knew was from her husband, so her hunger for Idgie would be tempered with the knowledge that there could be danger in so much need."

I felt the rumble-burn and throb in my crotch, my lips blood-heavy, swollen with the wet fire she'd lit, pressed into the now too-tight seam of my jeans. She raised her knee and pressed harder, then released, making my legs go weak, making me actually stagger towards the bed, my head swimming with her words.

"In that room, together, Ruth older, terrified, on fire for the first time in her life. And Idgie, this young butch rebel, she knew, she knew what to do, but never, never with someone she loved." Veronica turned me around to face her, to look deep into her sea-green eyes and go under. "I think in that quiet, green-scented, night-filled house, behind that locked door, those women would have burst into flame."

Veronica unbuttoned her camisole. My heart filled my throat as her breasts were freed. Her skin seemed illuminated, filled with the light that permeated everything in the room. Her mouth was slightly open, slightly smiling. Her breathing was shallow, fast and very hot. Her look pulled me in close—hunger hypnotizes, and I was her captive. Her hunger matched mine. It suspended us, beyond time, beyond geography. This wasn't California and it wasn't the twentieth century. We were outside of any given space, somewhere deep and old and far more gentle than where we actually lived.

My cunt was reaching meltdown as she slipped the camisole from her shoulders. Slowly, achingly, she opened each button on my work shirt, never taking her eyes from mine. Her fingers were educated in this maneuver; I smiled, thinking of all the butch shirts that had tumbled at their touch. She frowned again as if she could read my mind.

"You're wrong, you're very wrong, you know. Don't believe me. Don't believe this is different. I'll just have to show you."

As if in slow motion, she danced us down, moving the cambric fabric of the shirt across my breasts, chafing the nipples raw, and then licking them, making them ache even more at this tease.

"This night, this night is what I think happened." Veronica's mouth found mine as she raised the shirt and slid it and my arms over my head on the bed. Her tongue filled my mouth with the taste of peppermint. Again and again she thrust, her body now on top of mine on the comforter and pillows, her tongue creating the cadence.

A moan caught in my throat. This was almost too much. I tried to pull my mouth back, gasping for air, but this only exposed my neck to her lips, her teeth. Her tongue slid back to my ear, darting, quick as one of Idgie's charmed bees; I swear even her voice held a kind of buzz, a whispered but incoherent promise, the words finally unintelligible, unimportant. Perhaps language was her passion, but for now, mine was more primal; mine was flesh. Touch. Flame.

She pushed down and into me from above, straddling me with her weight, crushing the length of me with her long body and legs, holding my arms over my head, my hands still tangled in the cast-off shirt.

I was open, open and pressed, beneath my clothes—except for the shirt, I *was* still clothed. Delicious—I knew I could call off the surrender, could pry her away, peel her from me, but I was giving in, giving her this, and it made me laugh even under the fire, this stunning dare she was pulling off. Delicious shock, this femme riding me, wild, making me undone, taking my control, bucking and rolling and pressing me down, pulling flame from us both as she rose and sank and rose again. The sodden seam of my jeans bit into my clit more than I could take, so fast, we were moving so fast, but she wouldn't relent, not even allow the release of my cry.

"Sssshhh . . . remember . . . this would be all that Ruth would know, this hard, fast heat and ravage. And Idgie would be shocked and silent, they'd both have to be silent. The family was so close, all around them, now, sshhh." Veronica smothered me with her sandpaper whisper. Her searing lips brushed mine, sending another set of scalding waves over my skin.

Still. Be still. Had to fight everything that was natural in my response, in my soul. Fight all I thought I knew about myself. Keep my hands tangled and over my head, my legs wide and throbbing, my center molten, open to whatever this woman, this glorious, golden stranger had in store. Like Idgie, maybe this *was* my first surrender.

I closed my eyes. She was right. It had to be true. The movie, the book, here, in her bed. She knew every stroke, all the moves to get to the heart of me.

She pulled up and off and doffed her jeans. I lay motionless, watching her creamy body emerge from her clothes. I felt the rush of cold and hot air as she stripped my pants over my ass, then the press and burn as she thrust herself toward me, keeping my legs only wide enough, now, for her hands and face, keeping my ankles as tangled as my wrists, keeping me tangled and tied to her.

"All I could have known I would have learned from a man."
Veronica's voice was harsh and sharpened with the quick breaths
she inhaled. Almost a hiss. For a moment I was afraid. But then
her hand—that perfectly manicured, sculpted piece of awe-
inspiring woman, that hand that I'd watched for hours, dabbing at
tears, moving a wisp of hair gently back, buttoning and unbutton-
ing both her clothes and mine, caressing my face, my lips, my
breasts, caressing her own sex in between stroking my rock-hard
clit—that hand now paused and then slowly, unrelentingly, opened
me in a way that I'd never allowed anyone, in the way that I had
opened many women. And she watched my eyes, my mouth, my
body in the way that I'd watched when I'd felt my hand curve and
slide and flower inside the deep secret folds of my lovers.

Again and again, farther than I thought I could take her, she
took me, coaxed me, opened and split me and then pulled the
scream from me, coming like thunder, sparks from my gnashing
teeth, from my eyes, crying like some raging animal in heat, she
took me, pressed hard and deep and upon me, and she came too,
shuddering, calling my name out, elemental Eve, unbound, the
hidden warrior behind the Southern belle, all Amazon shock troop
and ripe love, all lace cast off and animal revealed. She called my
name as I came to her, totally undone, as surely Ruth and Idgie
must have come, each to the other, after so much longing, so many
years.

We held each other, recovering, sipping the cool mint tea she'd
made fresh. I was in awe: so long in California, jaded, not quite
Republican; I thought I'd seen or done it all.

Fat chance. Leave it to the South.

Veronica leaned over on one elbow, her lips glistening with the
fresh tea. She kissed me slow and full, full of soul and the taste of
green herbs and ice in summer. She sent shudders through me.

Not a stranger anymore, but still, a translator. I smiled through
our kiss.

Then I rolled on top of her, making her drop her tea to the floor.
Before she could react I slipped one hand to my lips, shushing
her, and with the other, I reached up and over us for the mason jar
with the flowered lid. For the honey.

AUTHOR BIOS

*BLAKE C. AARENS is the great-granddaughter of Hattie and Esther, the granddaughter of Dicy, and the daughter of Cobia. She is a survivor of childhood sexual abuse who writes award-winning erotic fiction. Her work has appeared in *Aché: A Journal for Lesbians of African Descent, Best American Erotica 1993, Penthouse,* and the anthology *Switch Hitters: Lesbians Write Gay Male Erotica and Gay Men Write Lesbian Erotica.* Blake is a working artist in search of her tribe.

KELLY CONWAY, a writer and musician, lives in Sacramento, California, with her divine butch and their three ill-mannered cats. You can find more of her work in *The Femme Mystique*, edited by Lesléa Newman; *Mother Lies*; *Write from the Heart, May/December*; and *Lesbian Short Fiction*. When not working on her novel, she's a booking agent whose company, Lavender Underground, produces concerts by women musicians and comics.

*WINN GILMORE grew up in the South, graduated from Smith College, and lives in California. Her writing has appeared in the magazines *Aché, On Our Backs*, and *frighten the horses*; the

---

*Contributors to previous *Herotica* collections.

anthologies *Unholy Alliances*, *Riding Desire*, and *Herotica 2*; and the journal *Sinister Wisdom*. She is seeking a publisher for her short story collection, *Trip to Nawlins*.

*JOLIE GRAHAM is a West Coast writer and artist presently at work on an erotic novel. She still wears the ear cuff.

GINU KAMANI is the author of *Junglee Girl*, a collection of short stories exploring the sensual recklessness of Indian women. Her work has been published in *On a Bed of Rice: An Asian-American Erotic Feast* and *Dick for a Day*. She is working on a novel and screenplays.

*SONJA KINDLEY's work has appeared in a number of publications, including *Elle*, *ZYZZYVA*, and *CutBank*.

*AURORA LIGHT has had erotica published in *Gallery*, *Hustler*, *Pillow Talk*, and *EIDOS*. She is a volunteer for the National EAR Foundation and publishes a poetry review.

*KAREN MARIE CHRISTA MINNS, author of *Bloodsong*, *Virago* and *Calling Rain*, is a thirty-nine-year-old Gemini novelist, exhibited painter, and general adventurer.

*SERENA MOLOCH lives in San Francisco. Her hobbies include improving her typing speed and trying on expensive clothing in stores. She has a story in *Virgin Territory 2* and is working on a script for an erotic feature called *Harmony's Party*.

FELICE NEWMAN is publisher of Cleis Press, where she is privileged to work with many cutting-edge authors of erotica. Her fiction appears in *The Second Coming*.

*CAROL QUEEN is a petite drag queen trapped in a woman's body. Her most recent books are *Exhibitionism for the Shy* (Down There Press), *Real Live Nude Girl*, and *Switch Hitters*, co-edited with Lawrence Schimel. She lives in San Francisco.

ADRIENNE RABINOV is a business consultant and professor at an East Coast university. She and her West Coast lover, for whom she wrote "In the Mood," think it's a hoot to be publishing their personal pornography.

JULIA RADER loves to make money from sex, especially from writing about it. For her mental health and global unity she makes performance rituals. She's studying to be an Alexander teacher while continuing to work on *The Dr. Angel Letters*, a novel that explains how S/M can save your life.

*STACY REED is a Houston writer and editor. She studied at the University of Texas at Austin and danced topless for several years. Reed has published essays, criticism, editorials, and features and has reported news. Her erotica appears in *First Person Sexual* (Down There Press) and the *Herotica* series. She is currently writing a novel.

*SUSAN ST. AUBIN reads cookbooks when she can't sleep. Her erotic stories have been anthologized in all five volumes of *Herotica, Yellow Silk: Erotic Arts and Letters, Erotic by Nature, Fever: Sensual Stories by Women Writers,* and *Best American Erotica 1995*.

KAREN A. SELZ is an assistant professor at a medical school, where she applies the conceptual and computational tools of mathematical physics to the study of brains and behavior. Sex-positive in her poetry and painting, she found it natural to design a machine that could compensate for and heal interpersonal deficits. Her story *The Hobby Horse* is the first entry in the smut category of her curriculum vitae.

MICHELE SERCHUK is a writer, photographer, and performer. Her work has been published in *Bust 'Zine* and *Australian Women's Forum*. She has adapted her stories and poems for the stage and has performed this work at New York's Dixon Place and in the Womenkind V and VI annual theater festivals. Her photography has been exhibited in a solo show at MBM Gallery in Soho and has appeared as cover art for several books of erotica.

CHRISTINE SOLANO is a bilingual and bisexual San Francisco writer, poet, and activist involved in deep ecology, human rights, and the abolition of the death penalty.

*MICHELLE STEVENS is a writer and teacher. She lives in Sherman Oaks, California, and highly recommends rechargeable batteries.

*CECILIA TAN is a writer, editor, and sexuality activist living and working in Boston. Her erotic fiction has appeared everywhere from *Penthouse* to *Ms.*, and in *Paramour, Taste of Latex, Black Sheets, Dark Angels: Lesbian Vampire Stories, On a Bed of Rice: Asian American Erotica, Looking for Mr. Preston, By Her Subdued, No Other Tribute, Noirotica, Backstage Passes,* and many more. She is the founder and publisher of Circlet Press (erotic science fiction and fantasy books) and has edited a "best of" Circlet collection entitled *SM Visions*.

*CATHERINE M. TAVEL lives with her firefighter husband in their native Brooklyn. Their many adventures take them to the tops of active volcanoes in Guatemala, river rafting during hailstorms in Wyoming, and, yes, even to perilous wrought-iron balconies in New Orleans. She considers herself very fortunate to be able to immortalize these experiences in print.

*JOAN LESLIE TAYLOR is a writer and accountant who lives in the woods of northern California with a large dog and a small cat. She is the author of *In the Light of Dying,* a book about her experiences as a hospice volunteer. In *Herotica 2* her story appeared under the name Maggie Brewster.

*MARCY SHEINER is the editor of *Herotica 4.* Her journalism and fiction have been published in magazines as diverse as *Penthouse* and *The Vegetarian Times, Mother Jones* and the Scandinavian *Cupido.* Her poetry, fiction, and nonfiction have also appeared in many literary journals and anthologies. She teaches erotic writing classes in the San Francisco Bay Area, where she lives, and is currently working on a collection of essays.